MOBY DICK

VOLUME ONE OF THREE

Moby Dick
Melville, Herman 1819 – 1891
First Published by Harper & Brothers in 1851
Irving, Washington 1783 – 1859
First Published by C. S. Van Winkle in 1819

Text edits © 2025 Grand Type Classics
Design © 2025 Grand Type Classics

Text set in 18 point Helvetica.
Chapter headings set in Helvetica Neue.

All rights reserved. All materials in this book are protected by copyright. No part of this publication may be reproduced, distributed, or transmitted in any form or by any means, including photocopying, recording, or other electronic or mechanical methods, without the prior written permission of the publisher.

ISBN: 978-1-83412-383-7 Volume One
ISBN: 978-1-83412-384-4 Volume Two
ISBN: 978-1-83412-385-1 Volume Three

MOBY DICK

VOLUME ONE OF THREE

HERMAN MELVILLE

GRAND TYPE CLASSICS

CONTENTS

VOLUME ONE

VOLUME TWO

ETYMOLOGY

(Supplied by a Late Consumptive Usher to a Grammar School)

THE PALE USHER – threadbare in coat, heart, body, and brain; I see him now. He was ever dusting his old lexicons and grammars, with a queer handkerchief, mockingly embellished with all the gay flags of all the known nations of the world. He loved to dust his old grammars; it somehow mildly reminded him of his mortality.

"While you take in hand to school others, and to teach them by what name a whale-fish is to be called in our tongue leaving out, through ignorance, the letter H, which almost alone maketh the signification of the word, you deliver that which is not true." – **Hackluyt**

"WHALE.... Sw. and Dan. **hval**. This animal is named from roundness or rolling; for in Dan. **hvalt** is arched or vaulted." – **Webster's Dictionary**

"WHALE.... It is more immediately from the Dut. and Ger. **Wallen**; A.S. **Walw-ian**, to roll, to wallow." – **Richardson's Dictionary**

KETOS,	Greek.
CETUS,	Latin.
WHOEL,	Anglo-Saxon.
HVALT,	Danish.
WAL,	Dutch.
HWAL,	Swedish.
WHALE,	Icelandic.
WHALE,	English.
BALEINE,	French.
BALLENA,	Spanish.
PEKEE-NUEE-NUEE,	Fegee.
PEHEE-NUEE-NUEE,	Erromangoan.

EXTRACTS

(Supplied by a Sub-Sub-Librarian)

IT WILL BE SEEN that this mere painstaking burrower and grub-worm of a poor devil of a Sub-Sub appears to have gone through the long Vaticans and street-stalls of the earth, picking up whatever random allusions to whales he could anyways find in any book whatsoever, sacred or profane. Therefore you must not, in every case at least, take the higgledy-piggledy whale statements, however authentic, in these extracts, for veritable gospel cetology. Far from it. As touching the ancient authors generally, as well as the poets here appearing, these extracts are solely valuable or entertaining, as affording a glancing bird's eye view of what has been promiscuously said, thought, fancied, and sung of Leviathan, by many nations and generations, including our own.

So fare thee well, poor devil of a Sub-Sub, whose commentator I am. Thou belongest to that hopeless, sallow tribe which no wine of this world will ever warm; and for whom even Pale Sherry would be too rosy-strong; but with whom one sometimes loves to sit, and feel poor-devilish, too; and grow convivial upon tears; and say to them bluntly, with full eyes and empty glasses, and in not altogether unpleasant sadness – Give it up, Sub-Subs! For by how much the more pains ye take to please the world, by so much the more shall ye for ever go thankless! Would that I could clear out Hampton Court and the Tuileries for ye! But gulp down your tears and hie aloft to the royal-mast with your hearts; for your friends who have gone before are clearing out the seven-storied heavens, and making refugees of long-pampered Gabriel, Michael, and Raphael, against your coming. Here ye strike but splintered hearts together – there, ye shall strike unsplinterable glasses!

EXTRACTS.

“And God created great whales.”

– **Genesis**.

“Leviathan maketh a path to shine after him; One would think the deep to be hoary.”

– **Job**.

“Now the Lord had prepared a great fish to swallow up Jonah.”

– **Jonah**.

“There go the ships; there is that Leviathan whom thou hast made to play therein.”

– **Psalms**.

"In that day, the Lord with his sore, and great, and strong sword, shall punish Leviathan the piercing serpent, even Leviathan that crooked serpent; and he shall slay the dragon that is in the sea."

– **Isaiah**.

"And what thing soever besides cometh within the chaos of this monster's mouth, be it beast, boat, or stone, down it goes all incontinently that foul great swallow of his, and perisheth in the bottomless gulf of his paunch."

– **Holland's Plutarch's Morals**.

"The Indian Sea breedeth the most and the biggest fishes that are: among which the Whales and Whirlpooles called Balaene, take up as much in length as four acres or arpens of land."

– **Holland's Pliny**.

"Scarcely had we proceeded two days on the sea, when about sunrise a great many Whales and other monsters of the sea, appeared. Among the former, one was of a most monstrous size.... This came towards us, open-mouthed, raising the waves on all sides, and beating the sea before him into a foam."

– **Tooke's Lucian**. "**The True History**."

"He visited this country also with a view of catching horse-whales, which had bones of very great value for their teeth, of which he brought some to the king.... The best whales were catched in his own country, of which some were forty-eight, some fifty yards long. He said that he was one of six who had killed sixty in two days."

– **Other or Other's verbal narrative taken down from his mouth by King Alfred, A.D.** 890.

"And whereas all the other things, whether beast or vessel, that enter into the dreadful gulf of this monster's (whale's) mouth, are immediately lost and swallowed up, the sea-gudgeon retires into it in great security, and there sleeps." – MONTAIGNE.

– **Apology for Raimond Sebond**.

"Let us fly, let us fly! Old Nick take me if is not Leviathan described by the noble prophet Moses in the life of patient Job."

– **Rabelais**.

"This whale's liver was two cartloads."

– **Stowe's Annals**.

"The great Leviathan that maketh the seas to seethe like boiling pan."

– **Lord Bacon's Version of the Psalms**.

"Touching that monstrous bulk of the whale or ork we have received nothing certain. They grow exceeding fat, insomuch that an incredible quantity of oil will be extracted out of one whale."

– **Ibid**. "**History of Life and Death**."

"The sovereignest thing on earth is parmacetti for an inward bruise."

– **King Henry**.

"Very like a whale."

– **Hamlet**.

"Which to secure, no skill of leach's art
Mote him availle, but to returne againe

To his wound's worker, that with lowly dart,
Dinting his breast, had bred his restless
paine,
Like as the wounded whale to shore flies
thro' the maine."
– **The Faerie Queen.**

"Immense as whales, the motion of whose vast bodies can in a peaceful calm trouble the ocean til it boil."
– **Sir William Davenant. Preface to Gondibert**.

"What spermacetti is, men might justly doubt, since the learned Hosmannus in his work of thirty years, saith plainly, **Nescio quid sit**."
– **Sir T. Browne. Of Sperma Ceti and the Sperma Ceti Whale. Vide his V. E.**

"Like Spencer's Talus with his modern flail
He threatens ruin with his ponderous tail.
Their fixed jav'lins in his side he wears,
And on his back a grove of pikes appears."

– **Waller's Battle of the Summer Islands**.

"By art is created that great Leviathan, called a Commonwealth or State – (in Latin, Civitas) which is but an artificial man."

– **Opening sentence of Hobbes's Leviathan**.

"Silly Mansoul swallowed it without chewing, as if it had been a sprat in the mouth of a whale."

– **Pilgrim's Progress**.

"That sea beast
Leviathan, which God of all his works
Created hugest that swim the ocean stream."

– **Paradise Lost**.

– -"There Leviathan,
Hugest of living creatures, in the deep
Stretched like a promontory sleeps or swims,
And seems a moving land; and at his gills

Draws in, and at his breath spouts out a
sea."

– **Ibid**.

"The mighty whales which swim in a sea of water, and have a sea of oil swimming in them."

– **Fuller's Profane and Holy State**.

"So close behind some promontory lie
The huge Leviathan to attend their prey,
And give no chance, but swallow in the fry,
Which through their gaping jaws mistake
the way."

– **Dryden's Annus Mirabilis**.

"While the whale is floating at the stern of the ship, they cut off his head, and tow it with a boat as near the shore as it will come; but it will be aground in twelve or thirteen feet water."

– **Thomas Edge's Ten Voyages to Spitzbergen, in Purchas**.

"In their way they saw many whales sporting in the ocean, and in wantonness fuzzing up the water through their pipes and vents, which nature has placed on their shoulders." – **Sir T. Herbert's Voyages into Asia and Africa. Harris Coll**.

"Here they saw such huge troops of whales, that they were forced to proceed with a great deal of caution for fear they should run their ship upon them." – **Schouten's Sixth Circumnavigation**.

"We set sail from the Elbe, wind N.E. in the ship called The Jonas-in-the-Whale.... Some say the whale can't open his mouth, but that is a fable.... They frequently climb up the masts to see whether they can see a whale, for the first discoverer has a ducat for his pains.... I was told of a whale taken near Shetland, that had above a barrel of herrings in his belly.... One of our harpooneers told me that he caught once a whale in Spitzbergen that was white all over."

– **A Voyage to Greenland, A.D.** 1671. **Harris Coll**.

"Several whales have come in upon this coast (Fife) Anno 1652, one eighty feet in length of the whale-bone kind came in, which (as I was informed), besides a vast quantity of oil, did afford 500 weight of baleen. The jaws of it stand for a gate in the garden of Pitferren." – **Sibbald's Fife and Kinross**.

"Myself have agreed to try whether I can master and kill this Sperma-ceti whale, for I could never hear of any of that sort that was killed by any man, such is his fierceness and swiftness." – **Richard Strafford's Letter from the Bermudas. Phil. Trans. A.D.** 1668.

"Whales in the sea God's voice obey." – **N. E. Primer**.

"We saw also abundance of large whales, there being more in those southern seas, as I may say, by a hundred to one; than we have to the northward of us." – **Captain Cowley's Voyage round the Globe, A.D.** 1729.

"... and the breath of the whale is frequently attended with such an insupportable smell, as to bring on a disorder of the brain."
– **Ulloa's South America**.

"To fifty chosen sylphs of special note,
We trust the important charge, the
petticoat.
Oft have we known that seven-fold fence
to fail,
Tho' stuffed with hoops and armed with
ribs of whale."
– **Rape of the Lock**.

"If we compare land animals in respect to magnitude, with those that take up their abode in the deep, we shall find they will appear contemptible in the comparison. The whale is doubtless the largest animal in creation." – **Goldsmith, Nat. Hist**.

"If you should write a fable for little fishes, you would make them speak like great wales." – **Goldsmith to Johnson**.

"In the afternoon we saw what was supposed to be a rock, but it was found to be a dead whale, which some Asiatics had killed, and were then towing ashore. They seemed to endeavor to conceal themselves behind the whale, in order to avoid being seen by us."
– **Cook's Voyages**.

"The larger whales, they seldom venture to attack. They stand in so great dread of some of them, that when out at sea they are afraid to mention even their names, and carry dung, lime-stone, juniper-wood, and some other articles of the same nature in their boats, in order to terrify and prevent their too near approach." – **Uno Von Troil's Letters on Banks's and Solander's Voyage to Iceland in** 1772.

"The Spermacetti Whale found by the Nantuckois, is an active, fierce animal, and requires vast address and boldness in the fishermen." – **Thomas Jefferson's Whale Memorial to the French minister in** 1778.

"And pray, sir, what in the world is equal to it?" – **Edmund Burke's reference in Parliament to the Nantucket Whale-Fishery**.

"Spain – a great whale stranded on the shores of Europe." – **Edmund Burke**. (**somewhere**.)

"A tenth branch of the king's ordinary revenue, said to be grounded on the consideration of his guarding and protecting the seas from pirates and robbers, is the right to **royal** fish, which are whale and sturgeon. And these, when either thrown ashore or caught near the coast, are the property of the king." – **Blackstone**.

"Soon to the sport of death the crews
    repair:
Rodmond unerring o'er his head suspends
The barbed steel, and every turn attends."
 – **Falconer's Shipwreck**.

"Bright shone the roofs, the domes, the
spires,
And rockets blew self driven,
To hang their momentary fire
Around the vault of heaven.
"So fire with water to compare,
The ocean serves on high,
Up-spouted by a whale in air,
To express unwieldy joy."
– **Cowper, on the Queen's Visit to London**.

"Ten or fifteen gallons of blood are thrown out of the heart at a stroke, with immense velocity." – **John Hunter's account of the dissection of a whale**. (**A small sized one**.)

"The aorta of a whale is larger in the bore than the main pipe of the water-works at London Bridge, and the water roaring in its passage through that pipe is inferior in impetus and velocity to the blood gushing from the whale's heart."

– **Paley's Theology**.

"The whale is a mammiferous animal without hind feet." – **Baron Cuvier**.

"In 40 degrees south, we saw Spermacetti Whales, but did not take any till the first of May, the sea being then covered with them." – **Colnett's Voyage for the Purpose of Extending the Spermaceti Whale Fishery**.

"In the free element beneath me swam,
Floundered and dived, in play, in chace, in
    battle,
Fishes of every colour, form, and kind;
Which language cannot paint, and mariner
Had never seen; from dread Leviathan
To insect millions peopling every wave:
Gather'd in shoals immense, like floating
    islands,
Led by mysterious instincts through that
    waste
And trackless region, though on every side
Assaulted by voracious enemies,
Whales, sharks, and monsters, arm'd in

front or jaw,
With swords, saws, spiral horns, or hooked fangs."
– **Montgomery's World before the Flood**.

"Io! Paean! Io! sing.
To the finny people's king.
Not a mightier whale than this
In the vast Atlantic is;
Not a fatter fish than he,
Flounders round the Polar Sea."
– **Charles Lamb's Triumph of the Whale**.

"In the year 1690 some persons were on a high hill observing the whales spouting and sporting with each other, when one observed: there – pointing to the sea – is a green pasture where our children's grand-children will go for bread." – **Obed Macy's History of Nantucket**.

"I built a cottage for Susan and myself and made a gateway in the form of a Gothic

Arch, by setting up a whale's jaw bones." – **Hawthorne's Twice Told Tales**.

"She came to bespeak a monument for her first love, who had been killed by a whale in the Pacific ocean, no less than forty years ago." – **Ibid**.

"No, Sir, 'tis a Right Whale," answered Tom; "I saw his sprout; he threw up a pair of as pretty rainbows as a Christian would wish to look at. He's a raal oil-butt, that fellow!" – **Cooper's Pilot**.

"The papers were brought in, and we saw in the Berlin Gazette that whales had been introduced on the stage there." – **Eckermann's Conversations with Goethe**.

"My God! Mr. Chace, what is the matter?" I answered, "we have been stove by a whale." – "**Narrative of the Shipwreck of the Whale Ship Essex of Nantucket, which was attacked and finally destroyed by a large Sperm Whale in the Pacific Ocean**." **By Owen Chace of Nantucket, first mate**

of said vessel. New York, 1821.

"A mariner sat in the shrouds one night,
The wind was piping free;
Now bright, now dimmed, was the
moonlight pale,
And the phospher gleamed in the wake of
the whale,
As it floundered in the sea."
– **Elizabeth Oakes Smith**.

"The quantity of line withdrawn from the boats engaged in the capture of this one whale, amounted altogether to 10,440 yards or nearly six English miles....

"Sometimes the whale shakes its tremendous tail in the air, which, cracking like a whip, resounds to the distance of three or four miles." – **Scoresby**.

"Mad with the agonies he endures from these fresh attacks, the infuriated Sperm Whale rolls over and over; he rears his enormous head, and with wide expanded jaws snaps at everything around him; he rushes at the boats with his head; they are propelled before him with vast swiftness, and sometimes utterly destroyed.... It is a matter of great astonishment that the consideration of the habits of so interesting, and, in a commercial point of view, so important an animal (as the Sperm Whale) should have been so entirely neglected, or should have excited so little curiosity among the numerous, and many of them competent observers, that of late years, must have possessed the most abundant and the most convenient opportunities of witnessing their habitudes." – **Thomas Beale's History of the Sperm Whale**, 1839.

"The Cachalot" (Sperm Whale) "is not only better armed than the True Whale" (Greenland or Right Whale) "in possessing a formidable weapon at either extremity of its body, but also more frequently displays a disposition to employ these weapons offensively and in manner at once so artful, bold, and mischievous, as to lead to its being regarded as the most dangerous to attack of all the known species of the whale tribe." – **Frederick Debell Bennett's Whaling Voyage Round the Globe**, 1840.

October 13. "There she blows," was sung out from the mast-head.
"Where away?" demanded the captain.
"Three points off the lee bow, sir."
"Raise up your wheel. Steady!"
"Steady, sir."
"Mast-head ahoy! Do you see that whale now?"
"Ay ay, sir! A shoal of Sperm Whales! There she blows! There she breaches!"
"Sing out! sing out every time!"
"Ay Ay, sir! There she blows! there – there – **thar** she blows – bowes – bo-o-os!"
"How far off?"
"Two miles and a half."
"Thunder and lightning! so near! Call all hands."

– **J. Ross Browne's Etchings of a Whaling Cruize**. 1846.

"The Whale-ship Globe, on board of which vessel occurred the horrid transactions we are about to relate, belonged to the island of Nantucket." – "**Narrative of the Globe Mutiny**," **by Lay and Hussey survivors. A.D.** 1828.

Being once pursued by a whale which he had wounded, he parried the assault for some time with a lance; but the furious monster at length rushed on the boat; himself and comrades only being preserved by leaping into the water when they saw the onset was inevitable." – **Missionary Journal of Tyerman and Bennett**.

"Nantucket itself," said Mr. Webster, "is a very striking and peculiar portion of the National interest. There is a population of eight or nine thousand persons living here in the sea, adding largely every year to the National wealth by the boldest and most persevering industry." – **Report of Daniel Webster's Speech in the U. S. Senate, on the application for the Erection of a Breakwater at Nantucket**. 1828.

"The whale fell directly over him, and probably killed him in a moment." – "**The Whale and his Captors, or The Whaleman's Adventures and the Whale's Biography, gathered on the Homeward Cruise of the Commodore Preble**." **By Rev. Henry T. Cheever**.

"If you make the least damn bit of noise," replied Samuel, "I will send you to hell." – **Life of Samuel Comstock** (**the mutineer**), **by his brother, William Comstock. Another Version of the whale-ship Globe narrative**.

"The voyages of the Dutch and English to the Northern Ocean, in order, if possible, to discover a passage through it to India, though they failed of their main object, laid-open the haunts of the whale." –

McCulloch's Commercial Dictionary.

"These things are reciprocal; the ball rebounds, only to bound forward again; for now in laying open the haunts of the whale, the whalemen seem to have indirectly hit upon new clews to that same mystic North-West Passage." – **From "Something" unpublished**.

"It is impossible to meet a whale-ship on the ocean without being struck by her near appearance. The vessel under short sail, with look-outs at the mast-heads, eagerly scanning the wide expanse around them, has a totally different air from those engaged in regular voyage." – **Currents and Whaling. U.S. Ex. Ex**.

"Pedestrians in the vicinity of London and elsewhere may recollect having seen large curved bones set upright in the earth, either to form arches over gateways, or entrances to alcoves, and they may perhaps have been told that these were the ribs of whales." – **Tales of a Whale Voyager to the Arctic**

Ocean.

"It was not till the boats returned from the pursuit of these whales, that the whites saw their ship in bloody possession of the savages enrolled among the crew." – **Newspaper Account of the Taking and Retaking of the Whale-Ship Hobomack**.

"It is generally well known that out of the crews of Whaling vessels (American) few ever return in the ships on board of which they departed." – **Cruise in a Whale Boat**.

"Suddenly a mighty mass emerged from the water, and shot up perpendicularly into the air. It was the whale." – **Miriam Coffin or the Whale Fisherman**.

"The Whale is harpooned to be sure; but bethink you, how you would manage a powerful unbroken colt, with the mere appliance of a rope tied to the root of his tail." – **A Chapter on Whaling in Ribs and Trucks**.

"On one occasion I saw two of these monsters (whales) probably male and female, slowly swimming, one after the other, within less than a stone's throw of the shore" (Terra Del Fuego), "over which the beech tree extended its branches." – **Darwin's Voyage of a Naturalist**.

"'Stern all!' exclaimed the mate, as upon turning his head, he saw the distended jaws of a large Sperm Whale close to the head of the boat, threatening it with instant destruction; – 'Stern all, for your lives!'" – **Wharton the Whale Killer**.

"So be cheery, my lads, let your hearts never fail, While the bold harpooneer is striking the whale!" – **Nantucket Song**.

"Oh, the rare old Whale, mid storm and
gale
In his ocean home will be
A giant in might, where might is right,
And King of the boundless sea."
– **Whale Song**.

CHAPTER ONE

Loomings

CALL ME ISHMAEL. Some years ago – never mind how long precisely – having little or no money in my purse, and nothing particular to interest me on shore, I thought I would sail about a little and see the watery part of the world. It is a way I have of driving off the spleen and regulating the circulation. Whenever I find myself growing grim about the mouth; whenever it is a damp, drizzly

November in my soul; whenever I find myself involuntarily pausing before coffin warehouses, and bringing up the rear of every funeral I meet; and especially whenever my hypos get such an upper hand of me, that it requires a strong moral principle to prevent me from deliberately stepping into the street, and methodically knocking people's hats off – then, I account it high time to get to sea as soon as I can. This is my substitute for pistol and ball. With a philosophical flourish Cato throws himself upon his sword; I quietly take to the ship. There is nothing surprising in this. If they but knew it, almost all men in their degree, some time or other, cherish very nearly the same feelings towards the ocean with me.

There now is your insular city of the Manhattoes, belted round by wharves as Indian isles by coral reefs – commerce surrounds it with her surf. Right and left, the streets take you waterward. Its extreme downtown is the battery, where that noble mole is washed by waves, and cooled by breezes, which a few hours previous were out of sight of land. Look at the crowds of water-gazers there.

Circumambulate the city of a dreamy Sabbath afternoon. Go from Corlears Hook to Coenties Slip, and from thence, by Whitehall, northward. What do you see? – Posted like silent sentinels all around the town, stand thousands upon thousands of mortal men fixed in ocean reveries. Some leaning against the spiles; some seated upon the pier-heads; some looking over the bulwarks of ships from China; some high aloft in the rigging, as if striving to get a still better seaward peep. But these are all landsmen; of week days pent up in lath and plaster – tied to counters, nailed to benches, clinched to desks. How then is this? Are the green fields gone? What do they here?

But look! here come more crowds, pacing straight for the water, and seemingly bound for a dive. Strange! Nothing will content them but the extremest limit of the land; loitering under the shady lee of yonder warehouses will not suffice. No. They must get just as nigh the water as they possibly can without falling in. And there they stand – miles of them – leagues. Inlanders all, they come from lanes and alleys, streets and avenues – north, east, south, and west. Yet here they all unite. Tell me, does the magnetic virtue of the needles of the compasses of all those ships attract them thither?

Once more. Say you are in the country; in some high land of lakes. Take almost any path you please, and ten to one it carries you down in a dale, and leaves you there by a pool in the stream. There is magic in it. Let the most absent-minded of men be plunged in his deepest reveries – stand that man on his legs, set his feet a-going, and he will infallibly lead you to water, if water there be in all that region. Should you ever be athirst in the great American desert, try this experiment, if your caravan happen to be supplied with a metaphysical professor. Yes, as every one knows, meditation and water are wedded for ever.

But here is an artist. He desires to paint you the dreamiest, shadiest, quietest, most enchanting bit of romantic landscape in all the valley of the Saco. What is the chief element he employs? There stand his trees, each with a hollow trunk, as if a hermit and a crucifix were within; and here sleeps his meadow, and there sleep his cattle; and up from yonder cottage goes a sleepy smoke. Deep into distant woodlands winds a mazy way, reaching to overlapping spurs of mountains bathed in their hill-side blue. But though the picture lies thus tranced, and though this pine-tree shakes down its sighs like leaves upon this shepherd's head, yet all were vain, unless the shepherd's eye were fixed upon the magic stream before him. Go visit the Prairies in June, when for scores on scores of miles you wade knee-deep among Tiger-lilies – what is the one charm wanting? – Water – there is not a drop of water there! Were Niagara but a cataract of sand, would you travel your thousand miles to see it? Why did the poor poet of Tennessee, upon suddenly receiving two handfuls of silver, deliberate whether to buy him a coat, which he sadly needed, or invest his money in a pedestrian trip to Rockaway Beach? Why is almost every robust healthy boy with a robust healthy soul in him, at some time or other crazy to go to sea? Why upon your first voyage as a passenger, did you yourself feel such a mystical vibration, when first told that you and your ship were now out of sight of land? Why did the old Persians hold the sea holy? Why did the Greeks give it a separate deity, and own brother of Jove? Surely all this is not without meaning. And still deeper the meaning of that story of Narcissus, who because he could not grasp the tormenting, mild image he saw in the fountain, plunged into it and was drowned. But that same image, we ourselves see in all rivers and oceans. It is the image of the ungraspable phantom of life; and this is the key to it all.

Now, when I say that I am in the habit of going to sea whenever I begin to grow hazy about the eyes, and begin to be over conscious of my lungs, I do not mean to have it inferred that I ever go to sea as a passenger. For to go as a passenger you must needs have a purse, and a purse is but a rag unless you have something in it. Besides, passengers get sea-sick – grow quarrelsome – don't sleep of nights – do not enjoy themselves much, as a general thing; – no, I never go as a passenger; nor, though I am something of a salt, do I ever go to sea as a Commodore, or a Captain, or a Cook. I abandon the glory and distinction of such offices to those who like them. For my part, I abominate all honourable respectable toils, trials, and tribulations of every kind whatsoever. It is quite as much as I can do to take care of myself, without taking care of ships, barques, brigs, schooners, and what not. And as for going as cook, – though I confess there is considerable glory in that, a cook being a sort of officer on ship-board – yet, somehow, I never fancied broiling fowls; – though once broiled, judiciously buttered, and judgmatically salted and peppered, there is no one who will speak more respectfully, not to say reverentially, of a broiled fowl than I will. It is out of the idolatrous dotings of the old Egyptians upon broiled ibis and roasted river horse, that you see the mummies of those creatures in their huge bake-houses the pyramids.

No, when I go to sea, I go as a simple sailor, right before the mast, plumb down into the forecastle, aloft there to the royal mast-head. True, they rather order me about some, and make me jump from spar to spar, like a grasshopper in a May meadow. And at first, this sort of thing is unpleasant enough. It touches one's sense of honour, particularly if you come of an old established family in the land, the Van Rensselaers, or Randolphs, or Hardicanutes. And more than all, if just previous to putting your hand into the tar-pot, you have been lording it as a country schoolmaster, making the tallest boys stand in awe of you. The transition is a keen one, I assure you, from a schoolmaster to a sailor, and requires a strong decoction of Seneca and the Stoics to enable you to grin and bear it. But even this wears off in time.

What of it, if some old hunks of a sea-captain orders me to get a broom and sweep down the decks? What does that indignity amount to, weighed, I mean, in the scales of the New Testament? Do you think the archangel Gabriel thinks anything the less of me, because I promptly and respectfully obey that old hunks in that particular instance? Who ain't a slave? Tell me that. Well, then, however the old sea-captains may order me about – however they may thump and punch me about, I have the satisfaction of knowing that it is all right; that everybody else is one way or other served in much the same way – either in a physical or metaphysical point of view, that is; and so the universal thump is passed round, and all hands should rub each other's shoulder-blades, and be content.

Again, I always go to sea as a sailor, because they make a point of paying me for my trouble, whereas they never pay passengers a single penny that I ever heard of. On the contrary, passengers themselves must pay. And there is all the difference in the world between paying and being paid. The act of paying is perhaps the most uncomfortable infliction that the two orchard thieves entailed upon us. But **being paid**, – what will compare with it? The urbane activity with which a man receives money is really marvellous, considering that we so earnestly believe money to be the root of all earthly ills, and that on no account can a monied man enter heaven. Ah! how cheerfully we consign ourselves to perdition!

Finally, I always go to sea as a sailor, because of the wholesome exercise and pure air of the fore-castle deck. For as in this world, head winds are far more prevalent than winds from astern (that is, if you never violate the Pythagorean maxim), so for the most part the Commodore on the quarter-deck gets his atmosphere at second hand from the sailors on the forecastle. He thinks he breathes it first; but not so. In much the same way do the commonalty lead their leaders in many other things, at the same time that the leaders little suspect it. But wherefore it was that after having repeatedly smelt the sea as a merchant sailor, I should now take it into my head to go on a whaling voyage; this the invisible police officer of the Fates, who has the constant surveillance of me, and secretly dogs me, and influences me in some unaccountable way – he can better answer than any one else. And, doubtless, my going on this whaling voyage, formed part of the grand programme of Providence that was drawn up a long time ago. It came in as a sort of brief interlude and solo between more extensive performances. I take it that this part of the bill must have run something like this:

"**Grand Contested Election for the Presidency of the United States.**
"WHALING VOYAGE BY ONE ISHMAEL.
"BLOODY BATTLE IN AFFGHANISTAN."

Though I cannot tell why it was exactly that those stage managers, the Fates, put me down for this shabby part of a whaling voyage, when others were set down for magnificent parts in high tragedies, and short and easy parts in genteel comedies, and jolly parts in farces – though I cannot tell why this was exactly; yet, now that I recall all the circumstances, I think I can see a little into the springs and motives which being cunningly presented to me under various disguises, induced me to set about performing the part I did, besides cajoling me into the delusion that it was a choice resulting from my own unbiased freewill and discriminating judgment.

Chief among these motives was the overwhelming idea of the great whale himself. Such a portentous and mysterious monster roused all my curiosity. Then the wild and distant seas where he rolled his island bulk; the undeliverable, nameless perils of the whale; these, with all the attending marvels of a thousand Patagonian sights and sounds, helped to sway me to my wish. With other men, perhaps, such things would not have been inducements; but as for me, I am tormented with an everlasting itch for things remote. I love to sail forbidden seas, and land on barbarous coasts. Not ignoring what is good, I am quick to perceive a horror, and could still be social with it – would they let me – since it is but well to be on friendly terms with all the inmates of the place one lodges in.

By reason of these things, then, the whaling

voyage was welcome; the great flood-gates of the wonder-world swung open, and in the wild conceits that swayed me to my purpose, two and two there floated into my inmost soul, endless processions of the whale, and, mid most of them all, one grand hooded phantom, like a snow hill in the air.

CHAPTER TWO

The Carpet-Bag

I STUFFED a shirt or two into my old carpet-bag, tucked it under my arm, and started for Cape Horn and the Pacific. Quitting the good city of old Manhatto, I duly arrived in New Bedford. It was a Saturday night in December. Much was I disappointed upon learning that the little packet for Nantucket had already sailed, and that no way of reaching that place would offer, till the following Monday.

As most young candidates for the pains and penalties of whaling stop at this same New Bedford, thence to embark on their voyage, it may as well be related that I, for one, had no idea of so doing. For my mind was made up to sail in no other than a Nantucket craft, because there was a fine, boisterous something about everything connected with that famous old island, which amazingly pleased me. Besides though New Bedford has of late been gradually monopolising the business of whaling, and though in this matter poor old Nantucket is now much behind her, yet Nantucket was her great original – the Tyre of this Carthage; – the place where the first dead American whale was stranded. Where else but from Nantucket did those aboriginal whalemen, the Red-Men, first sally out in canoes to give chase to the Leviathan? And where but from Nantucket, too, did that first adventurous little sloop put forth, partly laden with imported cobblestones – so goes the story – to throw at the whales, in order to discover when they were nigh enough to risk a harpoon from the bowsprit?

Now having a night, a day, and still another night following before me in New Bedford, ere I could embark for my destined port, it became a matter of concernment where I was to eat and sleep meanwhile. It was a very dubious-looking, nay, a very dark and dismal night, bitingly cold and cheerless. I knew no one in the place. With anxious grapnels I had sounded my pocket, and only brought up a few pieces of silver, – So, wherever you go, Ishmael, said I to myself, as I stood in the middle of a dreary street shouldering my bag, and comparing the gloom towards the north with the darkness towards the south – wherever in your wisdom you may conclude to lodge for the night, my dear Ishmael, be sure to inquire the price, and don't be too particular.

With halting steps I paced the streets,

and passed the sign of “The Crossed Harpoons” – but it looked too expensive and jolly there. Further on, from the bright red windows of the “Sword-Fish Inn,” there came such fervent rays, that it seemed to have melted the packed snow and ice from before the house, for everywhere else the congealed frost lay ten inches thick in a hard, asphaltic pavement, – rather weary for me, when I struck my foot against the flinty projections, because from hard, remorseless service the soles of my boots were in a most miserable plight. Too expensive and jolly, again thought I, pausing one moment to watch the broad glare in the street, and hear the sounds of the tinkling glasses within. But go on, Ishmael, said I at last; don’t you hear? get away from before the door; your patched boots are stopping the way. So on I went. I now by instinct followed the streets that took me waterward, for there, doubtless, were the cheapest, if not the cheeriest inns.

Such dreary streets! blocks of blackness, not houses, on either hand, and here and there a candle, like a candle moving about in a tomb. At this hour of the night, of the last day of the week, that quarter of the town proved all but deserted. But presently I came to a smoky light proceeding from a low, wide building, the door of which stood invitingly open. It had a careless look, as if it were meant for the uses of the public; so, entering, the first thing I did was to stumble over an ash-box in the porch. Ha! thought I, ha, as the flying particles almost choked me, are these ashes from that destroyed city, Gomorrah? But "The Crossed Harpoons," and "The Sword-Fish?" – this, then must needs be the sign of "The Trap." However, I picked myself up and hearing a loud voice within, pushed on and opened a second, interior door.

It seemed the great Black Parliament sitting in Tophet. A hundred black faces turned round in their rows to peer; and beyond, a black Angel of Doom was beating a book in a pulpit. It was a negro church; and the preacher's text was about the blackness of darkness, and the weeping and wailing and teeth-gnashing there. Ha, Ishmael, muttered I, backing out, Wretched entertainment at the sign of 'The Trap!'

Moving on, I at last came to a dim sort of light not far from the docks, and heard a forlorn creaking in the air; and looking up, saw a swinging sign over the door with a white painting upon it, faintly representing a tall straight jet of misty spray, and these words underneath – "The Spouter Inn: – Peter Coffin."

Coffin? – Spouter? – Rather ominous in that particular connexion, thought I. But it is a common name in Nantucket, they say, and I suppose this Peter here is an emigrant from there. As the light looked so dim, and the place, for the time, looked quiet enough, and the dilapidated little wooden house itself looked as if it might have been carted here from the ruins of some burnt district, and as the swinging sign had a poverty-stricken sort of creak to it, I thought that here was the very spot for cheap lodgings, and the best of pea coffee.

It was a queer sort of place – a gable-ended old house, one side palsied as it were, and leaning over sadly. It stood on a sharp bleak corner, where that tempestuous wind Euroclydon kept up a worse howling than ever it did about poor Paul's tossed craft. Euroclydon, nevertheless, is a mighty pleasant zephyr to any one in-doors, with his feet on the hob quietly toasting for bed. "In judging of that tempestuous wind called Euroclydon," says an old writer – of whose works I possess the only copy extant – "it maketh a marvellous difference, whether thou lookest out at it from a glass window where the frost is all on the outside, or whether thou observest it from that sashless window, where the frost is on both sides, and of which the wight Death is the only glazier." True enough, thought I, as this passage occurred to my mind – old black-letter, thou reasonest well. Yes, these eyes are windows, and this body of mine is the house. What a pity they didn't stop up the chinks and the crannies though, and thrust in a little lint here and there. But it's too late to make any improvements now. The universe is finished; the copestone is on, and the chips were carted off a million years ago. Poor Lazarus there, chattering his teeth against the curbstone for his pillow, and shaking off his tatters with his shiverings, he might plug up both ears with rags, and put a corn-cob into his mouth, and yet that would not keep out the tempestuous Euroclydon. Euroclydon! says old Dives, in his red silken wrapper – (he had a redder one afterwards) pooh, pooh! What a fine frosty night; how Orion glitters; what northern lights! Let them talk of their oriental summer climes of everlasting conservatories; give me the privilege of making my own summer with my own coals.

But what thinks Lazarus? Can he warm his blue hands by holding them up to the grand northern lights? Would not Lazarus rather be in Sumatra than here? Would he not far rather lay him down lengthwise along the line of the equator; yea, ye gods! go down to the fiery pit itself, in order to keep out this frost?

Now, that Lazarus should lie stranded there on the curbstone before the door of Dives, this is more wonderful than that an iceberg should be moored to one of the Moluccas. Yet Dives himself, he too lives like a Czar in an ice palace made of frozen sighs, and being a president of a temperance society, he only drinks the tepid tears of orphans.

But no more of this blubbering now, we are going a-whaling, and there is plenty of that yet to come. Let us scrape the ice from our frosted feet, and see what sort of a place this "Spouter" may be.

CHAPTER THREE

The Spouter-Inn

ENTERING THAT gable-ended Spouter-Inn, you found yourself in a wide, low, straggling entry with old-fashioned wainscots, reminding one of the bulwarks of some condemned old craft. On one side hung a very large oilpainting so thoroughly besmoked, and every way defaced, that in the unequal crosslights by which you viewed it, it was only by diligent study and a series of systematic visits to it, and careful inquiry of the neighbors, that you could any way arrive at an understanding of its purpose. Such unaccountable masses of shades and shadows, that at first you almost thought some ambitious young artist, in the time of the New England hags, had endeavored to delineate chaos bewitched. But by dint of much and earnest contemplation, and oft repeated ponderings, and especially by throwing open the little window towards the back of the entry, you at last come to the conclusion that such an idea, however wild, might not be altogether unwarranted.

But what most puzzled and confounded you was a long, limber, portentous, black mass of something hovering in the centre of the picture over three blue, dim, perpendicular lines floating in a nameless yeast. A boggy, soggy, squitchy picture truly, enough to drive a nervous man distracted. Yet was there a sort of indefinite, half-attained, unimaginable sublimity about it that fairly froze you to it, till you involuntarily took an oath with yourself to find out what that marvellous painting meant. Ever and anon a bright, but, alas, deceptive idea would dart you through. – It's the Black Sea in a midnight gale. – It's the unnatural combat of the four primal elements. – It's a blasted heath. – It's a Hyperborean winter scene. – It's the breaking-up of the icebound stream of Time. But at last all these fancies yielded to that one portentous something in the picture's midst. **That** once found out, and all the rest were plain. But stop; does it not bear a faint resemblance to a gigantic fish? even the great leviathan himself?

In fact, the artist's design seemed this: a final theory of my own, partly based upon the aggregated opinions of many aged persons with whom I conversed upon the subject. The picture represents a Cape-Horner in a great hurricane; the half-foundered ship weltering there with its three dismantled masts alone visible; and an exasperated whale, purposing to spring clean over the craft, is in the enormous act of impaling himself upon the three mast-heads.

The opposite wall of this entry was hung all over with a heathenish array of monstrous clubs and spears. Some were thickly set with glittering teeth resembling ivory saws; others were tufted with knots of human hair; and one was sickle-shaped, with a vast handle sweeping round like the segment made in the new-mown grass by a long-armed mower. You shuddered as you gazed, and wondered what monstrous cannibal and savage could ever have gone a death-harvesting with such a hacking, horrifying implement. Mixed with these were rusty old whaling lances and harpoons all broken and deformed. Some were storied weapons. With this once long lance, now wildly elbowed, fifty years ago did Nathan Swain kill fifteen whales between a sunrise and a sunset. And that harpoon – so like a corkscrew now – was flung in Javan seas, and run away with by a whale, years afterwards slain off the Cape of Blanco. The original iron entered nigh the tail, and, like a restless needle sojourning in the body of a man, travelled full forty feet, and at last was found imbedded in the hump.

Crossing this dusky entry, and on through yon low-arched way – cut through what in old times must have been a great central chimney with fireplaces all round – you enter the public room. A still duskier place is this, with such low ponderous beams above, and such old wrinkled planks beneath, that you would almost fancy you trod some old craft's cockpits, especially of such a howling night, when this corner-anchored old ark rocked so furiously. On one side stood a long, low, shelf-like table covered with cracked glass cases, filled with dusty rarities gathered from this wide world's remotest nooks. Projecting from the further angle of the room stands a dark-looking den – the bar – a rude attempt at a right whale's head. Be that how it may, there stands the vast arched bone of the whale's jaw, so wide, a coach might almost drive beneath it. Within are shabby shelves, ranged round with old decanters, bottles, flasks; and in those jaws of swift destruction, like another cursed Jonah (by which name indeed they called him), bustles a little withered old man, who, for their money, dearly sells the sailors deliriums and death.

Abominable are the tumblers into which he pours his poison. Though true cylinders without – within, the villanous green goggling glasses deceitfully tapered downwards to a cheating bottom. Parallel meridians rudely pecked into the glass, surround these footpads' goblets. Fill to **this** mark, and your charge is but a penny; to **this** a penny more; and so on to the full glass – the Cape Horn measure, which you may gulp down for a shilling.

Upon entering the place I found a number of young seamen gathered about a table, examining by a dim light divers specimens of **skrimshander**. I sought the landlord, and telling him I desired to be accommodated with a room, received for answer that his house was full – not a bed unoccupied. “But avast,” he added, tapping his forehead, “you haint no objections to sharing a harpooneer’s blanket, have ye? I s’pose you are goin’ a-whalin’, so you’d better get used to that sort of thing.”

I told him that I never liked to sleep two in a bed; that if I should ever do so, it would depend upon who the harpooneer might be, and that if he (the landlord) really had no other place for me, and the harpooneer was not decidedly objectionable, why rather than wander further about a strange town on so bitter a night, I would put up with the half of any decent man’s blanket.

“I thought so. All right; take a seat. Supper? – you want supper? Supper’ll be ready directly.”

I sat down on an old wooden settle, carved all over like a bench on the Battery.

At one end a ruminating tar was still further adorning it with his jack-knife, stooping over and diligently working away at the space between his legs. He was trying his hand at a ship under full sail, but he didn't make much headway, I thought.

At last some four or five of us were summoned to our meal in an adjoining room. It was cold as Iceland – no fire at all – the landlord said he couldn't afford it. Nothing but two dismal tallow candles, each in a winding sheet. We were fain to button up our monkey jackets, and hold to our lips cups of scalding tea with our half frozen fingers. But the fare was of the most substantial kind – not only meat and potatoes, but dumplings; good heavens! dumplings for supper! One young fellow in a green box coat, addressed himself to these dumplings in a most direful manner.

"My boy," said the landlord, "you'll have the nightmare to a dead sartainty."

"Landlord," I whispered, "that aint the

harpooneer is it?"

"Oh, no," said he, looking a sort of diabolically funny, "the harpooneer is a dark complexioned chap. He never eats dumplings, he don't – he eats nothing but steaks, and he likes 'em rare."

"The devil he does," says I. "Where is that harpooneer? Is he here?"

"He'll be here afore long," was the answer.

I could not help it, but I began to feel suspicious of this "dark complexioned" harpooneer. At any rate, I made up my mind that if it so turned out that we should sleep together, he must undress and get into bed before I did.

Supper over, the company went back to the bar-room, when, knowing not what else to do with myself, I resolved to spend the rest of the evening as a looker on.

Presently a rioting noise was heard without. Starting up, the landlord cried, "That's the Grampus's crew. I seed her reported in the offing this morning; a three years' voyage, and a full ship. Hurrah, boys; now we'll have the latest news from the Feegees."

A tramping of sea boots was heard in the entry; the door was flung open, and in rolled a wild set of mariners enough. Enveloped in their shaggy watch coats, and with their heads muffled in woollen comforters, all bedarned and ragged, and their beards stiff with icicles, they seemed an eruption of bears from Labrador. They had just landed from their boat, and this was the first house they entered. No wonder, then, that they made a straight wake for the whale's mouth – the bar – when the wrinkled little old Jonah, there officiating, soon poured them out brimmers all round. One complained of a bad cold in his head, upon which Jonah mixed him a pitch-like potion of gin and molasses, which he swore was a sovereign cure for all colds and catarrhs whatsoever, never mind of how long standing, or whether caught off the coast of Labrador, or on the weather side of an ice-island.

The liquor soon mounted into their heads, as it generally does even with the arrantest topers newly landed from sea, and they began capering about most obstreperously.

I observed, however, that one of them held somewhat aloof, and though he seemed desirous not to spoil the hilarity of his shipmates by his own sober face, yet upon the whole he refrained from making as much noise as the rest. This man interested me at once; and since the sea-gods had ordained that he should soon become my shipmate (though but a sleeping-partner one, so far as this narrative is concerned), I will here venture upon a little description of him. He stood full six feet in height, with noble shoulders, and a chest like a coffer-dam. I have seldom seen such brawn in a man. His face was deeply brown and burnt, making his white teeth dazzling by the contrast; while in the deep shadows of his eyes floated some reminiscences that did not seem to give him much joy. His voice at once announced that he was a Southerner, and from his fine stature, I thought he must be one of those tall mountaineers from the Alleghanian Ridge in Virginia. When the revelry of his companions had mounted to its height, this man slipped away unobserved, and I saw no more of him till he became my comrade on the sea. In a few minutes, however, he was missed by his shipmates, and being, it seems, for some reason a huge favourite with them, they raised a cry of “Bulkington! Bulkington! where’s Bulkington?” and darted out of the house in pursuit of him.

It was now about nine o’clock, and the room seeming almost supernaturally quiet after these orgies, I began to congratulate myself upon a little plan that had occurred to me just previous to the entrance of the seamen.

No man prefers to sleep two in a bed. In fact, you would a good deal rather not sleep with your own brother. I don’t know how it is, but people like to be private when they are sleeping. And when it comes to sleeping with an unknown stranger, in a strange inn, in a strange town, and that stranger a harpooneer, then your objections indefinitely multiply. Nor was there any earthly reason why I as a sailor should sleep two in a bed, more than anybody else; for sailors no more sleep two in a bed at sea, than bachelor Kings do ashore. To be sure they all sleep together in one apartment, but you have your own hammock, and cover yourself with your own blanket, and sleep in your own skin.

The more I pondered over this harpooneer, the more I abominated the thought of sleeping with him. It was fair to presume that being a harpooneer, his linen or woollen, as the case might be, would not be of the tidiest, certainly none of the finest. I began to twitch all over. Besides, it was getting late, and my decent harpooneer ought to be home and going bedwards. Suppose now, he should tumble in upon me at midnight – how could I tell from what vile hole he had been coming?

"Landlord! I've changed my mind about that harpooneer. – I shan't sleep with him. I'll try the bench here."

"Just as you please; I'm sorry I can't spare ye a tablecloth for a mattress, and it's a plaguy rough board here" – feeling of the knots and notches. "But wait a bit, Skrimshander; I've got a carpenter's plane there in the bar – wait, I say, and I'll make ye snug enough." So saying he procured the plane; and with his old silk handkerchief first dusting the bench, vigorously set to planing away at my bed, the while grinning like an ape. The shavings flew right and left; till at last the plane-iron came bump against an indestructible knot. The landlord was near spraining his wrist, and I told him for heaven's sake to quit – the bed was soft enough to suit me, and I did not know how all the planing in the world could make eider down of a pine plank. So gathering up the shavings with another grin, and throwing them into the great stove in the middle of the room, he went about his business, and left me in a brown study.

I now took the measure of the bench, and found that it was a foot too short; but that could be mended with a chair. But it was a foot too narrow, and the other bench in the room was about four inches higher than the planed one – so there was no yoking them. I then placed the first bench lengthwise along the only clear space against the wall, leaving a little interval between, for my back to settle down in. But I soon found that there came such a draught of cold air over me from under the sill of the window, that this plan would never do at all, especially as another current from the rickety door met the one from the window, and both together formed a series of small whirlwinds in the immediate vicinity of the spot where I had thought to spend the night.

The devil fetch that harpooneer, thought

I, but stop, couldn't I steal a march on him – bolt his door inside, and jump into his bed, not to be wakened by the most violent knockings? It seemed no bad idea; but upon second thoughts I dismissed it. For who could tell but what the next morning, so soon as I popped out of the room, the harpooneer might be standing in the entry, all ready to knock me down!

Still, looking round me again, and seeing no possible chance of spending a sufferable night unless in some other person's bed, I began to think that after all I might be cherishing unwarrantable prejudices against this unknown harpooneer. Thinks I, I'll wait awhile; he must be dropping in before long. I'll have a good look at him then, and perhaps we may become jolly good bedfellows after all – there's no telling.

But though the other boarders kept coming in by ones, twos, and threes, and going to bed, yet no sign of my harpooneer.

"Landlord!" said I, "what sort of a chap is

he – does he always keep such late hours?" It was now hard upon twelve o'clock.

The landlord chuckled again with his lean chuckle, and seemed to be mightily tickled at something beyond my comprehension. "No," he answered, "generally he's an early bird – airley to bed and airley to rise – yes, he's the bird what catches the worm. But to-night he went out a peddling, you see, and I don't see what on airth keeps him so late, unless, may be, he can't sell his head."

"Can't sell his head? – What sort of a bamboozingly story is this you are telling me?" getting into a towering rage. "Do you pretend to say, landlord, that this harpooneer is actually engaged this blessed Saturday night, or rather Sunday morning, in peddling his head around this town?"

"That's precisely it," said the landlord, "and I told him he couldn't sell it here, the market's overstocked."

"With what?" shouted I.

"With heads to be sure; ain't there too many heads in the world?"

"I tell you what it is, landlord," said I quite calmly, "you'd better stop spinning that yarn to me – I'm not green."

"May be not," taking out a stick and whittling a toothpick, "but I rayther guess you'll be done **brown** if that ere harpooneer hears you a slanderin' his head."

"I'll break it for him," said I, now flying into a passion again at this unaccountable farrago of the landlord's.

"It's broke a'ready," said he.

"Broke," said I – "**broke**, do you mean?"

"Sartain, and that's the very reason he can't sell it, I guess."

"Landlord," said I, going up to him as cool as Mt. Hecla in a snow-storm – "landlord, stop whittling. You and I must understand one another, and that too without delay. I come to your house and want a bed; you tell me you can only give me half a one; that the other half belongs to a certain harpooneer.

And about this harpooneer, whom I have not yet seen, you persist in telling me the most mystifying and exasperating stories tending to beget in me an uncomfortable feeling towards the man whom you design for my bedfellow – a sort of connexion, landlord, which is an intimate and confidential one in the highest degree. I now demand of you to speak out and tell me who and what this harpooneer is, and whether I shall be in all respects safe to spend the night with him. And in the first place, you will be so good as to unsay that story about selling his head, which if true I take to be good evidence that this harpooneer is stark mad, and I've no idea of sleeping with a madman; and you, sir, **you** I mean, landlord, **you**, sir, by trying to induce me to do so knowingly, would thereby render yourself liable to a criminal prosecution."

"Wall," said the landlord, fetching a long breath, "that's a purty long sarmon for a chap that rips a little now and then. But be easy, be easy, this here harpooneer I have been tellin' you of has just arrived from the south seas, where he bought up a lot of 'balmed New Zealand heads (great curios, you know), and he's sold all on 'em but one, and that one he's trying to sell to-night, cause to-morrow's Sunday, and it would not do to be sellin' human heads about the streets when folks is goin' to churches. He wanted to, last Sunday, but I stopped him just as he was goin' out of the door with four heads strung on a string, for all the airth like a string of inions."

This account cleared up the otherwise unaccountable mystery, and showed that the landlord, after all, had had no idea of fooling me – but at the same time what could I think of a harpooneer who stayed out of a Saturday night clean into the holy Sabbath, engaged in such a cannibal business as selling the heads of dead idolators?

"Depend upon it, landlord, that harpooneer is a dangerous man."

"He pays reg'lar," was the rejoinder. "But come, it's getting dreadful late, you had better be turning flukes – it's a nice bed; Sal and me slept in that ere bed the night we were spliced. There's plenty of room for two to kick about in that bed; it's an almighty big bed that. Why, afore we give it up, Sal used to put our Sam and little Johnny in the foot of it. But I got a dreaming and sprawling about one night, and somehow, Sam got pitched on the floor, and came near breaking his arm. Arter that, Sal said it wouldn't do. Come along here, I'll give ye a glim in a jiffy;" and so saying he lighted a candle and held it towards me, offering to lead the way. But I stood irresolute; when looking at a clock in the corner, he exclaimed "I vum it's Sunday – you won't see that harpooneer to-night; he's come to anchor somewhere – come along then; **do** come; **won't** ye come?"

I considered the matter a moment, and then up stairs we went, and I was ushered into a small room, cold as a clam, and furnished, sure enough, with a prodigious bed, almost big enough indeed for any four harpooneers to sleep abreast.

"There," said the landlord, placing the candle on a crazy old sea chest that did double duty as a wash-stand and centre table; "there, make yourself comfortable now, and good night to ye." I turned round from eyeing the bed, but he had disappeared.

Folding back the counterpane, I stooped over the bed. Though none of the most elegant, it yet stood the scrutiny tolerably well. I then glanced round the room; and besides the bedstead and centre table, could see no other furniture belonging to the place, but a rude shelf, the four walls, and a papered fireboard representing a man striking a whale. Of things not properly belonging to the room, there was a hammock lashed up, and thrown upon the floor in one corner; also a large seaman's bag, containing the harpooneer's wardrobe, no doubt in lieu of a land trunk. Likewise, there was a parcel of outlandish bone fish hooks on the shelf over the fire-place, and a tall harpoon standing at the head of the bed.

But what is this on the chest? I took it up, and held it close to the light, and felt it, and smelt it, and tried every way possible to arrive at some satisfactory conclusion concerning it. I can compare it to nothing but a large door mat, ornamented at the edges with little tinkling tags something like the stained porcupine quills round an Indian moccasin. There was a hole or slit in the middle of this mat, as you see the same in South American ponchos. But could it be possible that any sober harpooneer would get into a door mat, and parade the streets of any Christian town in that sort of guise? I put it on, to try it, and it weighed me down like a hamper, being uncommonly shaggy and thick, and I thought a little damp, as though this mysterious harpooneer had been wearing it of a rainy day. I went up in it to a bit of glass stuck against the wall, and I never saw such a sight in my life. I tore myself out of it in such a hurry that I gave myself a kink in the neck.

I sat down on the side of the bed, and commenced thinking about this head-peddling harpooneer, and his door mat. After thinking some time on the bed-side, I got up and took off my monkey jacket, and then stood in the middle of the room thinking. I then took off my coat, and thought a little more in my shirt sleeves. But beginning to feel very cold now, half undressed as I was, and remembering what the landlord said about the harpooneer's not coming home at all that night, it being so very late, I made no more ado, but jumped out of my pantaloons and boots, and then blowing out the light tumbled into bed, and commended myself to the care of heaven.

Whether that mattress was stuffed with corn-cobs or broken crockery, there is no telling, but I rolled about a good deal, and could not sleep for a long time. At last I slid off into a light doze, and had pretty nearly made a good offing towards the land of Nod, when I heard a heavy footfall in the passage, and saw a glimmer of light come into the room from under the door.

Lord save me, thinks I, that must be the harpooneer, the infernal head-peddler. But I lay perfectly still, and resolved not to say a word till spoken to. Holding a light in one hand, and that identical New Zealand head in the other, the stranger entered the room, and without looking towards the bed, placed his candle a good way off from me on the floor in one corner, and then began working away at the knotted cords of the large bag I before spoke of as being in the room. I was all eagerness to see his face, but he kept it averted for some time while employed in unlacing the bag's mouth. This accomplished, however, he turned round – when, good heavens! what a sight! Such a face! It was of a dark, purplish, yellow colour, here and there stuck over with large blackish looking squares. Yes, it's just as I thought, he's a terrible bedfellow; he's been in a fight, got dreadfully cut, and here he is, just from the surgeon. But at that moment he chanced to turn his face so towards the light, that I plainly saw they could not be sticking-plasters at all, those black squares on his cheeks. They were stains of some sort or other. At first I knew not what to make of this; but soon an inkling of the truth occurred to me. I remembered a story of a white man – a whaleman too – who, falling among the cannibals, had been tattooed by them. I concluded that this harpooneer, in the course of his distant voyages, must have met with a similar adventure. And what is it, thought I, after all! It's only his outside; a man can be honest in any sort of skin. But then, what to make of his unearthly complexion, that part of it, I mean, lying round about, and completely independent of the squares of tattooing. To be sure, it might be nothing but a good coat of tropical tanning; but I never heard of a hot sun's tanning a white man into a purplish yellow one. However, I had never been in the South Seas; and perhaps the sun there produced these extraordinary effects upon the skin. Now, while all these ideas were passing through me like lightning, this harpooneer never noticed me at all. But, after some difficulty having opened his bag, he commenced fumbling in it, and presently pulled out a sort of tomahawk, and a seal-skin wallet with the hair on. Placing these on the old chest in the middle of the room, he then took the New Zealand head – a ghastly thing enough – and crammed it down into the bag. He now took off his hat – a new beaver hat – when I came nigh singing out with fresh surprise. There was no hair on his head – none to speak of at least – nothing but a small scalp-knot twisted up on his forehead. His bald purplish head now looked for all the world like a mildewed skull. Had not the stranger stood between me and the door, I would have bolted out of it quicker than ever I bolted a dinner.

Even as it was, I thought something of slipping out of the window, but it was the second floor back. I am no coward, but what to make of this head-peddling purple rascal altogether passed my comprehension. Ignorance is the parent of fear, and being completely nonplussed and confounded about the stranger, I confess I was now as much afraid of him as if it was the devil himself who had thus broken into my room at the dead of night. In fact, I was so afraid of him that I was not game enough just then to address him, and demand a satisfactory answer concerning what seemed inexplicable in him.

Meanwhile, he continued the business of undressing, and at last showed his chest and arms. As I live, these covered parts of him were checkered with the same squares as his face; his back, too, was all over the same dark squares; he seemed to have been in a Thirty Years' War, and just escaped from it with a sticking-plaster shirt. Still more, his very legs were marked, as if a parcel of dark green frogs were running up the trunks of young palms. It was now quite plain that he must be some abominable savage or other shipped aboard of a whaleman in the South Seas, and so landed in this Christian country. I quaked to think of it. A peddler of heads too – perhaps the heads of his own brothers. He might take a fancy to mine – heavens! look at that tomahawk!

But there was no time for shuddering, for now the savage went about something that completely fascinated my attention, and convinced me that he must indeed be a heathen. Going to his heavy grego, or wrapall, or dreadnaught, which he had previously hung on a chair, he fumbled in the pockets, and produced at length a curious little deformed image with a hunch on its back, and exactly the colour of a three days' old Congo baby. Remembering the embalmed head, at first I almost thought that this black manikin was a real baby preserved in some similar manner. But seeing that it was not at all limber, and that it glistened a good deal like polished ebony, I concluded that it must be nothing but a wooden idol, which indeed it proved to be. For now the savage goes up to the empty fire-place, and removing the papered fire-board, sets up this little hunch-backed image, like a tenpin, between the andirons. The chimney jambs and all the bricks inside were very sooty, so that I thought this fire-place made a very appropriate little shrine or chapel for his Congo idol.

I now screwed my eyes hard towards the half hidden image, feeling but ill at ease meantime – to see what was next to follow. First he takes about a double handful of shavings out of his grego pocket, and places them carefully before the idol; then laying a bit of ship biscuit on top and applying the flame from the lamp, he kindled the shavings into a sacrificial blaze. Presently, after many hasty snatches into the fire, and still hastier withdrawals of his fingers (whereby he seemed to be scorching them badly), he at last succeeded in drawing out the biscuit; then blowing off the heat and ashes a little, he made a polite offer of it to the little negro. But the little devil did not seem to fancy such dry sort of fare at all; he never moved his lips. All these strange antics were accompanied by still stranger guttural noises from the devotee, who seemed to be praying in a sing-song or else singing some pagan psalmody or other, during which his face twitched about in the most unnatural manner. At last extinguishing the fire, he took the idol up very unceremoniously, and bagged it again in his grego pocket as carelessly as if he were a sportsman bagging a dead woodcock.

All these queer proceedings increased my

uncomfortableness, and seeing him now exhibiting strong symptoms of concluding his business operations, and jumping into bed with me, I thought it was high time, now or never, before the light was put out, to break the spell in which I had so long been bound.

But the interval I spent in deliberating what to say, was a fatal one. Taking up his tomahawk from the table, he examined the head of it for an instant, and then holding it to the light, with his mouth at the handle, he puffed out great clouds of tobacco smoke. The next moment the light was extinguished, and this wild cannibal, tomahawk between his teeth, sprang into bed with me. I sang out, I could not help it now; and giving a sudden grunt of astonishment he began feeling me.

Stammering out something, I knew not what, I rolled away from him against the wall, and then conjured him, whoever or whatever he might be, to keep quiet, and let me get up and light the lamp again. But his guttural responses satisfied me at once that he but ill comprehended my meaning.

"Who-e debel you?" – he at last said – "you no speak-e, dam-me, I kill-e." And so saying the lighted tomahawk began flourishing about me in the dark.

"Landlord, for God's sake, Peter Coffin!" shouted I. "Landlord! Watch! Coffin! Angels! save me!"

"Speak-e! tell-ee me who-ee be, or dam-me, I kill-e!" again growled the cannibal, while his horrid flourishings of the tomahawk scattered the hot tobacco ashes about me till I thought my linen would get on fire. But thank heaven, at that moment the landlord came into the room light in hand, and leaping from the bed I ran up to him.

"Don't be afraid now," said he, grinning again, "Queequeg here wouldn't harm a hair of your head."

"Stop your grinning," shouted I, "and why didn't you tell me that that infernal harpooneer was a cannibal?"

"I thought ye know'd it; – didn't I tell ye, he was a peddlin' heads around town? – but turn flukes again and go to sleep. Queequeg, look here – you sabbee me, I sabbee – you this man sleepe you – you sabbee?"

"Me sabbee plenty" – grunted Queequeg, puffing away at his pipe and sitting up in bed.

"You gettee in," he added, motioning to me with his tomahawk, and throwing the clothes to one side. He really did this in not only a civil but a really kind and charitable way. I stood looking at him a moment. For all his tattooings he was on the whole a clean, comely looking cannibal. What's all this fuss I have been making about, thought I to myself – the man's a human being just as I am: he has just as much reason to fear me, as I have to be afraid of him. Better sleep with a sober cannibal than a drunken Christian.

"Landlord," said I, "tell him to stash his tomahawk there, or pipe, or whatever you call it; tell him to stop smoking, in short, and I will turn in with him. But I don't fancy having a man smoking in bed with me. It's dangerous. Besides, I ain't insured."

This being told to Queequeg, he at once complied, and again politely motioned me to get into bed – rolling over to one side as much as to say – "I won't touch a leg of ye."

"Good night, landlord," said I, "you may go."

I turned in, and never slept better in my life.

CHAPTER FOUR

The Counterpane

UPON WAKING next morning about daylight, I found Queequeg's arm thrown over me in the most loving and affectionate manner. You had almost thought I had been his wife. The counterpane was of patchwork, full of odd little parti-coloured squares and triangles; and this arm of his tattooed all over with an interminable Cretan labyrinth of a figure, no two parts of which were of one precise shade – owing I suppose to his keeping his arm at sea unmethodically in sun and shade, his shirt sleeves irregularly rolled up at various times – this same arm of his, I say, looked for all the world like a strip of that same patchwork quilt. Indeed, partly lying on it as the arm did when I first awoke, I could hardly tell it from the quilt, they so blended their hues together; and it was only by the sense of weight and pressure that I could tell that Queequeg was hugging me.

My sensations were strange. Let me try to explain them. When I was a child, I well remember a somewhat similar circumstance that befell me; whether it was a reality or a dream, I never could entirely settle. The circumstance was this. I had been cutting up some caper or other – I think it was trying to crawl up the chimney, as I had seen a little sweep do a few days previous; and my stepmother who, somehow or other, was all the time whipping me, or sending me to bed supperless, – my mother dragged me by the legs out of the chimney and packed me off to bed, though it was only two o'clock in the afternoon of the 21st June, the longest day in the year in our hemisphere. I felt dreadfully. But there was no help for it, so up stairs I went to my little room in the third floor, undressed myself as slowly as possible so as to kill time, and with a bitter sigh got between the sheets.

I lay there dismally calculating that sixteen entire hours must elapse before I could hope for a resurrection. Sixteen hours in bed! the small of my back ached to think of it. And it was so light too; the sun shining in at the window, and a great rattling of coaches in the streets, and the sound of gay voices all over the house. I felt worse and worse – at last I got up, dressed, and softly going down in my stockinged feet, sought out my stepmother, and suddenly threw myself at her feet, beseeching her as a particular favour to give me a good slippering for my misbehaviour;

anything indeed but condemning me to lie abed such an unendurable length of time. But she was the best and most conscientious of stepmothers, and back I had to go to my room. For several hours I lay there broad awake, feeling a great deal worse than I have ever done since, even from the greatest subsequent misfortunes. At last I must have fallen into a troubled nightmare of a doze; and slowly waking from it – half steeped in dreams – I opened my eyes, and the before sun-lit room was now wrapped in outer darkness. Instantly I felt a shock running through all my frame; nothing was to be seen, and nothing was to be heard; but a supernatural hand seemed placed in mine. My arm hung over the counterpane, and the nameless, unimaginable, silent form or phantom, to which the hand belonged, seemed closely seated by my bed-side. For what seemed ages piled on ages, I lay there, frozen with the most awful fears, not daring to drag away my hand; yet ever thinking that if I could but stir it one single inch, the horrid spell would be broken. I knew not how this consciousness at last glided away from me; but waking in the morning, I shudderingly remembered it all, and for days and weeks and months afterwards I lost myself in confounding attempts to explain the mystery. Nay, to this very hour, I often puzzle myself with it.

Now, take away the awful fear, and my sensations at feeling the supernatural hand in mine were very similar, in their strangeness, to those which I experienced on waking up and seeing Queequeg's pagan arm thrown round me. But at length all the past night's events soberly recurred, one by one, in fixed reality, and then I lay only alive to the comical predicament. For though I tried to move his arm – unlock his bridegroom clasp – yet, sleeping as he was, he still hugged me tightly, as though naught but death should part us twain. I now strove to rouse him – "Queequeg!" – but his only answer was a snore. I then rolled over, my neck feeling as if it were in a horse-collar; and suddenly felt a slight scratch. Throwing aside the counterpane, there lay the tomahawk sleeping by the savage's side, as if it were a hatchet-faced baby. A pretty pickle, truly, thought I; abed here in a strange house in the broad day, with a cannibal and a tomahawk! "Queequeg! – in the name of goodness, Queequeg, wake!" At length, by dint of much wriggling, and loud and incessant expostulations upon the unbecomingness of his hugging a fellow male in that matrimonial sort of style, I succeeded in extracting a grunt; and presently, he drew back his arm, shook himself all over like a Newfoundland dog just from the water, and sat up in bed, stiff as a pike-staff, looking at me, and rubbing his eyes as if he did not altogether remember how I came to be there, though a dim consciousness of knowing something about me seemed slowly dawning over him. Meanwhile, I lay quietly eyeing him, having no serious misgivings now, and bent upon narrowly observing so curious a creature. When, at last, his mind seemed made up touching the character of his bedfellow, and he became, as it were, reconciled to the fact; he jumped out upon the floor, and by certain signs and sounds gave me to understand that, if it pleased me, he would dress first and then leave me to dress afterwards, leaving the whole apartment to myself. Thinks I, Queequeg, under the circumstances, this is a very civilized overture; but, the truth is, these savages have an innate sense of delicacy, say what you will; it is marvellous how essentially polite they are. I pay this particular compliment to Queequeg, because he treated me with so much civility and consideration, while I was guilty of great rudeness; staring at him from the bed, and watching all his toilette motions; for the time my curiosity getting the better of my breeding. Nevertheless, a man like Queequeg you don't see every day, he and his ways were well worth unusual regarding.

He commenced dressing at top by donning

his beaver hat, a very tall one, by the by, and then – still minus his trowsers – he hunted up his boots. What under the heavens he did it for, I cannot tell, but his next movement was to crush himself – boots in hand, and hat on – under the bed; when, from sundry violent gaspings and strainings, I inferred he was hard at work booting himself; though by no law of propriety that I ever heard of, is any man required to be private when putting on his boots. But Queequeg, do you see, was a creature in the transition stage – neither caterpillar nor butterfly. He was just enough civilized to show off his outlandishness in the strangest possible manners. His education was not yet completed. He was an undergraduate. If he had not been a small degree civilized, he very probably would not have troubled himself with boots at all; but then, if he had not been still a savage, he never would have dreamt of getting under the bed to put them on. At last, he emerged with his hat very much dented and crushed down over his eyes, and began creaking and limping about the room, as if, not being much accustomed to boots, his pair of damp, wrinkled cowhide ones – probably not made to order either – rather pinched and tormented him at the first go off of a bitter cold morning.

Seeing, now, that there were no curtains to the window, and that the street being very narrow, the house opposite commanded a plain view into the room, and observing more and more the indecorous figure that Queequeg made, staving about with little else but his hat and boots on; I begged him as well as I could, to accelerate his toilet somewhat, and particularly to get into his pantaloons as soon as possible. He complied, and then proceeded to wash himself. At that time in the morning any Christian would have washed his face; but Queequeg, to my amazement, contented himself with restricting his ablutions to his chest, arms, and hands. He then donned his waistcoat, and taking up a piece of hard soap on the wash-stand centre table, dipped it into water and commenced lathering his face. I was watching to see where he kept his razor, when lo and behold, he takes the harpoon from the bed corner, slips out the long wooden stock, unsheathes the head, whets it a little on his boot, and striding up to the bit of mirror against the wall, begins a vigorous scraping, or rather harpooning of his cheeks. Thinks I, Queequeg, this is using Rogers's best cutlery with a vengeance. Afterwards I wondered the less at this operation when I came to know of what fine steel the head of a harpoon is made, and how exceedingly sharp the long straight edges are always kept.

The rest of his toilet was soon achieved, and he proudly marched out of the room, wrapped up in his great pilot monkey jacket, and sporting his harpoon like a marshal's baton.

CHAPTER FIVE

Breakfast

I QUICKLY FOLLOWED suit, and descending into the bar-room accosted the grinning landlord very pleasantly. I cherished no malice towards him, though he had been skylarking with me not a little in the matter of my bedfellow.

However, a good laugh is a mighty good thing, and rather too scarce a good thing; the more's the pity. So, if any one man, in his own proper person, afford stuff for a good joke to anybody, let him not be backward, but let him cheerfully allow himself to spend and be spent in that way. And the man that has anything bountifully laughable about him, be sure there is more in that man than you perhaps think for.

The bar-room was now full of the boarders who had been dropping in the night previous, and whom I had not as yet had a good look at. They were nearly all whalemen; chief mates, and second mates, and third mates, and sea carpenters, and sea coopers, and sea blacksmiths, and harpooneers, and ship keepers; a brown and brawny company, with bosky beards; an unshorn, shaggy set, all wearing monkey jackets for morning gowns.

You could pretty plainly tell how long each one had been ashore. This young fellow's healthy cheek is like a sun-toasted pear in hue, and would seem to smell almost as musky; he cannot have been three days landed from his Indian voyage. That man next him looks a few shades lighter; you might say a touch of satin wood is in him. In the complexion of a third still lingers a tropic tawn, but slightly bleached withal; **he** doubtless has tarried whole weeks ashore. But who could show a cheek like Queequeg? which, barred with various tints, seemed like the Andes' western slope, to show forth in one array, contrasting climates, zone by zone.

"Grub, ho!" now cried the landlord, flinging open a door, and in we went to breakfast.

They say that men who have seen the world, thereby become quite at ease in manner, quite self-possessed in company. Not always, though: Ledyard, the great New England traveller, and Mungo Park, the Scotch one; of all men, they possessed the least assurance in the parlor. But perhaps the mere crossing of Siberia in a sledge drawn by dogs as Ledyard did, or the taking a long solitary walk on an empty stomach, in the negro heart of Africa, which was the sum of poor Mungo's performances – this kind of travel, I say, may not be the very best mode of attaining a high social polish. Still, for the most part, that sort of thing is to be had anywhere.

These reflections just here are occasioned by the circumstance that after we were all seated at the table, and I was preparing to hear some good stories about whaling; to my no small surprise, nearly every man maintained a profound silence. And not only that, but they looked embarrassed. Yes, here were a set of sea-dogs, many of whom without the slightest bashfulness had boarded great whales on the high seas – entire strangers to them – and duelled them dead without winking; and yet, here they sat at a social breakfast table – all of the same calling, all of kindred tastes – looking round as sheepishly at each other as though they had never been out of sight of some sheepfold among the Green Mountains. A curious sight; these bashful bears, these timid warrior whalemen!

But as for Queequeg – why, Queequeg sat there among them – at the head of the table, too, it so chanced; as cool as an icicle. To be sure I cannot say much for his breeding. His greatest admirer could not have cordially justified his bringing his harpoon into breakfast with him, and using it there without ceremony; reaching over the table with it, to the imminent jeopardy of many heads, and grappling the beefsteaks towards him. But **that** was certainly very coolly done by him, and every one knows that in most people's estimation, to do anything coolly is to do it genteelly.

We will not speak of all Queequeg's peculiarities here; how he eschewed coffee and hot rolls, and applied his undivided attention to beefsteaks, done rare. Enough, that when breakfast was over he withdrew like the rest into the public room, lighted his tomahawk-pipe, and was sitting there quietly digesting and smoking with his inseparable hat on, when I sallied out for a stroll.

CHAPTER SIX

The Street

IF I HAD BEEN astonished at first catching a glimpse of so outlandish an individual as Queequeg circulating among the polite society of a civilized town, that astonishment soon departed upon taking my first daylight stroll through the streets of New Bedford.

In thoroughfares nigh the docks, any considerable seaport will frequently offer to view the queerest looking nondescripts from foreign parts. Even in Broadway and

Chestnut streets, Mediterranean mariners will sometimes jostle the affrighted ladies. Regent Street is not unknown to Lascars and Malays; and at Bombay, in the Apollo Green, live Yankees have often scared the natives. But New Bedford beats all Water Street and Wapping. In these last-mentioned haunts you see only sailors; but in New Bedford, actual cannibals stand chatting at street corners; savages outright; many of whom yet carry on their bones unholy flesh. It makes a stranger stare.

But, besides the Feegeeans, Tongatobooarrs, Erromanggoans, Pannangians, and Brighggians, and, besides the wild specimens of the whaling-craft which unheeded reel about the streets, you will see other sights still more curious, certainly more comical. There weekly arrive in this town scores of green Vermonters and New Hampshire men, all athirst for gain and glory in the fishery. They are mostly young, of stalwart frames; fellows who have felled forests, and now seek to drop the axe and snatch the whale-lance. Many are as green as the Green Mountains whence they came. In some things you would think them but a few hours old. Look there! that chap strutting round the corner. He wears a beaver hat and swallow-tailed coat, girdled with a sailor-belt and sheath-knife. Here comes another with a sou'-wester and a bombazine cloak.

No town-bred dandy will compare with a country-bred one – I mean a downright bumpkin dandy – a fellow that, in the dog-days, will mow his two acres in buckskin gloves for fear of tanning his hands. Now when a country dandy like this takes it into his head to make a distinguished reputation, and joins the great whale-fishery, you should see the comical things he does upon reaching the seaport. In bespeaking his sea-outfit, he orders bell-buttons to his waistcoats; straps to his canvas trowsers. Ah, poor Hay-Seed! how bitterly will burst those straps in the first howling gale, when thou art driven, straps, buttons, and all, down the throat of the tempest.

But think not that this famous town has only harpooneers, cannibals, and bumpkins to show her visitors. Not at all. Still New Bedford is a queer place. Had it not been for us whalemen, that tract of land would this day perhaps have been in as howling condition as the coast of Labrador. As it is, parts of her back country are enough to frighten one, they look so bony. The town itself is perhaps the dearest place to live in, in all New England. It is a land of oil, true enough: but not like Canaan; a land, also, of corn and wine. The streets do not run with milk; nor in the spring-time do they pave them with fresh eggs. Yet, in spite of this, nowhere in all America will you find more patrician-like houses; parks and gardens more opulent, than in New Bedford. Whence came they? how planted upon this once scraggy scoria of a country?

Go and gaze upon the iron emblematical harpoons round yonder lofty mansion, and your question will be answered. Yes; all these brave houses and flowery gardens came from the Atlantic, Pacific, and Indian oceans. One and all, they were harpooned and dragged up hither from the bottom of the sea. Can Herr Alexander perform a feat like that?

In New Bedford, fathers, they say, give whales for dowers to their daughters, and portion off their nieces with a few porpoises a-piece. You must go to New Bedford to see a brilliant wedding; for, they say, they have reservoirs of oil in every house, and every night recklessly burn their lengths in spermaceti candles.

In summer time, the town is sweet to see; full of fine maples – long avenues of green and gold. And in August, high in air, the beautiful and bountiful horse-chestnuts, candelabra-wise, proffer the passer-by their tapering upright cones of congregated blossoms. So omnipotent is art; which in many a district of New Bedford has superinduced bright terraces of flowers upon the barren refuse rocks thrown aside at creation's final day.

And the women of New Bedford, they bloom like their own red roses. But roses only bloom in summer; whereas the fine carnation of their cheeks is perennial as sunlight in the seventh heavens. Elsewhere match that bloom of theirs, ye cannot, save in Salem, where they tell me the young girls breathe such musk, their sailor sweethearts smell them miles off shore, as though they were drawing nigh the odorous Moluccas instead of the Puritanic sands.

CHAPTER SEVEN

The Chapel

IN THIS SAME New Bedford there stands a Whaleman's Chapel, and few are the moody fishermen, shortly bound for the Indian Ocean or Pacific, who fail to make a Sunday visit to the spot. I am sure that I did not.

Returning from my first morning stroll, I again sallied out upon this special errand. The sky had changed from clear, sunny cold, to driving sleet and mist. Wrapping myself in my shaggy jacket of the cloth called bearskin, I fought my way against the stubborn storm. Entering, I found a small scattered congregation of sailors, and sailors' wives and widows. A muffled silence reigned, only broken at times by the shrieks of the storm. Each silent worshipper seemed purposely sitting apart from the other, as if each silent grief were insular and incommunicable. The chaplain had not yet arrived; and there these silent islands of men and women sat steadfastly eyeing several marble tablets, with black borders, masoned into the wall on either side the pulpit. Three of them ran something like the following, but I do not pretend to quote: –

SACRED TO THE MEMORY OF JOHN TALBOT, Who, at the age of eighteen, was lost overboard, Near the Isle of Desolation, off Patagonia, **November 1st**, 1836. THIS TABLET Is erected to his Memory BY HIS SISTER.

SACRED TO THE MEMORY OF ROBERT

LONG, WILLIS ELLERY, NATHAN COLEMAN, WALTER CANNY, SETH MACY, AND SAMUEL GLEIG, Forming one of the boats' crews OF THE SHIP ELIZA Who were towed out of sight by a Whale, On the Off-shore Ground in the PACIFIC, **December** 31**st**, 1839. THIS MARBLE Is here placed by their surviving SHIPMATES.

SACRED TO THE MEMORY OF The late CAPTAIN EZEKIEL HARDY, Who in the bows of his boat was killed by a Sperm Whale on the coast of Japan, **August** 3**d**, 1833. THIS TABLET Is erected to his Memory BY HIS WIDOW.

Shaking off the sleet from my ice-glazed hat and jacket, I seated myself near the door, and turning sideways was surprised to see Queequeg near me. Affected by the solemnity of the scene, there was a wondering gaze of incredulous curiosity in his countenance. This savage was the only person present who seemed to notice my entrance; because he was the only one who could not read, and, therefore, was not reading those frigid inscriptions on the wall. Whether any of the relatives of the seamen whose names appeared there were now among the congregation, I knew not; but so many are the unrecorded accidents in the fishery, and so plainly did several women present wear the countenance if not the trappings of some unceasing grief, that I feel sure that here before me were assembled those, in whose unhealing hearts the sight of those bleak tablets sympathetically caused the old wounds to bleed afresh.

Oh! ye whose dead lie buried beneath the green grass; who standing among flowers can say – here, **here** lies my beloved; ye know not the desolation that broods in bosoms like these. What bitter blanks in those black-bordered marbles which cover no ashes! What despair in those immovable inscriptions! What deadly voids and unbidden infidelities in the lines that seem to gnaw upon all Faith, and refuse resurrections to the beings who have placelessly perished without a grave. As well might those tablets stand in the cave of Elephanta as here.

In what census of living creatures, the dead of mankind are included; why it is that a universal proverb says of them, that they tell no tales, though containing more secrets than the Goodwin Sands; how it is that to his name who yesterday departed for the other world, we prefix so significant and infidel a word, and yet do not thus entitle him, if he but embarks for the remotest Indies of this living earth; why the Life Insurance Companies pay death-forfeitures upon immortals; in what eternal, unstirring paralysis, and deadly, hopeless trance, yet lies antique Adam who died sixty round centuries ago; how it is that we still refuse to be comforted for those who we nevertheless maintain are dwelling in unspeakable bliss; why all the living so strive to hush all the dead; wherefore but the rumor of a knocking in a tomb will terrify a whole city. All these things are not without their meanings.

But Faith, like a jackal, feeds among the tombs, and even from these dead doubts she gathers her most vital hope.

It needs scarcely to be told, with what feelings, on the eve of a Nantucket voyage, I regarded those marble tablets, and by the murky light of that darkened, doleful day read the fate of the whalemen who had gone before me. Yes, Ishmael, the same fate may be thine. But somehow I grew merry again. Delightful inducements to embark, fine chance for promotion, it seems – aye, a stove boat will make me an immortal by brevet. Yes, there is death in this business of whaling – a speechlessly quick chaotic bundling of a man into Eternity. But what then? Methinks we have hugely mistaken this matter of Life and Death. Methinks that what they call my shadow here on earth is my true substance. Methinks that in looking at things spiritual, we are too much like oysters observing the sun through the water, and thinking that thick water the thinnest of air. Methinks my body is but the lees of my better being. In fact take my body who will, take it I say, it is not me. And therefore three cheers for Nantucket; and come a stove boat and stove body when they will, for stave my soul, Jove himself cannot.

CHAPTER EIGHT

The Pulpit

I HAD NOT BEEN seated very long ere a man of a certain venerable robustness entered; immediately as the storm-pelted door flew back upon admitting him, a quick regardful eyeing of him by all the congregation, sufficiently attested that this fine old man was the chaplain. Yes, it was the famous Father Mapple, so called by the whalemen, among whom he was a very great favourite. He had been a sailor and a harpooneer in his youth, but for many years past had dedicated his life to the ministry. At the time I now write of, Father Mapple was in the hardy winter of a healthy old age; that sort of old age which seems merging into a second flowering youth, for among all the fissures of his wrinkles, there shone certain mild gleams of a newly developing bloom – the spring verdure peeping forth even beneath February's snow. No one having previously heard his history, could for the first time behold Father Mapple without the utmost interest, because there were certain engrafted clerical peculiarities about him, imputable to that adventurous maritime life he had led. When he entered I observed that he carried no umbrella, and certainly had not come in his carriage, for his tarpaulin hat ran down with melting sleet, and his great pilot cloth jacket seemed almost to drag him to the floor with the weight of the water it had absorbed. However, hat and coat and overshoes were one by one removed, and hung up in a little space in an adjacent corner; when, arrayed in a decent suit, he quietly approached the pulpit.

Like most old fashioned pulpits, it was a very lofty one, and since a regular stairs to such a height would, by its long angle with the floor, seriously contract the already small area of the chapel, the architect, it seemed, had acted upon the hint of Father Mapple, and finished the pulpit without a stairs, substituting a perpendicular side ladder, like those used in mounting a ship from a boat at sea. The wife of a whaling captain had provided the chapel with a handsome pair of red worsted man-ropes for this ladder, which, being itself nicely headed, and stained with a mahogany colour, the whole contrivance, considering what manner of chapel it was, seemed by no means in bad taste. Halting for an instant at the foot of the ladder, and with both hands grasping the ornamental knobs of the man-ropes, Father Mapple cast a look upwards, and then with a truly sailor-like but still reverential dexterity, hand over hand, mounted the steps as if ascending the main-top of his vessel.

The perpendicular parts of this side ladder, as is usually the case with swinging ones, were of cloth-covered rope, only the rounds were of wood, so that at every step there was a joint. At my first glimpse of the pulpit, it had not escaped me that however convenient for a ship, these joints in the present instance seemed unnecessary. For I was not prepared to see Father Mapple after gaining the height, slowly turn round, and stooping over the pulpit, deliberately drag up the ladder step by step, till the whole was deposited within, leaving him impregnable in his little Quebec.

I pondered some time without fully comprehending the reason for this. Father Mapple enjoyed such a wide reputation for sincerity and sanctity, that I could not suspect him of courting notoriety by any mere tricks of the stage. No, thought I, there must be some sober reason for this thing; furthermore, it must symbolize something unseen. Can it be, then, that by that act of physical isolation, he signifies his spiritual withdrawal for the time, from all outward worldly ties and connexions? Yes, for replenished with the meat and wine of the word, to the faithful man of God, this pulpit, I see, is a self-containing stronghold – a lofty Ehrenbreitstein, with a perennial well of water within the walls.

But the side ladder was not the only strange feature of the place, borrowed from the chaplain's former sea-farings. Between the marble cenotaphs on either hand of the pulpit, the wall which formed its back was adorned with a large painting representing a gallant ship beating against a terrible storm off a lee coast of black rocks and snowy breakers. But high above the flying scud and dark-rolling clouds, there floated a little isle of sunlight, from which beamed forth an angel's face; and this bright face shed a distinct spot of radiance upon the ship's tossed deck, something like that silver plate now inserted into the Victory's plank where Nelson fell. "Ah, noble ship," the angel seemed to say, "beat on, beat on, thou noble ship, and bear a hardy helm; for lo! the sun is breaking through; the clouds are rolling off – serenest azure is at hand."

Nor was the pulpit itself without a trace of the same sea-taste that had achieved the ladder and the picture. Its panelled front was in the likeness of a ship's bluff bows, and the Holy Bible rested on a projecting piece of scroll work, fashioned after a ship's fiddle-headed beak.

What could be more full of meaning? – for the pulpit is ever this earth's foremost part; all the rest comes in its rear; the pulpit leads the world. From thence it is the storm of God's quick wrath is first descried, and the bow must bear the earliest brunt. From thence it is the God of breezes fair or foul is first invoked for favourable winds. Yes, the world's a ship on its passage out, and not a voyage complete; and the pulpit is its prow.

CHAPTER NINE

The Sermon

FATHER MAPPLE ROSE, and in a mild voice of unassuming authority ordered the scattered people to condense. “Starboard gangway, there! side away to larboard – larboard gangway to starboard! Midships! midships!”

There was a low rumbling of heavy sea-boots among the benches, and a still slighter shuffling of women’s shoes, and all was quiet again, and every eye on the preacher.

He paused a little; then kneeling in the pulpit's bows, folded his large brown hands across his chest, uplifted his closed eyes, and offered a prayer so deeply devout that he seemed kneeling and praying at the bottom of the sea.

This ended, in prolonged solemn tones, like the continual tolling of a bell in a ship that is foundering at sea in a fog – in such tones he commenced reading the following hymn; but changing his manner towards the concluding stanzas, burst forth with a pealing exultation and joy –

"The ribs and terrors in the whale,
Arched over me a dismal gloom,
While all God's sun-lit waves rolled by,
And lift me deepening down to doom.
"I saw the opening maw of hell,
With endless pains and sorrows there;
Which none but they that feel can tell –
Oh, I was plunging to despair.

"In black distress, I called my God,
When I could scarce believe him mine,
He bowed his ear to my complaints –
No more the whale did me confine.
"With speed he flew to my relief,
As on a radiant dolphin borne;
Awful, yet bright, as lightning shone
The face of my Deliverer God.
"My song for ever shall record
That terrible, that joyful hour;
I give the glory to my God,
His all the mercy and the power."

Nearly all joined in singing this hymn, which swelled high above the howling of the storm. A brief pause ensued; the preacher slowly turned over the leaves of the Bible, and at last, folding his hand down upon the proper page, said: "Beloved shipmates, clinch the last verse of the first chapter of Jonah – 'And God had prepared a great fish to swallow up Jonah.'"

"Shipmates, this book, containing only

four chapters – four yarns – is one of the smallest strands in the mighty cable of the Scriptures. Yet what depths of the soul does Jonah's deep sealine sound! what a pregnant lesson to us is this prophet! What a noble thing is that canticle in the fish's belly! How billow-like and boisterously grand! We feel the floods surging over us; we sound with him to the kelpy bottom of the waters; sea-weed and all the slime of the sea is about us! But **what** is this lesson that the book of Jonah teaches? Shipmates, it is a two-stranded lesson; a lesson to us all as sinful men, and a lesson to me as a pilot of the living God. As sinful men, it is a lesson to us all, because it is a story of the sin, hard-heartedness, suddenly awakened fears, the swift punishment, repentance, prayers, and finally the deliverance and joy of Jonah. As with all sinners among men, the sin of this son of Amittai was in his wilful disobedience of the command of God – never mind now what that command was, or how conveyed –

which he found a hard command. But all the things that God would have us do are hard for us to do – remember that – and hence, he oftener commands us than endeavors to persuade. And if we obey God, we must disobey ourselves; and it is in this disobeying ourselves, wherein the hardness of obeying God consists.

"With this sin of disobedience in him, Jonah still further flouts at God, by seeking to flee from Him. He thinks that a ship made by men will carry him into countries where God does not reign, but only the Captains of this earth. He skulks about the wharves of Joppa, and seeks a ship that's bound for Tarshish. There lurks, perhaps, a hitherto unheeded meaning here. By all accounts Tarshish could have been no other city than the modern Cadiz. That's the opinion of learned men. And where is Cadiz, shipmates? Cadiz is in Spain; as far by water, from Joppa, as Jonah could possibly have sailed in those ancient days, when the Atlantic was an almost unknown sea. Because Joppa, the modern Jaffa, shipmates, is on the most easterly coast of the Mediterranean, the Syrian; and Tarshish or Cadiz more than two thousand miles to the westward from that, just outside the Straits of Gibraltar. See ye not then, shipmates, that Jonah sought to flee world-wide from God? Miserable man! Oh! most contemptible and worthy of all scorn; with slouched hat and guilty eye, skulking from his God; prowling among the shipping like a vile burglar hastening to cross the seas. So disordered, self-condemning is his look, that had there been policemen in those days, Jonah, on the mere suspicion of something wrong, had been arrested ere he touched a deck. How plainly he's a fugitive! no baggage, not a hat-box, valise, or carpet-bag, – no friends accompany him to the wharf with their adieux. At last, after much dodging search, he finds the Tarshish ship receiving the last items of her cargo; and as he steps on board to see its Captain in the cabin, all the sailors for the moment desist from hoisting in the goods, to mark the stranger's evil eye. Jonah sees this; but in vain he tries to look all ease and confidence; in vain essays his wretched smile. Strong intuitions of the man assure the mariners he can be no innocent. In their gamesome but still serious way, one whispers to the other – "Jack, he's robbed a widow;" or, "Joe, do you mark him; he's a bigamist;" or, "Harry lad, I guess he's the adulterer that broke jail in old Gomorrah, or belike, one of the missing murderers from Sodom." Another runs to read the bill that's stuck against the spile upon the wharf to which the ship is moored, offering five hundred gold coins for the apprehension of a parricide, and containing a description of his person. He reads, and looks from Jonah to the bill; while all his sympathetic shipmates now crowd round Jonah, prepared to lay their hands upon him. Frighted Jonah trembles, and summoning all his boldness to his face, only looks so much the more a coward. He will not confess himself suspected; but that itself is strong suspicion. So he makes the best of it; and when the sailors find him not to be the man that is advertised, they let him pass, and he descends into the cabin.

"'Who's there?' cries the Captain at his busy desk, hurriedly making out his papers for the Customs – 'Who's there?' Oh! how that harmless question mangles Jonah! For the instant he almost turns to flee again. But he rallies. 'I seek a passage in this ship to Tarshish; how soon sail ye, sir?' Thus far the busy Captain had not looked up to Jonah, though the man now stands before him; but no sooner does he hear that hollow voice, than he darts a scrutinizing glance. 'We sail with the next coming tide,' at last he slowly answered, still intently eyeing him. 'No sooner, sir?' – 'Soon enough for any honest man that goes a passenger.' Ha! Jonah, that's another stab. But he swiftly calls away the Captain from that scent. 'I'll sail with ye,' – he says, – 'the passage money how much is that? – I'll pay now.' For it is particularly written, shipmates, as if it were a thing not to be overlooked in this history, 'that he paid the fare thereof' ere the craft did sail. And taken with the context, this is full of meaning.

"Now Jonah's Captain, shipmates, was one whose discernment detects crime in any, but whose cupidity exposes it only in the penniless. In this world, shipmates, sin that pays its way can travel freely, and without a passport; whereas Virtue, if a pauper, is stopped at all frontiers. So Jonah's Captain prepares to test the length of Jonah's purse, ere he judge him openly. He charges him thrice the usual sum; and it's assented to. Then the Captain knows that Jonah is a fugitive; but at the same time resolves to help a flight that paves its rear with gold. Yet when Jonah fairly takes out his purse, prudent suspicions still molest the Captain.

He rings every coin to find a counterfeit. Not a forger, any way, he mutters; and Jonah is put down for his passage. 'Point out my state-room, Sir,' says Jonah now, 'I'm travel-weary; I need sleep.' 'Thou lookest like it,' says the Captain, 'there's thy room.' Jonah enters, and would lock the door, but the lock contains no key. Hearing him foolishly fumbling there, the Captain laughs lowly to himself, and mutters something about the doors of convicts' cells being never allowed to be locked within. All dressed and dusty as he is, Jonah throws himself into his berth, and finds the little state-room ceiling almost resting on his forehead. The air is close, and Jonah gasps. Then, in that contracted hole, sunk, too, beneath the ship's water-line, Jonah feels the heralding presentiment of that stifling hour, when the whale shall hold him in the smallest of his bowels' wards.

"Screwed at its axis against the side, a swinging lamp slightly oscillates in Jonah's room; and the ship, heeling over towards the wharf with the weight of the last bales received, the lamp, flame and all, though in slight motion, still maintains a permanent obliquity with reference to the room; though, in truth, infallibly straight itself, it but made obvious the false, lying levels among which it hung. The lamp alarms and frightens Jonah; as lying in his berth his tormented eyes roll round the place, and this thus far successful fugitive finds no refuge for his restless glance. But that contradiction in the lamp more and more appals him. The floor, the ceiling, and the side, are all awry. 'Oh! so my conscience hangs in me!' he groans, 'straight upwards, so it burns; but the chambers of my soul are all in crookedness!'

"Like one who after a night of drunken revelry hies to his bed, still reeling, but with conscience yet pricking him, as the plungings of the Roman race-horse but so much the more strike his steel tags into him; as one who in that miserable plight still turns and turns in giddy anguish, praying

God for annihilation until the fit be passed; and at last amid the whirl of woe he feels, a deep stupor steals over him, as over the man who bleeds to death, for conscience is the wound, and there's naught to staunch it; so, after sore wrestlings in his berth, Jonah's prodigy of ponderous misery drags him drowning down to sleep.

"And now the time of tide has come; the ship casts off her cables; and from the deserted wharf the uncheered ship for Tarshish, all careening, glides to sea. That ship, my friends, was the first of recorded smugglers! the contraband was Jonah. But the sea rebels; he will not bear the wicked burden. A dreadful storm comes on, the ship is like to break. But now when the boatswain calls all hands to lighten her; when boxes, bales, and jars are clattering overboard; when the wind is shrieking, and the men are yelling, and every plank thunders with trampling feet right over Jonah's head; in all this raging tumult, Jonah sleeps his hideous sleep. He sees no black sky and raging sea, feels not the reeling timbers, and little hears he or heeds he the far rush of the mighty whale, which even now with open mouth is cleaving the seas after him. Aye, shipmates, Jonah was gone down into the sides of the ship – a berth in the cabin as I have taken it, and was fast asleep. But the frightened master comes to him, and shrieks in his dead ear, 'What meanest thou, O, sleeper! arise!' Startled from his lethargy by that direful cry, Jonah staggers to his feet, and stumbling to the deck, grasps a shroud, to look out upon the sea. But at that moment he is sprung upon by a panther billow leaping over the bulwarks. Wave after wave thus leaps into the ship, and finding no speedy vent runs roaring fore and aft, till the mariners come nigh to drowning while yet afloat. And ever, as the white moon shows her affrighted face from the steep gullies in the blackness overhead, aghast Jonah sees the rearing bowsprit pointing high upward, but soon beat downward again towards the tormented deep.

"Terrors upon terrors run shouting through his soul. In all his cringing attitudes, the God-fugitive is now too plainly known. The sailors mark him; more and more certain grow their suspicions of him, and at last, fully to test the truth, by referring the whole matter to high Heaven, they fall to casting lots, to see for whose cause this great tempest was upon them. The lot is Jonah's; that discovered, then how furiously they mob him with their questions. 'What is thine occupation? Whence comest thou? Thy country? What people? But mark now, my shipmates, the behavior of poor Jonah. The eager mariners but ask him who he is, and where from; whereas, they not only receive an answer to those questions, but likewise another answer to a question not put by them, but the unsolicited answer is forced from Jonah by the hard hand of God that is upon him.

"'I am a Hebrew,' he cries – and then – 'I

fear the Lord the God of Heaven who hath made the sea and the dry land!' Fear him, O Jonah? Aye, well mightest thou fear the Lord God **then!** Straightway, he now goes on to make a full confession; whereupon the mariners became more and more appalled, but still are pitiful. For when Jonah, not yet supplicating God for mercy, since he but too well knew the darkness of his deserts, – when wretched Jonah cries out to them to take him and cast him forth into the sea, for he knew that for **his** sake this great tempest was upon them; they mercifully turn from him, and seek by other means to save the ship. But all in vain; the indignant gale howls louder; then, with one hand raised invokingly to God, with the other they not unreluctantly lay hold of Jonah.

"And now behold Jonah taken up as an anchor and dropped into the sea; when instantly an oily calmness floats out from the east, and the sea is still, as Jonah carries down the gale with him, leaving smooth water behind. He goes down in the whirling heart of such a masterless commotion that he scarce heeds the moment when he drops seething into the yawning jaws awaiting him; and the whale shoots-to all his ivory teeth, like so many white bolts, upon his prison. Then Jonah prayed unto the Lord out of the fish's belly. But observe his prayer, and learn a weighty lesson. For sinful as he is, Jonah does not weep and wail for direct deliverance. He feels that his dreadful punishment is just. He leaves all his deliverance to God, contenting himself with this, that spite of all his pains and pangs, he will still look towards His holy temple. And here, shipmates, is true and faithful repentance; not clamorous for pardon, but grateful for punishment. And how pleasing to God was this conduct in Jonah, is shown in the eventual deliverance of him from the sea and the whale. Shipmates, I do not place Jonah before you to be copied for his sin but I do place him before you as a model for repentance. Sin not; but if you do, take heed to repent of it like Jonah."

While he was speaking these words, the howling of the shrieking, slanting storm without seemed to add new power to the preacher, who, when describing Jonah's sea-storm, seemed tossed by a storm himself. His deep chest heaved as with a ground-swell; his tossed arms seemed the warring elements at work; and the thunders that rolled away from off his swarthy brow, and the light leaping from his eye, made all his simple hearers look on him with a quick fear that was strange to them.

There now came a lull in his look, as he silently turned over the leaves of the Book once more; and, at last, standing motionless, with closed eyes, for the moment, seemed communing with God and himself.

But again he leaned over towards the people, and bowing his head lowly, with an aspect of the deepest yet manliest humility, he spake these words:

"Shipmates, God has laid but one hand upon you; both his hands press upon me. I have read ye by what murky light may be mine the lesson that Jonah teaches to all sinners; and therefore to ye, and still more to me, for I am a greater sinner than ye. And now how gladly would I come down from this mast-head and sit on the hatches there where you sit, and listen as you listen, while some one of you reads **me** that other and more awful lesson which Jonah teaches to **me**, as a pilot of the living God. How being an anointed pilot-prophet, or speaker of true things, and bidden by the Lord to sound those unwelcome truths in the ears of a wicked Nineveh, Jonah, appalled at the hostility he should raise, fled from his mission, and sought to escape his duty and his God by taking ship at Joppa. But God is everywhere; Tarshish he never reached. As we have seen, God came upon him in the whale, and swallowed him down to living gulfs of doom, and with swift slantings tore him along 'into the midst of the seas,' where the eddying depths sucked him ten thousand fathoms down, and 'the weeds were wrapped about his head,' and all the watery world of woe bowled over him. Yet even then beyond the reach of any plummet – 'out of the belly of hell' – when the whale grounded upon the ocean's utmost bones, even then, God heard the engulphed, repenting prophet when he cried. Then God spake unto the fish; and from the shuddering cold and blackness of the sea, the whale came breeching up towards the warm and pleasant sun, and all the delights of air and earth; and 'vomited out Jonah upon the dry land;' when the word of the Lord came a second time; and Jonah, bruised and beaten – his ears, like two sea-shells, still multitudinously murmuring of the ocean – Jonah did the Almighty's bidding. And what was that, shipmates? To preach the Truth to the face of Falsehood! That was it!

"This, shipmates, this is that other lesson; and woe to that pilot of the living God who slights it. Woe to him whom this world charms from Gospel duty! Woe to him who seeks to pour oil upon the waters when God has brewed them into a gale! Woe to him who seeks to please rather than to appal! Woe to him whose good name is more to him than goodness! Woe to him who, in this world, courts not dishonour! Woe to him who would not be true, even though to be false were salvation! Yea, woe to him who, as the great Pilot Paul has it, while preaching to others is himself a castaway!"

He dropped and fell away from himself for a moment; then lifting his face to them again, showed a deep joy in his eyes, as he cried out with a heavenly enthusiasm, – "But oh! shipmates! on the starboard hand of every woe, there is a sure delight; and higher the top of that delight, than the bottom of the woe is deep. Is not the main-truck higher than the kelson is low? Delight is to him – a far, far upward, and inward delight – who against the proud gods and commodores of this earth, ever stands forth his own inexorable self. Delight is to him whose strong arms yet support him, when the ship of this base treacherous world has gone down beneath him. Delight is to him, who gives no quarter in the truth, and kills, burns, and destroys all sin though he pluck it out from under the robes of Senators and Judges. Delight, – top-gallant delight is to him, who acknowledges no law or lord, but the Lord his God, and is only a patriot to heaven. Delight is to him, whom all the waves of the billows of the seas of the boisterous mob can never shake from this sure Keel of the Ages. And eternal delight and deliciousness will be his, who coming to lay him down, can say with his final breath – O Father! – chiefly known to me by Thy rod – mortal or immortal, here I die. I have striven to be Thine, more than to be this world's, or mine own. Yet this is nothing: I leave eternity to Thee; for what is man that he should live out the lifetime of his God?"

He said no more, but slowly waving a benediction, covered his face with his hands, and so remained kneeling, till all the people had departed, and he was left alone in the place.

CHAPTER TEN

A Bosom Friend

RETURNING TO THE Spouter-Inn from the Chapel, I found Queequeg there quite alone; he having left the Chapel before the benediction some time. He was sitting on a bench before the fire, with his feet on the stove hearth, and in one hand was holding close up to his face that little negro idol of his; peering hard into its face, and with a jack-knife gently whittling away at its nose, meanwhile humming to himself in his heathenish way.

But being now interrupted, he put up the image; and pretty soon, going to the table, took up a large book there, and placing it on his lap began counting the pages with deliberate regularity; at every fiftieth page – as I fancied – stopping a moment, looking vacantly around him, and giving utterance to a long-drawn gurgling whistle of astonishment. He would then begin again at the next fifty; seeming to commence at number one each time, as though he could not count more than fifty, and it was only by such a large number of fifties being found together, that his astonishment at the multitude of pages was excited.

With much interest I sat watching him. Savage though he was, and hideously marred about the face – at least to my taste – his countenance yet had a something in it which was by no means disagreeable. You cannot hide the soul. Through all his unearthly tattooings, I thought I saw the traces of a simple honest heart; and in his large, deep eyes, fiery black and bold, there seemed tokens of a spirit that would dare a thousand devils. And besides all this, there was a certain lofty bearing about the Pagan, which even his uncouthness could not altogether maim. He looked like a man who had never cringed and never had had a creditor. Whether it was, too, that his head being shaved, his forehead was drawn out in freer and brighter relief, and looked more expansive than it otherwise would, this I will not venture to decide; but certain it was his head was phrenologically an excellent one. It may seem ridiculous, but it reminded me of General Washington's head, as seen in the popular busts of him. It had the same long regularly graded retreating slope from above the brows, which were likewise very projecting, like two long promontories thickly wooded on top. Queequeg was George Washington cannibalistically developed.

Whilst I was thus closely scanning him, half-pretending meanwhile to be looking out at the storm from the casement, he never heeded my presence, never troubled himself with so much as a single glance; but appeared wholly occupied with counting the pages of the marvellous book. Considering how sociably we had been sleeping together the night previous, and especially considering the affectionate arm I had found thrown over me upon waking in the morning, I thought this indifference of his very strange. But savages are strange beings; at times you do not know exactly how to take them. At first they are overawing; their calm self-collectedness of simplicity seems a Socratic wisdom. I had noticed also that Queequeg never consorted at all, or but very little, with the other seamen in the inn. He made no advances whatever; appeared to have no desire to enlarge the circle of his acquaintances. All this struck me as mighty singular; yet, upon second thoughts, there was something almost sublime in it. Here was a man some twenty thousand miles from home, by the way of Cape Horn, that is – which was the only way he could get there – thrown among people as strange to him as though he were in the planet Jupiter; and yet he seemed entirely at his ease; preserving the utmost serenity; content with his own companionship; always equal to himself. Surely this was a touch of fine philosophy; though no doubt he had never heard there was such a thing as that. But, perhaps, to be true philosophers, we mortals should not be conscious of so living or so striving. So soon as I hear that such or such a man gives himself out for a philosopher, I conclude that, like the dyspeptic old woman, he must have "broken his digester."

As I sat there in that now lonely room; the fire burning low, in that mild stage when, after its first intensity has warmed the air, it then only glows to be looked at; the evening shades and phantoms gathering round the casements, and peering in upon us silent, solitary twain; the storm booming without in solemn swells; I began to be sensible of strange feelings. I felt a melting in me. No more my splintered heart and maddened hand were turned against the wolfish world. This soothing savage had redeemed it. There he sat, his very indifference speaking a nature in which there lurked no civilized hypocrisies and bland deceits. Wild he was; a very sight of sights to see; yet I began to feel myself mysteriously drawn towards him. And those same things that would have repelled most others, they were the very magnets that thus drew me. I'll try a pagan friend, thought I, since Christian kindness has proved but hollow courtesy. I drew my bench near him, and made some friendly signs and hints, doing my best to talk with him meanwhile. At first he little noticed these advances; but presently, upon my referring to his last night's hospitalities, he made out to ask me whether we were again to be bedfellows. I told him yes; whereat I thought he looked pleased, perhaps a little complimented.

We then turned over the book together, and I endeavored to explain to him the purpose of the printing, and the meaning of the few pictures that were in it. Thus I soon engaged his interest; and from that we went to jabbering the best we could about the various outer sights to be seen in this famous town. Soon I proposed a social smoke; and, producing his pouch and tomahawk, he quietly offered me a puff. And then we sat exchanging puffs from that wild pipe of his, and keeping it regularly passing between us.

If there yet lurked any ice of indifference towards me in the Pagan's breast, this pleasant, genial smoke we had, soon thawed it out, and left us cronies. He seemed to take to me quite as naturally and unbiddenly as I to him; and when our smoke was over, he pressed his forehead against mine, clasped me round the waist, and said that henceforth we were married; meaning, in his country's phrase, that we were bosom friends; he would gladly die for me, if need should be. In a countryman, this sudden flame of friendship would have seemed far too premature, a thing to be much distrusted; but in this simple savage those old rules would not apply.

After supper, and another social chat and smoke, we went to our room together. He made me a present of his embalmed head; took out his enormous tobacco wallet, and groping under the tobacco, drew out some thirty dollars in silver; then spreading them on the table, and mechanically dividing them into two equal portions, pushed one of them towards me, and said it was mine. I was going to remonstrate; but he silenced me by pouring them into my trowsers' pockets. I let them stay. He then went about his evening prayers, took out his idol, and removed the paper fireboard. By certain signs and symptoms, I thought he seemed anxious for me to join him; but well knowing what was to follow, I deliberated a moment whether, in case he invited me, I would comply or otherwise.

I was a good Christian; born and bred in the bosom of the infallible Presbyterian Church. How then could I unite with this wild idolator in worshipping his piece of wood? But what is worship? thought I. Do you suppose now, Ishmael, that the magnanimous God of heaven and earth – pagans and all included – can possibly be jealous of an insignificant bit of black wood? Impossible! But what is worship? – to do the will of God – **that** is worship. And what is the will of God? – to do to my fellow man what I would have my fellow man to do to me – **that** is the will of God. Now, Queequeg is my fellow man. And what do I wish that this Queequeg would do to me? Why, unite with me in my particular Presbyterian form of worship. Consequently, I must then unite with him in his; ergo, I must turn idolator. So I kindled the shavings; helped prop up the innocent little idol; offered him burnt biscuit with Queequeg; salamed before him twice or thrice; kissed his nose; and that done, we undressed and went to bed, at peace with our own consciences and all the world. But we did not go to sleep without some little chat.

How it is I know not; but there is no place like a bed for confidential disclosures between friends. Man and wife, they say, there open the very bottom of their souls to each other; and some old couples often lie and chat over old times till nearly morning. Thus, then, in our hearts' honeymoon, lay I and Queequeg – a cosy, loving pair.

CHAPTER ELEVEN

Nightgown

WE HAD LAIN thus in bed, chatting and napping at short intervals, and Queequeg now and then affectionately throwing his brown tattooed legs over mine, and then drawing them back; so entirely sociable and free and easy were we; when, at last, by reason of our confabulations, what little nappishness remained in us altogether departed, and we felt like getting up again, though day-break was yet some way down the future.

Yes, we became very wakeful; so much so that our recumbent position began to grow wearisome, and by little and little we found ourselves sitting up; the clothes well tucked around us, leaning against the head-board with our four knees drawn up close together, and our two noses bending over them, as if our kneepans were warming-pans. We felt very nice and snug, the more so since it was so chilly out of doors; indeed out of bed-clothes too, seeing that there was no fire in the room. The more so, I say, because truly to enjoy bodily warmth, some small part of you must be cold, for there is no quality in this world that is not what it is merely by contrast. Nothing exists in itself. If you flatter yourself that you are all over comfortable, and have been so a long time, then you cannot be said to be comfortable any more. But if, like Queequeg and me in the bed, the tip of your nose or the crown of your head be slightly chilled, why then, indeed, in the general consciousness you feel most delightfully and unmistakably warm. For this reason a sleeping apartment should never be furnished with a fire, which is one of the luxurious discomforts of the rich. For the height of this sort of deliciousness is to have nothing but the blanket between you and your snugness and the cold of the outer air. Then there you lie like the one warm spark in the heart of an arctic crystal.

We had been sitting in this crouching manner for some time, when all at once I thought I would open my eyes; for when between sheets, whether by day or by night, and whether asleep or awake, I have a way of always keeping my eyes shut, in order the more to concentrate the snugness of being in bed. Because no man can ever feel his own identity aright except his eyes be closed; as if darkness were indeed the proper element of our essences, though light be more congenial to our clayey part. Upon opening my eyes then, and coming out of my own pleasant and self-created darkness into the imposed and coarse outer gloom of the unilluminated twelve-o'clock-at-night, I experienced a disagreeable revulsion. Nor did I at all object to the hint from Queequeg that perhaps it were best to strike a light, seeing that we were so wide awake; and besides he felt a strong desire to have a few quiet puffs from his Tomahawk. Be it said, that though I had felt such a strong repugnance to his smoking in the bed the night before, yet see how elastic our stiff prejudices grow when love once comes to bend them. For now I liked nothing better than to have Queequeg smoking by me, even in bed, because he seemed to be full of such serene household joy then. I no more felt unduly concerned for the landlord's policy of insurance. I was only alive to the condensed confidential comfortableness of sharing a pipe and a blanket with a real friend. With our shaggy jackets drawn about our shoulders, we now passed the Tomahawk from one to the other, till slowly there grew over us a blue hanging tester of smoke, illuminated by the flame of the new-lit lamp.

Whether it was that this undulating tester rolled the savage away to far distant scenes, I know not, but he now spoke of his native island; and, eager to hear his history, I begged him to go on and tell it. He gladly complied. Though at the time I but ill comprehended not a few of his words, yet subsequent disclosures, when I had become more familiar with his broken phraseology, now enable me to present the whole story such as it may prove in the mere skeleton I give.

CHAPTER TWELVE

Biographical

QUEEQUEG WAS a native of Rokovoko, an island far away to the West and South. It is not down in any map; true places never are.

When a new-hatched savage running wild about his native woodlands in a grass clout, followed by the nibbling goats, as if he were a green sapling; even then, in Queequeg's ambitious soul, lurked a strong desire to see something more of Christendom than a specimen whaler or two. His father was a High Chief, a King; his uncle a High Priest; and on the maternal side he boasted aunts who were the wives of unconquerable warriors. There was excellent blood in his veins – royal stuff; though sadly vitiated, I fear, by the cannibal propensity he nourished in his untutored youth.

A Sag Harbor ship visited his father's bay, and Queequeg sought a passage to Christian lands. But the ship, having her full complement of seamen, spurned his suit; and not all the King his father's influence could prevail. But Queequeg vowed a vow. Alone in his canoe, he paddled off to a distant strait, which he knew the ship must pass through when she quitted the island. On one side was a coral reef; on the other a low tongue of land, covered with mangrove thickets that grew out into the water. Hiding his canoe, still afloat, among these thickets, with its prow seaward, he sat down in the stern, paddle low in hand; and when the ship was gliding by, like a flash he darted out; gained her side; with one backward dash of his foot capsized and sank his canoe; climbed up the chains; and throwing himself at full length upon the deck, grappled a ring-bolt there, and swore not to let it go, though hacked in pieces.

In vain the captain threatened to throw him overboard; suspended a cutlass over his naked wrists; Queequeg was the son of a King, and Queequeg budged not. Struck by his desperate dauntlessness, and his wild desire to visit Christendom, the captain at last relented, and told him he might make himself at home. But this fine young savage – this sea Prince of Wales, never saw the Captain's cabin. They put him down among the sailors, and made a whaleman of him. But like Czar Peter content to toil in the shipyards of foreign cities, Queequeg disdained no seeming ignominy, if thereby he might happily gain the power of enlightening his untutored countrymen. For at bottom – so he told me – he was actuated by a profound desire to learn among the Christians, the arts whereby to make his people still happier than they were; and more than that, still better than they were. But, alas! the practices of whalemen soon convinced him that even Christians could be both miserable and wicked; infinitely more so, than all his father's heathens. Arrived at last in old Sag Harbor; and seeing what the sailors did there; and then going on to Nantucket, and seeing how they spent their wages in **that** place also, poor Queequeg gave it up for lost. Thought he, it's a wicked world in all meridians; I'll die a pagan.

And thus an old idolator at heart, he yet lived among these Christians, wore their clothes, and tried to talk their gibberish. Hence the queer ways about him, though now some time from home.

By hints, I asked him whether he did not propose going back, and having a coronation; since he might now consider his father dead and gone, he being very old and feeble at the last accounts. He answered no, not yet;

and added that he was fearful Christianity, or rather Christians, had unfitted him for ascending the pure and undefiled throne of thirty pagan Kings before him. But by and by, he said, he would return, – as soon as he felt himself baptized again. For the nonce, however, he proposed to sail about, and sow his wild oats in all four oceans. They had made a harpooneer of him, and that barbed iron was in lieu of a sceptre now.

I asked him what might be his immediate purpose, touching his future movements. He answered, to go to sea again, in his old vocation. Upon this, I told him that whaling was my own design, and informed him of my intention to sail out of Nantucket, as being the most promising port for an adventurous whaleman to embark from. He at once resolved to accompany me to that island, ship aboard the same vessel, get into the same watch, the same boat, the same mess with me, in short to share my every hap; with both my hands in his, boldly dip into the

Potluck of both worlds. To all this I joyously assented; for besides the affection I now felt for Queequeg, he was an experienced harpooneer, and as such, could not fail to be of great usefulness to one, who, like me, was wholly ignorant of the mysteries of whaling, though well acquainted with the sea, as known to merchant seamen.

His story being ended with his pipe's last dying puff, Queequeg embraced me, pressed his forehead against mine, and blowing out the light, we rolled over from each other, this way and that, and very soon were sleeping.

CHAPTER THIRTEEN

Wheelbarrow

NEXT MORNING, Monday, after disposing of the embalmed head to a barber, for a block, I settled my own and comrade's bill; using, however, my comrade's money. The grinning landlord, as well as the boarders, seemed amazingly tickled at the sudden friendship which had sprung up between me and Queequeg – especially as Peter Coffin's cock and bull stories about him had previously so much alarmed me concerning the very person whom I now companied with.

We borrowed a wheelbarrow, and embarking our things, including my own poor carpet-bag, and Queequeg's canvas sack and hammock, away we went down to "the Moss," the little Nantucket packet schooner moored at the wharf. As we were going along the people stared; not at Queequeg so much – for they were used to seeing cannibals like him in their streets, – but at seeing him and me upon such confidential terms. But we heeded them not, going along wheeling the barrow by turns, and Queequeg now and then stopping to adjust the sheath on his harpoon barbs. I asked him why he carried such a troublesome thing with him ashore, and whether all whaling ships did not find their own harpoons. To this, in substance, he replied, that though what I hinted was true enough, yet he had a particular affection for his own harpoon, because it was of assured stuff, well tried in many a mortal combat, and deeply intimate with the hearts of whales. In short, like many inland reapers and mowers, who go into the farmers' meadows armed with their own scythes – though in no wise obliged to furnish them – even so, Queequeg, for his own private reasons, preferred his own harpoon.

Shifting the barrow from my hand to his, he told me a funny story about the first wheelbarrow he had ever seen. It was in Sag Harbor. The owners of his ship, it seems, had lent him one, in which to carry his heavy chest to his boarding house. Not to seem ignorant about the thing – though in truth he was entirely so, concerning the precise way in which to manage the barrow – Queequeg puts his chest upon it; lashes it fast; and then shoulders the barrow and marches up the wharf. "Why," said I, "Queequeg, you might have known better than that, one would think. Didn't the people laugh?"

Upon this, he told me another story. The people of his island of Rokovoko, it seems, at their wedding feasts express the fragrant water of young cocoanuts into a large stained calabash like a punchbowl; and this punchbowl always forms the great central ornament on the braided mat where the feast is held. Now a certain grand merchant ship once touched at Rokovoko, and its commander – from all accounts, a very stately punctilious gentleman, at least for a sea captain – this commander was invited to the wedding feast of Queequeg's sister, a pretty young princess just turned of ten. Well; when all the wedding guests were assembled at the bride's bamboo cottage, this Captain marches in, and being assigned the post of honour, placed himself over against the punchbowl, and between the High Priest and his majesty the King, Queequeg's father. Grace being said, – for those people have their grace as well as we – though Queequeg told me that unlike us, who at such times look downwards to our platters, they, on the contrary, copying the ducks, glance upwards to the great Giver of all feasts – Grace, I say, being said, the High Priest opens the banquet by the immemorial ceremony of the island; that is, dipping his consecrated and consecrating fingers into the bowl before the blessed beverage circulates. Seeing himself placed next the Priest, and noting the ceremony, and thinking himself – being Captain of a ship – as having plain precedence over a mere island King, especially in the King's own house – the Captain coolly proceeds to wash his hands in the punchbowl; – taking it I suppose for a huge finger-glass. "Now," said Queequeg, "what you tink now? – Didn't our people laugh?"

At last, passage paid, and luggage safe, we stood on board the schooner. Hoisting sail, it glided down the Acushnet river. On one side, New Bedford rose in terraces of streets, their ice-covered trees all glittering in the clear, cold air. Huge hills and mountains of casks on casks were piled upon her wharves, and side by side the world-wandering whale ships lay silent and safely moored at last; while from others came a sound of carpenters and coopers, with blended noises of fires and forges to melt the pitch, all betokening that new cruises were on the start; that one most perilous and long voyage ended, only begins a second; and a second ended, only begins a third, and so on, for ever and for aye. Such is the endlessness, yea, the intolerableness of all earthly effort.

Gaining the more open water, the bracing breeze waxed fresh; the little Moss tossed the quick foam from her bows, as a young colt his snortings. How I snuffed that Tartar air! – how I spurned that turnpike earth! – that common highway all over dented with the marks of slavish heels and hoofs; and turned me to admire the magnanimity of the sea which will permit no records.

At the same foam-fountain, Queequeg seemed to drink and reel with me. His dusky nostrils swelled apart; he showed his filed and pointed teeth. On, on we flew; and our offing gained, the Moss did homage to the blast; ducked and dived her bows as a slave before the Sultan. Sideways leaning, we sideways darted; every ropeyarn tingling like a wire; the two tall masts buckling like Indian canes in land tornadoes. So full of this reeling scene were we, as we stood by the plunging bowsprit, that for some time we did not notice the jeering glances of the passengers, a lubber-like assembly, who marvelled that two fellow beings should be so companionable; as though a white man were anything more dignified than a whitewashed negro. But there were some boobies and bumpkins there, who, by their intense greenness, must have come from the heart and centre of all verdure.

Queequeg caught one of these young saplings mimicking him behind his back. I thought the bumpkin's hour of doom was come. Dropping his harpoon, the brawny savage caught him in his arms, and by an almost miraculous dexterity and strength, sent him high up bodily into the air; then slightly tapping his stern in mid-somerset, the fellow landed with bursting lungs upon his feet, while Queequeg, turning his back upon him, lighted his tomahawk pipe and passed it to me for a puff.

"Capting! Capting!" yelled the bumpkin, running towards that officer; "Capting, Capting, here's the devil."

"Hallo, **you** sir," cried the Captain, a gaunt rib of the sea, stalking up to Queequeg, "what in thunder do you mean by that? Don't you know you might have killed that chap?"

"What him say?" said Queequeg, as he mildly turned to me.

"He say," said I, "that you came near kill-e that man there," pointing to the still shivering greenhorn.

"Kill-e," cried Queequeg, twisting his tattooed face into an unearthly expression of disdain, "ah! him bevy small-e fish-e; Queequeg no kill-e so small-e fish-e; Queequeg kill-e big whale!"

"Look you," roared the Captain, "I'll kill-e **you**, you cannibal, if you try any more of your tricks aboard here; so mind your eye."

But it so happened just then, that it was high time for the Captain to mind his own eye. The prodigious strain upon the mainsail had parted the weather-sheet, and the tremendous boom was now flying from side to side, completely sweeping the entire after part of the deck. The poor fellow whom Queequeg had handled so roughly, was swept overboard; all hands were in a panic; and to attempt snatching at the boom to stay it, seemed madness. It flew from right to left, and back again, almost in one ticking of a watch, and every instant seemed on the point of snapping into splinters. Nothing was done, and nothing seemed capable of being done; those on deck rushed towards the bows, and stood eyeing the boom as if it were the lower jaw of an exasperated whale. In the midst of this consternation, Queequeg dropped deftly to his knees, and crawling under the path of the boom, whipped hold of a rope, secured one end to the bulwarks, and then flinging the other like a lasso, caught it round the boom as it swept over his head, and at the next jerk, the spar was that way trapped, and all was safe. The schooner was run into the wind, and while the hands were clearing away the stern boat, Queequeg, stripped to the waist, darted from the side with a long living arc of a leap. For three minutes or more he was seen swimming like a dog, throwing his long arms straight out before him, and by turns revealing his brawny shoulders through the freezing foam. I looked at the grand and glorious fellow, but saw no one to be saved. The greenhorn had gone down. Shooting himself perpendicularly from the water, Queequeg, now took an instant's glance around him, and seeming to see just how matters were, dived down and disappeared. A few minutes more, and he rose again, one arm still striking out, and with the other dragging a lifeless form. The boat soon picked them up. The poor bumpkin was restored. All hands voted Queequeg a noble trump; the captain begged his pardon. From that hour I clove to Queequeg like a barnacle; yea, till poor Queequeg took his last long dive.

Was there ever such unconsciousness? He did not seem to think that he at all deserved a medal from the Humane and Magnanimous Societies. He only asked for water – fresh water – something to wipe the brine off; that done, he put on dry clothes, lighted his pipe, and leaning against the bulwarks, and mildly eyeing those around him, seemed to be saying to himself – "It's a mutual, joint-stock world, in all meridians. We cannibals must help these Christians."

CHAPTER FOURTEEN

Nantucket

NOTHING MORE happened on the passage worthy the mentioning; so, after a fine run, we safely arrived in Nantucket.

Nantucket! Take out your map and look at it. See what a real corner of the world it occupies; how it stands there, away off shore, more lonely than the Eddystone lighthouse. Look at it – a mere hillock, and elbow of sand; all beach, without a background. There is more sand there than you would use in twenty years as a substitute for blotting paper. Some gamesome wights will tell you that they have to plant weeds there, they don't grow naturally; that they import Canada thistles; that they have to send beyond seas for a spile to stop a leak in an oil cask; that pieces of wood in Nantucket are carried about like bits of the true cross in Rome; that people there plant toadstools before their houses, to get under the shade in summer time; that one blade of grass makes an oasis, three blades in a day's walk a prairie; that they wear quicksand shoes, something like Laplander snow-shoes; that they are so shut up, belted about, every way inclosed, surrounded, and made an utter island of by the ocean, that to their very chairs and tables small clams will sometimes be found adhering, as to the backs of sea turtles. But these extravaganzas only show that Nantucket is no Illinois.

Look now at the wondrous traditional story of how this island was settled by the red-men. Thus goes the legend. In olden times an eagle swooped down upon the New England coast, and carried off an infant Indian in his talons. With loud lament the parents saw their child borne out of sight over the wide waters. They resolved to follow in the same direction. Setting out in their canoes, after a perilous passage they discovered the island, and there they found an empty ivory casket, – the poor little Indian's skeleton.

What wonder, then, that these Nantucketers, born on a beach, should take to the sea for a livelihood! They first caught crabs and quohogs in the sand; grown bolder, they waded out with nets for mackerel; more experienced, they pushed off in boats and captured cod; and at last, launching a navy of great ships on the sea, explored this watery world; put an incessant belt of circumnavigations round it; peeped in at Behring's Straits; and in all seasons and all oceans declared everlasting war with the mightiest animated mass that has survived the flood; most monstrous and most mountainous! That Himmalehan, salt-sea Mastodon, clothed with such portentousness of unconscious power, that his very panics are more to be dreaded than his most fearless and malicious assaults!

And thus have these naked Nantucketers, these sea hermits, issuing from their ant-hill in the sea, overrun and conquered the watery world like so many Alexanders; parcelling out among them the Atlantic, Pacific, and Indian oceans, as the three pirate powers did Poland. Let America add Mexico to Texas, and pile Cuba upon Canada; let the English overswarm all India, and hang out their blazing banner from the sun; two thirds of this terraqueous globe are the Nantucketer's. For the sea is his; he owns it, as Emperors own empires; other seamen having but a right of way through it.

Merchant ships are but extension bridges; armed ones but floating forts; even pirates and privateers, though following the sea as highwaymen the road, they but plunder other ships, other fragments of the land like themselves, without seeking to draw their living from the bottomless deep itself. The Nantucketer, he alone resides and riots on the sea; he alone, in Bible language, goes down to it in ships; to and fro ploughing it as his own special plantation. **There** is his home; **there** lies his business, which a Noah's flood would not interrupt, though it overwhelmed all the millions in China. He lives on the sea, as prairie cocks in the prairie; he hides among the waves, he climbs them as chamois hunters climb the Alps. For years he knows not the land; so that when he comes to it at last, it smells like another world, more strangely than the moon would to an Earthsman. With the landless gull, that at sunset folds her wings and is rocked to sleep between billows; so at nightfall, the Nantucketer, out of sight of land, furls his sails, and lays him to his rest, while under his very pillow rush herds of walruses and whales.

CHAPTER FIFTEEN

Chowder

IT WAS QUITE late in the evening when the little Moss came snugly to anchor, and Queequeg and I went ashore; so we could attend to no business that day, at least none but a supper and a bed. The landlord of the Spouter-Inn had recommended us to his cousin Hosea Hussey of the Try Pots, whom he asserted to be the proprietor of one of the best kept hotels in all Nantucket, and moreover he had assured us that Cousin Hosea, as he called him, was famous for his chowders. In short, he plainly hinted that we could not possibly do better than try pot-luck at the Try Pots. But the directions he had given us about keeping a yellow warehouse on our starboard hand till we opened a white church to the larboard, and then keeping that on the larboard hand till we made a corner three points to the starboard, and that done, then ask the first man we met where the place was: these crooked directions of his very much puzzled us at first, especially as, at the outset, Queequeg insisted that the yellow warehouse – our first point of departure – must be left on the larboard hand, whereas I had understood Peter Coffin to say it was on the starboard. However, by dint of beating about a little in the dark, and now and then knocking up a peaceable inhabitant to inquire the way, we at last came to something which there was no mistaking.

Two enormous wooden pots painted black, and suspended by asses' ears, swung from the cross-trees of an old top-mast, planted in front of an old doorway. The horns of the cross-trees were sawed off on the other side, so that this old top-mast looked not a little like a gallows. Perhaps I was over sensitive to such impressions at the time, but I could not help staring at this gallows with a vague misgiving. A sort of crick was in my neck as I gazed up to the two remaining horns; yes, **two** of them, one for Queequeg, and one for me. It's ominous, thinks I. A Coffin my Innkeeper upon landing in my first whaling port; tombstones staring at me in the whalemen's chapel; and here a gallows! and a pair of prodigious black pots too! Are these last throwing out oblique hints touching Tophet?

I was called from these reflections by the sight of a freckled woman with yellow hair and a yellow gown, standing in the porch of the inn, under a dull red lamp swinging there, that looked much like an injured eye, and carrying on a brisk scolding with a man in a purple woollen shirt.

"Get along with ye," said she to the man, "or I'll be combing ye!"

"Come on, Queequeg," said I, "all right. There's Mrs. Hussey."

And so it turned out; Mr. Hosea Hussey being from home, but leaving Mrs. Hussey entirely competent to attend to all his affairs. Upon making known our desires for a supper and a bed, Mrs. Hussey, postponing further scolding for the present, ushered us into a little room, and seating us at a table spread with the relics of a recently concluded repast, turned round to us and said – "Clam or Cod?"

"What's that about Cods, ma'am?" said I, with much politeness.

"Clam or Cod?" she repeated.

"A clam for supper? a cold clam; is **that** what you mean, Mrs. Hussey?" says I, "but that's a rather cold and clammy reception in the winter time, ain't it, Mrs. Hussey?"

But being in a great hurry to resume scolding the man in the purple Shirt, who was waiting for it in the entry, and seeming to hear nothing but the word "clam," Mrs. Hussey hurried towards an open door leading to the kitchen, and bawling out "clam for two," disappeared.

"Queequeg," said I, "do you think that we can make out a supper for us both on one clam?"

However, a warm savory steam from the kitchen served to belie the apparently cheerless prospect before us. But when that smoking chowder came in, the mystery was delightfully explained. Oh, sweet friends! hearken to me. It was made of small juicy clams, scarcely bigger than hazel nuts, mixed with pounded ship biscuit, and salted pork cut up into little flakes; the whole enriched with butter, and plentifully seasoned with pepper and salt.

Our appetites being sharpened by the frosty voyage, and in particular, Queequeg seeing his favourite fishing food before him, and the chowder being surpassingly excellent, we despatched it with great expedition: when leaning back a moment and bethinking me of Mrs. Hussey's clam and cod announcement, I thought I would try a little experiment. Stepping to the kitchen door, I uttered the word "cod" with great emphasis, and resumed my seat. In a few moments the savoury steam came forth again, but with a different flavor, and in good time a fine cod-chowder was placed before us.

We resumed business; and while plying our spoons in the bowl, thinks I to myself, I wonder now if this here has any effect on the head? What's that stultifying saying about chowder-headed people? "But look, Queequeg, ain't that a live eel in your bowl? Where's your harpoon?"

Fishiest of all fishy places was the Try

Pots, which well deserved its name; for the pots there were always boiling chowders. Chowder for breakfast, and chowder for dinner, and chowder for supper, till you began to look for fish-bones coming through your clothes. The area before the house was paved with clam-shells. Mrs. Hussey wore a polished necklace of codfish vertebra; and Hosea Hussey had his account books bound in superior old shark-skin. There was a fishy flavor to the milk, too, which I could not at all account for, till one morning happening to take a stroll along the beach among some fishermen's boats, I saw Hosea's brindled cow feeding on fish remnants, and marching along the sand with each foot in a cod's decapitated head, looking very slip-shod, I assure ye.

Supper concluded, we received a lamp, and directions from Mrs. Hussey concerning the nearest way to bed; but, as Queequeg was about to precede me up the stairs, the lady reached forth her arm, and demanded his harpoon; she allowed no harpoon in her chambers. “Why not?” said I; “every true whaleman sleeps with his harpoon – but why not?” “Because it’s dangerous,” says she. “Ever since young Stiggs coming from that unfort’nt v’y’ge of his, when he was gone four years and a half, with only three barrels of **ile**, was found dead in my first floor back, with his harpoon in his side; ever since then I allow no boarders to take sich dangerous weepons in their rooms at night. So, Mr. Queequeg” (for she had learned his name), “I will just take this here iron, and keep it for you till morning. But the chowder; clam or cod to-morrow for breakfast, men?”

“Both,” says I; “and let’s have a couple of smoked herring by way of variety.”

CHAPTER SIXTEEN

The Ship

IN BED WE concocted our plans for the morrow. But to my surprise and no small concern, Queequeg now gave me to understand, that he had been diligently consulting Yojo – the name of his black little god – and Yojo had told him two or three times over, and strongly insisted upon it everyway, that instead of our going together among the whaling-fleet in harbor, and in concert selecting our craft; instead of this, I say, Yojo earnestly enjoined that the selection of the ship should rest wholly with me, inasmuch as Yojo purposed befriending us; and, in order to do so, had already pitched upon a vessel, which, if left to myself, I, Ishmael, should infallibly light upon, for all the world as though it had turned out by chance; and in that vessel I must immediately ship myself, for the present irrespective of Queequeg.

I have forgotten to mention that, in many things, Queequeg placed great confidence in the excellence of Yojo's judgment and surprising forecast of things; and cherished Yojo with considerable esteem, as a rather good sort of god, who perhaps meant well enough upon the whole, but in all cases did not succeed in his benevolent designs.

Now, this plan of Queequeg's, or rather Yojo's, touching the selection of our craft; I did not like that plan at all. I had not a little relied upon Queequeg's sagacity to point out the whaler best fitted to carry us and our fortunes securely. But as all my remonstrances produced no effect upon Queequeg, I was obliged to acquiesce; and accordingly prepared to set about this business with a determined rushing sort of energy and vigor, that should quickly settle that trifling little affair. Next morning early, leaving Queequeg shut up with Yojo in our little bedroom – for it seemed that it was some sort of Lent or Ramadan, or day of fasting, humiliation, and prayer with Queequeg and Yojo that day; **how** it was I never could find out, for, though I applied myself to it several times, I never could master his liturgies and XXXIX Articles – leaving Queequeg, then, fasting on his tomahawk pipe, and Yojo warming himself at his sacrificial fire of shavings, I sallied out among the shipping. After much prolonged sauntering and many random inquiries, I learnt that there were three ships up for three-years' voyages – The Devil-dam, the Tit-bit, and the Pequod. **Devil-Dam**, I do not know the origin of; **Tit-**

bit is obvious; **Pequod**, you will no doubt remember, was the name of a celebrated tribe of Massachusetts Indians; now extinct as the ancient Medes. I peered and pryed about the Devil-dam; from her, hopped over to the Tit-bit; and finally, going on board the Pequod, looked around her for a moment, and then decided that this was the very ship for us.

You may have seen many a quaint craft in your day, for aught I know; – square-toed luggers; mountainous Japanese junks; butter-box galliots, and what not; but take my word for it, you never saw such a rare old craft as this same rare old Pequod. She was a ship of the old school, rather small if anything; with an old-fashioned claw-footed look about her. Long seasoned and weather-stained in the typhoons and calms of all four oceans, her old hull's complexion was darkened like a French grenadier's, who has alike fought in Egypt and Siberia. Her venerable bows looked bearded. Her masts – cut somewhere on the coast of Japan, where her original ones were lost overboard in a gale – her masts stood stiffly up like the spines of the three old kings of Cologne. Her ancient decks were worn and wrinkled, like the pilgrim-worshipped flag-stone in Canterbury Cathedral where Becket bled. But to all these her old antiquities, were added new and marvellous features, pertaining to the wild business that for more than half a century she had followed. Old Captain Peleg, many years her chief-mate, before he commanded another vessel of his own, and now a retired seaman, and one of the principal owners of the Pequod, – this old Peleg, during the term of his chief-mateship, had built upon her original grotesqueness, and inlaid it, all over, with a quaintness both of material and device, unmatched by anything except it be Thorkill-Hake's carved buckler or bedstead. She was apparelled like any barbaric Ethiopian emperor, his neck heavy with pendants of polished ivory. She was a thing of trophies. A cannibal of a craft, tricking herself forth in the chased bones of her enemies. All round, her unpanelled, open bulwarks were garnished like one continuous jaw, with the long sharp teeth of the sperm whale, inserted there for pins, to fasten her old hempen thews and tendons to. Those thews ran not through base blocks of land wood, but deftly travelled over sheaves of sea-ivory. Scorning a turnstile wheel at her reverend helm, she sported there a tiller; and that tiller was in one mass, curiously carved from the long narrow lower jaw of her hereditary foe. The helmsman who steered by that tiller in a tempest, felt like the Tartar, when he holds back his fiery steed by clutching its jaw. A noble craft, but somehow a most melancholy! All noble things are touched with that.

Now when I looked about the quarter-deck, for some one having authority, in order to propose myself as a candidate for the voyage, at first I saw nobody; but I could not well overlook a strange sort of tent, or rather wigwam, pitched a little behind the main-mast. It seemed only a temporary erection used in port. It was of a conical shape, some ten feet high; consisting of the long, huge slabs of limber black bone taken from the middle and highest part of the jaws of the right-whale. Planted with their broad ends on the deck, a circle of these slabs laced together, mutually sloped towards each other, and at the apex united in a tufted point, where the loose hairy fibres waved to and fro like the top-knot on some old Pottowottamie Sachem's head. A triangular opening faced towards the bows of the ship, so that the insider commanded a complete view forward.

And half concealed in this queer tenement, I at length found one who by his aspect seemed to have authority; and who, it being noon, and the ship's work suspended, was now enjoying respite from the burden of command. He was seated on an old-fashioned oaken chair, wriggling all over with curious carving; and the bottom of which was formed of a stout interlacing of the same elastic stuff of which the wigwam was constructed.

There was nothing so very particular, perhaps, about the appearance of the elderly man I saw; he was brown and brawny, like most old seamen, and heavily rolled up in blue pilot-cloth, cut in the Quaker style; only there was a fine and almost microscopic net-work of the minutest wrinkles interlacing round his eyes, which must have arisen from his continual sailings in many hard gales, and always looking to windward; – for this causes the muscles about the eyes to become pursed together. Such eye-wrinkles are very effectual in a scowl.

"Is this the Captain of the Pequod?" said I, advancing to the door of the tent.

"Supposing it be the captain of the Pequod, what dost thou want of him?" he demanded.

"I was thinking of shipping."

"Thou wast, wast thou? I see thou art no Nantucketer – ever been in a stove boat?"

"No, Sir, I never have."

"Dost know nothing at all about whaling, I dare say – eh?

"Nothing, Sir; but I have no doubt I shall soon learn. I've been several voyages in the merchant service, and I think that – "

"Merchant service be damned. Talk not that lingo to me. Dost see that leg? – I'll take that leg away from thy stern, if ever thou talkest of the marchant service to me again. Marchant service indeed! I suppose now ye feel considerable proud of having served in those marchant ships. But flukes! man, what makes thee want to go a whaling, eh? – it looks a little suspicious, don't it, eh? – Hast not been a pirate, hast thou? – Didst not rob thy last Captain, didst thou? – Dost not think of murdering the officers when thou gettest to sea?"

I protested my innocence of these things.

I saw that under the mask of these half humorous innuendoes, this old seaman, as an insulated Quakerish Nantucketer, was full of his insular prejudices, and rather distrustful of all aliens, unless they hailed from Cape Cod or the Vineyard.

"But what takes thee a-whaling? I want to know that before I think of shipping ye."

"Well, sir, I want to see what whaling is. I want to see the world."

"Want to see what whaling is, eh? Have ye clapped eye on Captain Ahab?"

"Who is Captain Ahab, sir?"

"Aye, aye, I thought so. Captain Ahab is the Captain of this ship."

"I am mistaken then. I thought I was speaking to the Captain himself."

"Thou art speaking to Captain Peleg – that's who ye are speaking to, young man. It belongs to me and Captain Bildad to see the Pequod fitted out for the voyage, and supplied with all her needs, including crew. We are part owners and agents. But as I was going to say, if thou wantest to know what whaling is, as thou tellest ye do, I can put ye in a way of finding it out before ye bind yourself to it, past backing out. Clap eye on Captain Ahab, young man, and thou wilt find that he has only one leg."

"What do you mean, sir? Was the other one lost by a whale?"

"Lost by a whale! Young man, come nearer to me: it was devoured, chewed up, crunched by the monstrousest parmacetty that ever chipped a boat! – ah, ah!"

I was a little alarmed by his energy, perhaps also a little touched at the hearty grief in his concluding exclamation, but said as calmly as I could, "What you say is no doubt true enough, sir; but how could I know there was any peculiar ferocity in that particular whale, though indeed I might have inferred as much from the simple fact of the accident."

"Look ye now, young man, thy lungs are a sort of soft, d'ye see; thou dost not talk shark a bit. **Sure**, ye've been to sea before now; sure of that?"

"Sir," said I, "I thought I told you that I had been four voyages in the merchant – "

"Hard down out of that! Mind what I said about the marchant service – don't aggravate me – I won't have it. But let us understand each other. I have given thee a hint about what whaling is; do ye yet feel inclined for it?"

"I do, sir."

"Very good. Now, art thou the man to pitch a harpoon down a live whale's throat, and then jump after it? Answer, quick!"

"I am, sir, if it should be positively indispensable to do so; not to be got rid of, that is; which I don't take to be the fact."

"Good again. Now then, thou not only wantest to go a-whaling, to find out by experience what whaling is, but ye also want to go in order to see the world? Was not that what ye said? I thought so. Well then, just step forward there, and take a peep over the weather-bow, and then back to me and tell me what ye see there."

For a moment I stood a little puzzled by this curious request, not knowing exactly how to take it, whether humorously or in earnest. But concentrating all his crow's feet into one scowl, Captain Peleg started me on the errand.

Going forward and glancing over the weather bow, I perceived that the ship swinging to her anchor with the flood-tide, was now obliquely pointing towards the open ocean. The prospect was unlimited, but exceedingly monotonous and forbidding; not the slightest variety that I could see.

"Well, what's the report?" said Peleg when I came back; "what did ye see?"

"Not much," I replied – "nothing but water; considerable horizon though, and there's a squall coming up, I think."

"Well, what does thou think then of seeing the world? Do ye wish to go round Cape Horn to see any more of it, eh? Can't ye see the world where you stand?"

I was a little staggered, but go a-whaling I must, and I would; and the Pequod was as good a ship as any – I thought the best – and all this I now repeated to Peleg. Seeing me so determined, he expressed his willingness to ship me.

"And thou mayest as well sign the papers right off," he added – "come along with ye." And so saying, he led the way below deck into the cabin.

Seated on the transom was what seemed to me a most uncommon and surprising figure. It turned out to be Captain Bildad, who along with Captain Peleg was one of the largest owners of the vessel; the other shares, as is sometimes the case in these ports, being held by a crowd of old annuitants; widows, fatherless children, and chancery wards; each owning about the value of a timber head, or a foot of plank, or a nail or two in the ship. People in Nantucket invest their money in whaling vessels, the same way that you do yours in approved state stocks bringing in good interest.

Now, Bildad, like Peleg, and indeed many other Nantucketers, was a Quaker, the island having been originally settled by that sect; and to this day its inhabitants in general retain in an uncommon measure the peculiarities of the Quaker, only variously and anomalously modified by things altogether alien and heterogeneous. For some of these same Quakers are the most sanguinary of all sailors and whale-hunters. They are fighting Quakers; they are Quakers with a vengeance.

So that there are instances among them of men, who, named with Scripture names – a singularly common fashion on the island – and in childhood naturally imbibing the stately dramatic thee and thou of the Quaker idiom; still, from the audacious, daring, and boundless adventure of their subsequent lives, strangely blend with these unoutgrown peculiarities, a thousand bold dashes of character, not unworthy a Scandinavian sea-king, or a poetical Pagan Roman. And when these things unite in a man of greatly superior natural force, with a globular brain and a ponderous heart; who has also by the stillness and seclusion of many long night-watches in the remotest waters, and beneath constellations never seen here at the north, been led to think untraditionally and independently; receiving all nature's sweet or savage impressions fresh from her own virgin voluntary and confiding breast, and thereby chiefly, but with some help from accidental advantages, to learn a bold and nervous lofty language – that man makes one in a whole nation's census – a mighty pageant creature, formed for noble tragedies. Nor will it at all detract from him, dramatically regarded, if either by birth or other circumstances, he have what seems a half wilful overruling morbidness at the bottom of his nature. For all men tragically great are made so through a certain morbidness. Be sure of this, O young ambition, all mortal greatness is but disease. But, as yet we have not to do with such an one, but with quite another; and still a man, who, if indeed peculiar, it only results again from another phase of the Quaker, modified by individual circumstances.

Like Captain Peleg, Captain Bildad was a well-to-do, retired whaleman. But unlike Captain Peleg – who cared not a rush for what are called serious things, and indeed deemed those self-same serious things the veriest of all trifles – Captain Bildad had not only been originally educated according to the strictest sect of Nantucket Quakerism, but all his subsequent ocean life, and the sight of many unclad, lovely island creatures, round the Horn – all that had not moved this native born Quaker one single jot, had not so much as altered one angle of his vest. Still, for all this immutableness, was there some lack of common consistency about worthy Captain Peleg. Though refusing, from conscientious scruples, to bear arms against land invaders, yet himself had illimitably invaded the Atlantic and Pacific; and though a sworn foe to human bloodshed, yet had he in his straight-bodied coat, spilled tuns upon tuns of leviathan gore. How now in the contemplative evening of his days, the pious Bildad reconciled these things in the reminiscence, I do not know; but it did not seem to concern him much, and very probably he had long since come to the sage and sensible conclusion that a man's religion is one thing, and this practical world quite another. This world pays dividends. Rising from a little cabin-boy in short clothes of the drabbest drab, to a harpooneer in a broad shad-bellied waistcoat; from that becoming boat-header, chief-mate, and captain, and finally a ship owner; Bildad, as I hinted before, had concluded his adventurous career by wholly retiring from active life at the goodly age of sixty, and dedicating his remaining days to the quiet receiving of his well-earned income.

Now, Bildad, I am sorry to say, had the reputation of being an incorrigible old hunks, and in his sea-going days, a bitter, hard task-master. They told me in Nantucket, though it certainly seems a curious story, that when he sailed the old Categut whaleman, his crew, upon arriving home, were mostly all carried ashore to the hospital, sore exhausted and worn out. For a pious man, especially for a Quaker, he was certainly rather hard-hearted, to say the least. He never used to swear, though, at his men, they said; but somehow he got an inordinate quantity of cruel, unmitigated hard work out of them. When Bildad was a chief-mate, to have his drab-coloured eye intently looking at you, made you feel completely nervous, till you could clutch something – a hammer or a marling-spike, and go to work like mad, at something or other, never mind what. Indolence and idleness perished before him. His own person was the exact embodiment of his utilitarian character. On his long, gaunt body, he carried no spare flesh, no superfluous beard, his chin having a soft, economical nap to it, like the worn nap of his broad-brimmed hat.

Such, then, was the person that I saw seated on the transom when I followed Captain Peleg down into the cabin. The space between the decks was small; and there, bolt-upright, sat old Bildad, who always sat so, and never leaned, and this to save his coat tails. His broad-brim was placed beside him; his legs were stiffly crossed; his drab vesture was buttoned up to his chin; and spectacles on nose, he seemed absorbed in reading from a ponderous volume.

"Bildad," cried Captain Peleg, "at it again, Bildad, eh? Ye have been studying those Scriptures, now, for the last thirty years, to my certain knowledge. How far ye got, Bildad?"

As if long habituated to such profane talk from his old shipmate, Bildad, without noticing his present irreverence, quietly looked up, and seeing me, glanced again inquiringly towards Peleg.

"He says he's our man, Bildad," said Peleg, "he wants to ship."

"Dost thee?" said Bildad, in a hollow tone, and turning round to me.

"I **dost**," said I unconsciously, he was so intense a Quaker.

"What do ye think of him, Bildad?" said Peleg.

"He'll do," said Bildad, eyeing me, and then went on spelling away at his book in a mumbling tone quite audible.

I thought him the queerest old Quaker I ever saw, especially as Peleg, his friend and old shipmate, seemed such a blusterer. But I said nothing, only looking round me sharply. Peleg now threw open a chest, and drawing forth the ship's articles, placed pen and ink before him, and seated himself at a little table. I began to think it was high time to settle with myself at what terms I would be willing to engage for the voyage. I was already aware that in the whaling business they paid no wages; but all hands, including the captain, received certain shares of the profits called **lays**, and that these lays were proportioned to the degree of importance pertaining to the respective duties of the ship's company. I was also aware that being a green hand at whaling, my own lay would not be very large; but considering that I was used to the sea, could steer a ship, splice a rope, and all that, I made no doubt that from all I had heard I should be offered at least the 275th lay – that is, the 275th part of the clear net proceeds of the voyage, whatever that might eventually amount to. And though the 275th lay was what they call a rather **long lay**, yet it was better than nothing; and if we had a lucky voyage, might pretty nearly pay for the clothing I would wear out on it, not to speak of my three years' beef and board, for which I would not have to pay one stiver.

It might be thought that this was a poor way to accumulate a princely fortune – and so it was, a very poor way indeed. But I am one of those that never take on about princely fortunes, and am quite content if the world is ready to board and lodge me, while I am putting up at this grim sign of the Thunder Cloud. Upon the whole, I thought that the 275th lay would be about the fair thing, but would not have been surprised had I been offered the 200th, considering I was of a broad-shouldered make.

But one thing, nevertheless, that made me a little distrustful about receiving a generous share of the profits was this: Ashore, I had heard something of both Captain Peleg and his unaccountable old crony Bildad; how that they being the principal proprietors of the Pequod, therefore the other and more inconsiderable and scattered owners, left nearly the whole management of the ship's affairs to these two. And I did not know but what the stingy old Bildad might have a mighty deal to say about shipping hands, especially as I now found him on board the Pequod, quite at home there in the cabin, and reading his Bible as if at his own fireside. Now while Peleg was vainly trying to mend a pen with his jack-knife, old Bildad, to my no small surprise, considering that he was such an interested party in these proceedings; Bildad never heeded us, but went on mumbling to himself out of his book, "**Lay** not up for yourselves treasures upon earth, where moth – "

"Well, Captain Bildad," interrupted Peleg, "what d'ye say, what lay shall we give this young man?"

"Thou knowest best," was the sepulchral reply, "the seven hundred and seventy-seventh wouldn't be too much, would it? – 'where moth and rust do corrupt, but **lay** – '"

Lay, indeed, thought I, and such a lay!

the seven hundred and seventy-seventh! Well, old Bildad, you are determined that I, for one, shall not **lay** up many **lays** here below, where moth and rust do corrupt. It was an exceedingly **long lay** that, indeed; and though from the magnitude of the figure it might at first deceive a landsman, yet the slightest consideration will show that though seven hundred and seventy-seven is a pretty large number, yet, when you come to make a **teenth** of it, you will then see, I say, that the seven hundred and seventy-seventh part of a farthing is a good deal less than seven hundred and seventy-seven gold doubloons; and so I thought at the time.

"Why, blast your eyes, Bildad," cried Peleg, "thou dost not want to swindle this young man! he must have more than that."

"Seven hundred and seventy-seventh," again said Bildad, without lifting his eyes; and then went on mumbling – "for where your treasure is, there will your heart be also."

"I am going to put him down for the three hundredth," said Peleg, "do ye hear that, Bildad! The three hundredth lay, I say."

Bildad laid down his book, and turning solemnly towards him said, "Captain Peleg, thou hast a generous heart; but thou must consider the duty thou owest to the other owners of this ship – widows and orphans, many of them – and that if we too abundantly reward the labors of this young man, we may be taking the bread from those widows and those orphans. The seven hundred and seventy-seventh lay, Captain Peleg."

"Thou Bildad!" roared Peleg, starting up and clattering about the cabin. "Blast ye, Captain Bildad, if I had followed thy advice in these matters, I would afore now had a conscience to lug about that would be heavy enough to founder the largest ship that ever sailed round Cape Horn."

"Captain Peleg," said Bildad steadily, "thy

conscience may be drawing ten inches of water, or ten fathoms, I can't tell; but as thou art still an impenitent man, Captain Peleg, I greatly fear lest thy conscience be but a leaky one; and will in the end sink thee foundering down to the fiery pit, Captain Peleg."

"Fiery pit! fiery pit! ye insult me, man; past all natural bearing, ye insult me. It's an all-fired outrage to tell any human creature that he's bound to hell. Flukes and flames! Bildad, say that again to me, and start my soul-bolts, but I'll – I'll – yes, I'll swallow a live goat with all his hair and horns on. Out of the cabin, ye canting, drab-coloured son of a wooden gun – a straight wake with ye!"

As he thundered out this he made a rush at Bildad, but with a marvellous oblique, sliding celerity, Bildad for that time eluded him.

Alarmed at this terrible outburst between the two principal and responsible owners of the ship, and feeling half a mind to give up all idea of sailing in a vessel so questionably owned and temporarily commanded, I stepped aside from the door to give egress to Bildad, who, I made no doubt, was all eagerness to vanish from before the awakened wrath of Peleg. But to my astonishment, he sat down again on the transom very quietly, and seemed to have not the slightest intention of withdrawing. He seemed quite used to impenitent Peleg and his ways. As for Peleg, after letting off his rage as he had, there seemed no more left in him, and he, too, sat down like a lamb, though he twitched a little as if still nervously agitated. "Whew!" he whistled at last – "the squall's gone off to leeward, I think. Bildad, thou used to be good at sharpening a lance, mend that pen, will ye. My jack-knife here needs the grindstone. That's he; thank ye, Bildad. Now then, my young man, Ishmael's thy name, didn't ye say? Well then, down ye go here, Ishmael, for the three hundredth lay."

"Captain Peleg," said I, "I have a friend with me who wants to ship too – shall I bring him down to-morrow?"

"To be sure," said Peleg. "Fetch him along, and we'll look at him."

"What lay does he want?" groaned Bildad, glancing up from the book in which he had again been burying himself.

"Oh! never thee mind about that, Bildad," said Peleg. "Has he ever whaled it any?" turning to me.

"Killed more whales than I can count, Captain Peleg."

"Well, bring him along then."

And, after signing the papers, off I went; nothing doubting but that I had done a good morning's work, and that the Pequod was the identical ship that Yojo had provided to carry Queequeg and me round the Cape.

But I had not proceeded far, when I began to bethink me that the Captain with whom I was to sail yet remained unseen by me; though, indeed, in many cases, a whale-ship will be completely fitted out, and receive all her crew on board, ere the captain makes himself visible by arriving to take command; for sometimes these voyages are so prolonged, and the shore intervals at home so exceedingly brief, that if the captain have a family, or any absorbing concernment of that sort, he does not trouble himself much about his ship in port, but leaves her to the owners till all is ready for sea. However, it is always as well to have a look at him before irrevocably committing yourself into his hands. Turning back I accosted Captain Peleg, inquiring where Captain Ahab was to be found.

"And what dost thou want of Captain Ahab? It's all right enough; thou art shipped."

"Yes, but I should like to see him."

"But I don't think thou wilt be able to at present. I don't know exactly what's the matter with him; but he keeps close inside the house; a sort of sick, and yet he don't look so. In fact, he ain't sick; but no, he isn't well either. Any how, young man, he won't always see me, so I don't suppose he will thee. He's a queer man, Captain Ahab – so some think – but a good one. Oh, thou'lt like him well enough; no fear, no fear. He's a grand, ungodly, god-like man, Captain Ahab; doesn't speak much; but, when he does speak, then you may well listen. Mark ye, be forewarned; Ahab's above the common; Ahab's been in colleges, as well as 'mong the cannibals; been used to deeper wonders than the waves; fixed his fiery lance in mightier, stranger foes than whales. His lance! aye, the keenest and the surest that out of all our isle! Oh! he ain't Captain Bildad; no, and he ain't Captain Peleg; **he's Ahab**, boy; and Ahab of old, thou knowest, was a crowned king!"

"And a very vile one. When that wicked king was slain, the dogs, did they not lick his blood?"

"Come hither to me – hither, hither," said Peleg, with a significance in his eye that almost startled me. "Look ye, lad; never say that on board the Pequod. Never say it anywhere. Captain Ahab did not name himself. 'Twas a foolish, ignorant whim of his crazy, widowed mother, who died when he was only a twelvemonth old. And yet the old squaw Tistig, at Gayhead, said that the name would somehow prove prophetic. And, perhaps, other fools like her may tell thee the same. I wish to warn thee. It's a lie. I know Captain Ahab well; I've sailed with him as mate years ago; I know what he is – a good man – not a pious, good man, like Bildad, but a swearing good man – something like me – only there's a good deal more of him. Aye, aye, I know that he was never very jolly; and I know that on the passage home, he was a little out of his mind for a spell; but it was the sharp shooting pains in his bleeding stump that brought that about, as any one might see. I know, too, that ever since he lost his leg last voyage by that accursed whale, he's been a kind of moody – desperate moody, and savage sometimes; but that will all pass off. And once for all, let me tell thee and assure thee, young man, it's better to sail with a moody good captain than a laughing bad one. So good-bye to thee – and wrong not Captain Ahab, because he happens to have a wicked name. Besides, my boy, he has a wife – not three voyages wedded – a sweet, resigned girl. Think of that; by that sweet girl that old man has a child: hold ye then there can be any utter, hopeless harm in Ahab? No, no, my lad; stricken, blasted, if he be, Ahab has his humanities!"

As I walked away, I was full of thoughtfulness; what had been incidentally revealed to me of Captain Ahab, filled me with a certain wild vagueness of painfulness concerning him. And somehow, at the time, I felt a sympathy and a sorrow for him, but for I don't know what, unless it was the cruel loss of his leg. And yet I also felt a strange awe of him; but that sort of awe, which I cannot at all describe, was not exactly awe; I do not know what it was. But I felt it; and it did not disincline me towards him; though I felt impatience at what seemed like mystery in him, so imperfectly as he was known to me then. However, my thoughts were at length carried in other directions, so that for the present dark Ahab slipped my mind.

CHAPTER SEVENTEEN

The Ramadan

AS QUEEQUEG'S Ramadan, or Fasting and Humiliation, was to continue all day, I did not choose to disturb him till towards night-fall; for I cherish the greatest respect towards everybody's religious obligations, never mind how comical, and could not find it in my heart to undervalue even a congregation of ants worshipping a toad-stool; or those other creatures in certain parts of our earth, who with a degree of footmanism quite unprecedented in other planets, bow down before the torso of a deceased landed proprietor merely on account of the inordinate possessions yet owned and rented in his name.

I say, we good Presbyterian Christians should be charitable in these things, and not fancy ourselves so vastly superior to other mortals, pagans and what not, because of their half-crazy conceits on these subjects. There was Queequeg, now, certainly entertaining the most absurd notions about Yojo and his Ramadan; – but what of that? Queequeg thought he knew what he was about, I suppose; he seemed to be content; and there let him rest. All our arguing with him would not avail; let him be, I say: and Heaven have mercy on us all – Presbyterians and Pagans alike – for we are all somehow dreadfully cracked about the head, and sadly need mending.

Towards evening, when I felt assured that

all his performances and rituals must be over, I went up to his room and knocked at the door; but no answer. I tried to open it, but it was fastened inside. "Queequeg," said I softly through the key-hole: – all silent. "I say, Queequeg! why don't you speak? It's I – Ishmael." But all remained still as before. I began to grow alarmed. I had allowed him such abundant time; I thought he might have had an apoplectic fit. I looked through the key-hole; but the door opening into an odd corner of the room, the key-hole prospect was but a crooked and sinister one. I could only see part of the foot-board of the bed and a line of the wall, but nothing more. I was surprised to behold resting against the wall the wooden shaft of Queequeg's harpoon, which the landlady the evening previous had taken from him, before our mounting to the chamber. That's strange, thought I; but at any rate, since the harpoon stands yonder, and he seldom or never goes abroad without it, therefore he must be inside here, and no possible mistake.

"Queequeg! – Queequeg!" – all still. Something must have happened. Apoplexy! I tried to burst open the door; but it stubbornly resisted. Running down stairs, I quickly stated my suspicions to the first person I met – the chamber-maid. "La! la!" she cried, "I thought something must be the matter. I went to make the bed after breakfast, and the door was locked; and not a mouse to be heard; and it's been just so silent ever since. But I thought, may be, you had both gone off and locked your baggage in for safe keeping. La! la, ma'am! – Mistress! murder! Mrs. Hussey! apoplexy!" – and with these cries, she ran towards the kitchen, I following.

Mrs. Hussey soon appeared, with a mustard-pot in one hand and a vinegar-cruet in the other, having just broken away from the occupation of attending to the castors, and scolding her little black boy meantime.

"Wood-house!" cried I, "which way to it?

Run for God's sake, and fetch something to pry open the door – the axe! – the axe! he's had a stroke; depend upon it!" – and so saying I was unmethodically rushing up stairs again empty-handed, when Mrs. Hussey interposed the mustard-pot and vinegar-cruet, and the entire castor of her countenance.

"What's the matter with you, young man?"

"Get the axe! For God's sake, run for the doctor, some one, while I pry it open!"

"Look here," said the landlady, quickly putting down the vinegar-cruet, so as to have one hand free; "look here; are you talking about prying open any of my doors?" – and with that she seized my arm. "What's the matter with you? What's the matter with you, shipmate?"

In as calm, but rapid a manner as possible, I gave her to understand the whole case. Unconsciously clapping the vinegar-cruet to one side of her nose, she ruminated for an instant; then exclaimed – "No! I haven't seen it since I put it there." Running to a little closet under the landing of the stairs, she glanced in, and returning, told me that Queequeg's harpoon was missing. "He's killed himself," she cried. "It's unfort'nate Stiggs done over again – there goes another counterpane – God pity his poor mother! – it will be the ruin of my house. Has the poor lad a sister? Where's that girl? – there, Betty, go to Snarles the Painter, and tell him to paint me a sign, with – "no suicides permitted here, and no smoking in the parlor;" – might as well kill both birds at once. Kill? The Lord be merciful to his ghost! What's that noise there? You, young man, avast there!"

And running up after me, she caught me as I was again trying to force open the door.

"I don't allow it; I won't have my premises spoiled. Go for the locksmith, there's one about a mile from here. But avast!" putting her hand in her side-pocket, "here's a key that'll fit, I guess; let's see." And with that, she turned it in the lock; but, alas! Queequeg's supplemental bolt remained unwithdrawn within.

"Have to burst it open," said I, and was running down the entry a little, for a good start, when the landlady caught at me, again vowing I should not break down her premises; but I tore from her, and with a sudden bodily rush dashed myself full against the mark.

With a prodigious noise the door flew open, and the knob slamming against the wall, sent the plaster to the ceiling; and there, good heavens! there sat Queequeg, altogether cool and self-collected; right in the middle of the room; squatting on his hams, and holding Yojo on top of his head. He looked neither one way nor the other way, but sat like a carved image with scarce a sign of active life.

"Queequeg," said I, going up to him, "Queequeg, what's the matter with you?"

"He hain't been a sittin' so all day, has he?"

said the landlady.

But all we said, not a word could we drag out of him; I almost felt like pushing him over, so as to change his position, for it was almost intolerable, it seemed so painfully and unnaturally constrained; especially, as in all probability he had been sitting so for upwards of eight or ten hours, going too without his regular meals.

"Mrs. Hussey," said I, "he's **alive** at all events; so leave us, if you please, and I will see to this strange affair myself."

Closing the door upon the landlady, I endeavored to prevail upon Queequeg to take a chair; but in vain. There he sat; and all he could do – for all my polite arts and blandishments – he would not move a peg, nor say a single word, nor even look at me, nor notice my presence in the slightest way.

I wonder, thought I, if this can possibly be a part of his Ramadan; do they fast on their hams that way in his native island. It must be so; yes, it's part of his creed, I suppose;

well, then, let him rest; he'll get up sooner or later, no doubt. It can't last for ever, thank God, and his Ramadan only comes once a year; and I don't believe it's very punctual then.

I went down to supper. After sitting a long time listening to the long stories of some sailors who had just come from a plum-pudding voyage, as they called it (that is, a short whaling-voyage in a schooner or brig, confined to the north of the line, in the Atlantic Ocean only); after listening to these plum-puddingers till nearly eleven o'clock, I went up stairs to go to bed, feeling quite sure by this time Queequeg must certainly have brought his Ramadan to a termination. But no; there he was just where I had left him; he had not stirred an inch. I began to grow vexed with him; it seemed so downright senseless and insane to be sitting there all day and half the night on his hams in a cold room, holding a piece of wood on his head.

"For heaven's sake, Queequeg, get up

and shake yourself; get up and have some supper. You'll starve; you'll kill yourself, Queequeg." But not a word did he reply.

Despairing of him, therefore, I determined to go to bed and to sleep; and no doubt, before a great while, he would follow me. But previous to turning in, I took my heavy bearskin jacket, and threw it over him, as it promised to be a very cold night; and he had nothing but his ordinary round jacket on. For some time, do all I would, I could not get into the faintest doze. I had blown out the candle; and the mere thought of Queequeg – not four feet off – sitting there in that uneasy position, stark alone in the cold and dark; this made me really wretched. Think of it; sleeping all night in the same room with a wide awake pagan on his hams in this dreary, unaccountable Ramadan!

But somehow I dropped off at last, and knew nothing more till break of day; when, looking over the bedside, there squatted Queequeg, as if he had been screwed down to the floor. But as soon as the first glimpse of sun entered the window, up he got, with stiff and grating joints, but with a cheerful look; limped towards me where I lay; pressed his forehead again against mine; and said his Ramadan was over.

Now, as I before hinted, I have no objection to any person's religion, be it what it may, so long as that person does not kill or insult any other person, because that other person don't believe it also. But when a man's religion becomes really frantic; when it is a positive torment to him; and, in fine, makes this earth of ours an uncomfortable inn to lodge in; then I think it high time to take that individual aside and argue the point with him.

And just so I now did with Queequeg. "Queequeg," said I, "get into bed now, and lie and listen to me." I then went on, beginning with the rise and progress of the primitive religions, and coming down to the various religions of the present time, during which time I labored to show Queequeg that all these Lents, Ramadans, and prolonged ham-squattings in cold, cheerless rooms were stark nonsense; bad for the health; useless for the soul; opposed, in short, to the obvious laws of Hygiene and common sense. I told him, too, that he being in other things such an extremely sensible and sagacious savage, it pained me, very badly pained me, to see him now so deplorably foolish about this ridiculous Ramadan of his. Besides, argued I, fasting makes the body cave in; hence the spirit caves in; and all thoughts born of a fast must necessarily be half-starved. This is the reason why most dyspeptic religionists cherish such melancholy notions about their hereafters. In one word, Queequeg, said I, rather digressively; hell is an idea first born on an undigested apple-dumpling; and since then perpetuated through the hereditary dyspepsias nurtured by Ramadans.

I then asked Queequeg whether he

himself was ever troubled with dyspepsia; expressing the idea very plainly, so that he could take it in. He said no; only upon one memorable occasion. It was after a great feast given by his father the king, on the gaining of a great battle wherein fifty of the enemy had been killed by about two o'clock in the afternoon, and all cooked and eaten that very evening.

"No more, Queequeg," said I, shuddering; "that will do;" for I knew the inferences without his further hinting them. I had seen a sailor who had visited that very island, and he told me that it was the custom, when a great battle had been gained there, to barbecue all the slain in the yard or garden of the victor; and then, one by one, they were placed in great wooden trenchers, and garnished round like a pilau, with breadfruit and cocoanuts; and with some parsley in their mouths, were sent round with the victor's compliments to all his friends, just as though these presents were so many

Christmas turkeys.

After all, I do not think that my remarks about religion made much impression upon Queequeg. Because, in the first place, he somehow seemed dull of hearing on that important subject, unless considered from his own point of view; and, in the second place, he did not more than one third understand me, couch my ideas simply as I would; and, finally, he no doubt thought he knew a good deal more about the true religion than I did. He looked at me with a sort of condescending concern and compassion, as though he thought it a great pity that such a sensible young man should be so hopelessly lost to evangelical pagan piety.

At last we rose and dressed; and Queequeg, taking a prodigiously hearty breakfast of chowders of all sorts, so that the landlady should not make much profit by reason of his Ramadan, we sallied out to board the Pequod, sauntering along, and picking our teeth with halibut bones.

CHAPTER EIGHTEEN

His Mark

AS WE WERE walking down the end of the wharf towards the ship, Queequeg carrying his harpoon, Captain Peleg in his gruff voice loudly hailed us from his wigwam, saying he had not suspected my friend was a cannibal, and furthermore announcing that he let no cannibals on board that craft, unless they previously produced their papers.

"What do you mean by that, Captain

Peleg?" said I, now jumping on the bulwarks, and leaving my comrade standing on the wharf.

"I mean," he replied, "he must show his papers."

"Yes," said Captain Bildad in his hollow voice, sticking his head from behind Peleg's, out of the wigwam. "He must show that he's converted. Son of darkness," he added, turning to Queequeg, "art thou at present in communion with any Christian church?"

"Why," said I, "he's a member of the first Congregational Church." Here be it said, that many tattooed savages sailing in Nantucket ships at last come to be converted into the churches.

"First Congregational Church," cried Bildad, "what! that worships in Deacon Deuteronomy Coleman's meeting-house?" and so saying, taking out his spectacles, he rubbed them with his great yellow bandana handkerchief, and putting them on very carefully, came out of the wigwam, and leaning stiffly over the bulwarks, took a good long look at Queequeg.

"How long hath he been a member?" he then said, turning to me; "not very long, I rather guess, young man."

"No," said Peleg, "and he hasn't been baptized right either, or it would have washed some of that devil's blue off his face."

"Do tell, now," cried Bildad, "is this Philistine a regular member of Deacon Deuteronomy's meeting? I never saw him going there, and I pass it every Lord's day."

"I don't know anything about Deacon Deuteronomy or his meeting," said I; "all I know is, that Queequeg here is a born member of the First Congregational Church. He is a deacon himself, Queequeg is."

"Young man," said Bildad sternly, "thou art skylarking with me – explain thyself, thou young Hittite. What church dost thee mean? answer me."

Finding myself thus hard pushed, I replied. "I mean, sir, the same ancient Catholic Church to which you and I, and Captain Peleg there, and Queequeg here, and all of us, and every mother's son and soul of us belong; the great and everlasting First Congregation of this whole worshipping world; we all belong to that; only some of us cherish some queer crotchets no ways touching the grand belief; in **that** we all join hands."

"Splice, thou mean'st **splice** hands," cried Peleg, drawing nearer. "Young man, you'd better ship for a missionary, instead of a fore-mast hand; I never heard a better sermon. Deacon Deuteronomy – why Father Mapple himself couldn't beat it, and he's reckoned something. Come aboard, come aboard; never mind about the papers. I say, tell Quohog there – what's that you call him? tell Quohog to step along. By the great anchor, what a harpoon he's got there! looks like good stuff that; and he handles it about right. I say, Quohog, or whatever your name is, did you ever stand in the head of a whale-boat? did you ever strike a fish?"

Without saying a word, Queequeg, in his wild sort of way, jumped upon the bulwarks, from thence into the bows of one of the whale-boats hanging to the side; and then bracing his left knee, and poising his harpoon, cried out in some such way as this: –

“Cap’ain, you see him small drop tar on water dere? You see him? well, spose him one whale eye, well, den!” and taking sharp aim at it, he darted the iron right over old Bildad’s broad brim, clean across the ship’s decks, and struck the glistening tar spot out of sight.

“Now,” said Queequeg, quietly hauling in the line, “spos-ee him whale-e eye; why, dad whale dead.”

“Quick, Bildad,” said Peleg, his partner, who, aghast at the close vicinity of the flying harpoon, had retreated towards the cabin gangway. “Quick, I say, you Bildad, and get the ship’s papers. We must have Hedgehog there, I mean Quohog, in one of our boats.

Look ye, Quohog, we'll give ye the ninetieth lay, and that's more than ever was given a harpooneer yet out of Nantucket."

So down we went into the cabin, and to my great joy Queequeg was soon enrolled among the same ship's company to which I myself belonged.

When all preliminaries were over and Peleg had got everything ready for signing, he turned to me and said, "I guess, Quohog there don't know how to write, does he? I say, Quohog, blast ye! dost thou sign thy name or make thy mark?"

But at this question, Queequeg, who had twice or thrice before taken part in similar ceremonies, looked no ways abashed; but taking the offered pen, copied upon the paper, in the proper place, an exact counterpart of a queer round figure which was tattooed upon his arm; so that through Captain Peleg's obstinate mistake touching his appellative, it stood something like this: –

Quohog. his X mark.

Meanwhile Captain Bildad sat earnestly and steadfastly eyeing Queequeg, and at last rising solemnly and fumbling in the huge pockets of his broad-skirted drab coat, took out a bundle of tracts, and selecting one entitled "The Latter Day Coming; or No Time to Lose," placed it in Queequeg's hands, and then grasping them and the book with both his, looked earnestly into his eyes, and said, "Son of darkness, I must do my duty by thee; I am part owner of this ship, and feel concerned for the souls of all its crew; if thou still clingest to thy Pagan ways, which I sadly fear, I beseech thee, remain not for aye a Belial bondsman. Spurn the idol Bell, and the hideous dragon; turn from the wrath to come; mind thine eye, I say; oh! goodness gracious! steer clear of the fiery pit!"

Something of the salt sea yet lingered in old Bildad's language, heterogeneously mixed with Scriptural and domestic phrases.

"Avast there, avast there, Bildad, avast

now spoiling our harpooneer," cried Peleg. "Pious harpooneers never make good voyagers – it takes the shark out of 'em; no harpooneer is worth a straw who aint pretty sharkish. There was young Nat Swaine, once the bravest boat-header out of all Nantucket and the Vineyard; he joined the meeting, and never came to good. He got so frightened about his plaguy soul, that he shrinked and sheered away from whales, for fear of after-claps, in case he got stove and went to Davy Jones."

"Peleg! Peleg!" said Bildad, lifting his eyes and hands, "thou thyself, as I myself, hast seen many a perilous time; thou knowest, Peleg, what it is to have the fear of death; how, then, can'st thou prate in this ungodly guise. Thou beliest thine own heart, Peleg. Tell me, when this same Pequod here had her three masts overboard in that typhoon on Japan, that same voyage when thou went mate with Captain Ahab, did'st thou not think of Death and the Judgment then?"

"Hear him, hear him now," cried Peleg, marching across the cabin, and thrusting his hands far down into his pockets, – "hear him, all of ye. Think of that! When every moment we thought the ship would sink! Death and the Judgment then? What? With all three masts making such an everlasting thundering against the side; and every sea breaking over us, fore and aft. Think of Death and the Judgment then? No! no time to think about Death then. Life was what Captain Ahab and I was thinking of; and how to save all hands – how to rig jury-masts – how to get into the nearest port; that was what I was thinking of."

Bildad said no more, but buttoning up his coat, stalked on deck, where we followed him. There he stood, very quietly overlooking some sailmakers who were mending a top-sail in the waist. Now and then he stooped to pick up a patch, or save an end of tarred twine, which otherwise might have been wasted.

CHAPTER NINETEEN

The Prophet

"SHIPMATES, have ye shipped in that ship?"

Queequeg and I had just left the Pequod, and were sauntering away from the water, for the moment each occupied with his own thoughts, when the above words were put to us by a stranger, who, pausing before us, levelled his massive forefinger at the vessel in question. He was but shabbily apparelled in faded jacket and patched trowsers; a rag of a black handkerchief investing his neck. A confluent small-pox had in all directions flowed over his face, and left it like the complicated ribbed bed of a torrent, when the rushing waters have been dried up.

"Have ye shipped in her?" he repeated.

"You mean the ship Pequod, I suppose," said I, trying to gain a little more time for an uninterrupted look at him.

"Aye, the Pequod – that ship there," he said, drawing back his whole arm, and then rapidly shoving it straight out from him, with the fixed bayonet of his pointed finger darted full at the object.

"Yes," said I, "we have just signed the articles."

"Anything down there about your souls?"

"About what?"

"Oh, perhaps you hav'n't got any," he said quickly. "No matter though, I know many chaps that hav'n't got any, – good luck to 'em; and they are all the better off for it. A soul's a sort of a fifth wheel to a wagon."

"What are you jabbering about, shipmate?" said I.

"**He's** got enough, though, to make up for all deficiencies of that sort in other chaps," abruptly said the stranger, placing a nervous emphasis upon the word **he**.

"Queequeg," said I, "let's go; this fellow has broken loose from somewhere; he's talking about something and somebody we don't know."

"Stop!" cried the stranger. "Ye said true – ye hav'n't seen Old Thunder yet, have ye?"

"Who's Old Thunder?" said I, again riveted with the insane earnestness of his manner.

"Captain Ahab."

"What! the captain of our ship, the Pequod?"

"Aye, among some of us old sailor chaps, he goes by that name. Ye hav'n't seen him yet, have ye?"

"No, we hav'n't. He's sick they say, but is getting better, and will be all right again before long."

"All right again before long!" laughed the stranger, with a solemnly derisive sort of laugh. "Look ye; when Captain Ahab is all right, then this left arm of mine will be all right; not before."

"What do you know about him?"

"What did they **tell** you about him? Say that!"

"They didn't tell much of anything about him; only I've heard that he's a good whale-hunter, and a good captain to his crew."

"That's true, that's true – yes, both true enough. But you must jump when he gives an order. Step and growl; growl and go – that's the word with Captain Ahab. But nothing about that thing that happened to him off Cape Horn, long ago, when he lay like dead for three days and nights; nothing about that deadly skrimmage with the Spaniard afore the altar in Santa? – heard nothing about that, eh? Nothing about the silver calabash he spat into? And nothing about his losing his leg last voyage, according to the prophecy. Didn't ye hear a word about them matters and something more, eh? No, I don't think ye did; how could ye? Who knows it? Not all Nantucket, I guess. But hows'ever, mayhap, ye've heard tell about the leg, and how he lost it; aye, ye have heard of that, I dare say. Oh yes, **that** every one knows a'most – I mean they know he's only one leg; and that a parmacetti took the other off."

"My friend," said I, "what all this gibberish of yours is about, I don't know, and I don't much care; for it seems to me that you must be a little damaged in the head. But if you are speaking of Captain Ahab, of that ship there, the Pequod, then let me tell you, that I know all about the loss of his leg."

"**All** about it, eh – sure you do? – all?"

"Pretty sure."

With finger pointed and eye levelled at the Pequod, the beggar-like stranger stood a moment, as if in a troubled reverie; then starting a little, turned and said: – "Ye've shipped, have ye? Names down on the papers? Well, well, what's signed, is signed; and what's to be, will be; and then again, perhaps it won't be, after all. Anyhow, it's all fixed and arranged a'ready; and some sailors or other must go with him, I suppose; as well these as any other men, God pity 'em! Morning to ye, shipmates, morning; the ineffable heavens bless ye; I'm sorry I stopped ye."

"Look here, friend," said I, "if you have anything important to tell us, out with it; but if you are only trying to bamboozle us, you are mistaken in your game; that's all I have to say."

"And it's said very well, and I like to hear a chap talk up that way; you are just the man for him – the likes of ye. Morning to ye, shipmates, morning! Oh! when ye get there, tell 'em I've concluded not to make one of 'em."

"Ah, my dear fellow, you can't fool us that

way – you can't fool us. It is the easiest thing in the world for a man to look as if he had a great secret in him."

"Morning to ye, shipmates, morning."

"Morning it is," said I. "Come along, Queequeg, let's leave this crazy man. But stop, tell me your name, will you?"

"Elijah."

Elijah! thought I, and we walked away, both commenting, after each other's fashion, upon this ragged old sailor; and agreed that he was nothing but a humbug, trying to be a bugbear. But we had not gone perhaps above a hundred yards, when chancing to turn a corner, and looking back as I did so, who should be seen but Elijah following us, though at a distance. Somehow, the sight of him struck me so, that I said nothing to Queequeg of his being behind, but passed on with my comrade, anxious to see whether the stranger would turn the same corner that we did. He did; and then it seemed to me that he was dogging us, but with what intent

I could not for the life of me imagine. This circumstance, coupled with his ambiguous, half-hinting, half-revealing, shrouded sort of talk, now begat in me all kinds of vague wonderments and half-apprehensions, and all connected with the Pequod; and Captain Ahab; and the leg he had lost; and the Cape Horn fit; and the silver calabash; and what Captain Peleg had said of him, when I left the ship the day previous; and the prediction of the squaw Tistig; and the voyage we had bound ourselves to sail; and a hundred other shadowy things.

I was resolved to satisfy myself whether this ragged Elijah was really dogging us or not, and with that intent crossed the way with Queequeg, and on that side of it retraced our steps. But Elijah passed on, without seeming to notice us. This relieved me; and once more, and finally as it seemed to me, I pronounced him in my heart, a humbug.

CHAPTER TWENTY

All Astir

A DAY OR TWO passed, and there was great activity aboard the Pequod. Not only were the old sails being mended, but new sails were coming on board, and bolts of canvas, and coils of rigging; in short, everything betokened that the ship's preparations were hurrying to a close. Captain Peleg seldom or never went ashore, but sat in his wigwam keeping a sharp look-out upon the hands:

Bildad did all the purchasing and providing at the stores; and the men employed in the hold and on the rigging were working till long after night-fall.

On the day following Queequeg's signing the articles, word was given at all the inns where the ship's company were stopping, that their chests must be on board before night, for there was no telling how soon the vessel might be sailing. So Queequeg and I got down our traps, resolving, however, to sleep ashore till the last. But it seems they always give very long notice in these cases, and the ship did not sail for several days. But no wonder; there was a good deal to be done, and there is no telling how many things to be thought of, before the Pequod was fully equipped.

Every one knows what a multitude of things – beds, sauce-pans, knives and forks, shovels and tongs, napkins, nut-crackers, and what not, are indispensable to the business of housekeeping. Just so with whaling, which necessitates a three-years' housekeeping upon the wide ocean, far from all grocers, costermongers, doctors, bakers, and bankers. And though this also holds true of merchant vessels, yet not by any means to the same extent as with whalemen. For besides the great length of the whaling voyage, the numerous articles peculiar to the prosecution of the fishery, and the impossibility of replacing them at the remote harbors usually frequented, it must be remembered, that of all ships, whaling vessels are the most exposed to accidents of all kinds, and especially to the destruction and loss of the very things upon which the success of the voyage most depends. Hence, the spare boats, spare spars, and spare lines and harpoons, and spare everythings, almost, but a spare Captain and duplicate ship.

At the period of our arrival at the Island, the heaviest storage of the Pequod had been almost completed; comprising her beef, bread, water, fuel, and iron hoops and staves. But, as before hinted, for some time there was a continual fetching and carrying on board of divers odds and ends of things, both large and small.

Chief among those who did this fetching and carrying was Captain Bildad's sister, a lean old lady of a most determined and indefatigable spirit, but withal very kindhearted, who seemed resolved that, if **she** could help it, nothing should be found wanting in the Pequod, after once fairly getting to sea. At one time she would come on board with a jar of pickles for the steward's pantry; another time with a bunch of quills for the chief mate's desk, where he kept his log; a third time with a roll of flannel for the small of some one's rheumatic back. Never did any woman better deserve her name, which was Charity – Aunt Charity, as everybody called her. And like a sister of charity did this charitable Aunt Charity bustle about hither and thither, ready to turn her hand and heart to anything that promised to yield safety, comfort, and consolation to all on board a ship in which her beloved brother Bildad was concerned, and in which she herself owned a score or two of well-saved dollars.

But it was startling to see this excellent hearted Quakeress coming on board, as she did the last day, with a long oil-ladle in one hand, and a still longer whaling lance in the other. Nor was Bildad himself nor Captain Peleg at all backward. As for Bildad, he carried about with him a long list of the articles needed, and at every fresh arrival, down went his mark opposite that article upon the paper. Every once in a while Peleg came hobbling out of his whalebone den, roaring at the men down the hatchways, roaring up to the riggers at the mast-head, and then concluded by roaring back into his wigwam.

During these days of preparation,

Queequeg and I often visited the craft, and as often I asked about Captain Ahab, and how he was, and when he was going to come on board his ship. To these questions they would answer, that he was getting better and better, and was expected aboard every day; meantime, the two captains, Peleg and Bildad, could attend to everything necessary to fit the vessel for the voyage. If I had been downright honest with myself, I would have seen very plainly in my heart that I did but half fancy being committed this way to so long a voyage, without once laying my eyes on the man who was to be the absolute dictator of it, so soon as the ship sailed out upon the open sea. But when a man suspects any wrong, it sometimes happens that if he be already involved in the matter, he insensibly strives to cover up his suspicions even from himself. And much this way it was with me. I said nothing, and tried to think nothing.

At last it was given out that some time next day the ship would certainly sail. So next morning, Queequeg and I took a very early start.

CHAPTER TWENTY ONE

Going Aboard

IT WAS NEARLY six o'clock, but only grey imperfect misty dawn, when we drew nigh the wharf.

"There are some sailors running ahead there, if I see right," said I to Queequeg, "it can't be shadows; she's off by sunrise, I guess; come on!"

"Avast!" cried a voice, whose owner at the same time coming close behind us, laid a hand upon both our shoulders, and then insinuating himself between us, stood stooping forward a little, in the uncertain twilight, strangely peering from Queequeg to me. It was Elijah.

"Going aboard?"

"Hands off, will you," said I.

"Lookee here," said Queequeg, shaking himself, "go 'way!"

"Ain't going aboard, then?"

"Yes, we are," said I, "but what business is that of yours? Do you know, Mr. Elijah, that I consider you a little impertinent?"

"No, no, no; I wasn't aware of that," said Elijah, slowly and wonderingly looking from me to Queequeg, with the most unaccountable glances.

"Elijah," said I, "you will oblige my friend and me by withdrawing. We are going to the Indian and Pacific Oceans, and would prefer not to be detained."

"Ye be, be ye? Coming back afore breakfast?"

"He's cracked, Queequeg," said I, "come on."

"Holloa!" cried stationary Elijah, hailing us when we had removed a few paces.

"Never mind him," said I, "Queequeg, come on."

But he stole up to us again, and suddenly clapping his hand on my shoulder, said – "Did ye see anything looking like men going towards that ship a while ago?"

Struck by this plain matter-of-fact question, I answered, saying, "Yes, I thought I did see four or five men; but it was too dim to be sure."

"Very dim, very dim," said Elijah. "Morning to ye."

Once more we quitted him; but once more he came softly after us; and touching my shoulder again, said, "See if you can find 'em now, will ye?

"Find who?"

"Morning to ye! morning to ye!" he rejoined, again moving off. "Oh! I was going to warn ye against – but never mind, never mind – it's all one, all in the family too; – sharp frost this morning, ain't it? Good-bye to ye. Shan't see ye again very soon, I guess; unless it's before the Grand Jury." And with these cracked words he finally departed, leaving me, for the moment, in no small wonderment at his frantic impudence.

At last, stepping on board the Pequod, we found everything in profound quiet, not a soul moving. The cabin entrance was locked within; the hatches were all on, and lumbered with coils of rigging. Going forward to the forecastle, we found the slide of the scuttle open. Seeing a light, we went down, and found only an old rigger there, wrapped in a tattered pea-jacket. He was thrown at whole length upon two chests, his face downwards and inclosed in his folded arms. The profoundest slumber slept upon him.

"Those sailors we saw, Queequeg, where can they have gone to?" said I, looking dubiously at the sleeper. But it seemed that, when on the wharf, Queequeg had not at all noticed what I now alluded to; hence I would have thought myself to have been optically deceived in that matter, were it not for Elijah's otherwise inexplicable question. But I beat the thing down; and again marking the sleeper, jocularly hinted to Queequeg that perhaps we had best sit up with the body; telling him to establish himself accordingly. He put his hand upon the sleeper's rear, as though feeling if it was soft enough; and then, without more ado, sat quietly down there.

"Gracious! Queequeg, don't sit there," said I.

"Oh! perry dood seat," said Queequeg, "my country way; won't hurt him face."

"Face!" said I, "call that his face? very benevolent countenance then; but how hard he breathes, he's heaving himself; get off, Queequeg, you are heavy, it's grinding the face of the poor. Get off, Queequeg! Look, he'll twitch you off soon. I wonder he don't wake."

Queequeg removed himself to just beyond the head of the sleeper, and lighted his tomahawk pipe. I sat at the feet. We kept the pipe passing over the sleeper, from one to the other. Meanwhile, upon questioning him in his broken fashion, Queequeg gave me to understand that, in his land, owing to the absence of settees and sofas of all sorts, the king, chiefs, and great people generally, were in the custom of fattening some of the lower orders for ottomans; and to furnish a house comfortably in that respect, you had only to buy up eight or ten lazy fellows, and lay them round in the piers and alcoves. Besides, it was very convenient on an excursion; much better than those garden-chairs which are convertible into walking-sticks; upon occasion, a chief calling his attendant, and desiring him to make a settee of himself under a spreading tree, perhaps in some damp marshy place.

While narrating these things, every time Queequeg received the tomahawk from me, he flourished the hatchet-side of it over the sleeper's head.

"What's that for, Queequeg?"

"Perry easy, kill-e; oh! perry easy!"

He was going on with some wild reminiscences about his tomahawk-pipe, which, it seemed, had in its two uses both brained his foes and soothed his soul, when we were directly attracted to the sleeping rigger. The strong vapour now completely filling the contracted hole, it began to tell upon him. He breathed with a sort of muffledness; then seemed troubled in the nose; then revolved over once or twice; then sat up and rubbed his eyes.

"Holloa!" he breathed at last, "who be ye smokers?"

"Shipped men," answered I, "when does she sail?"

"Aye, aye, ye are going in her, be ye? She sails to-day. The Captain came aboard last night."

"What Captain? – Ahab?"

"Who but him indeed?"

I was going to ask him some further questions concerning Ahab, when we heard a noise on deck.

"Holloa! Starbuck's astir," said the rigger. "He's a lively chief mate, that; good man, and a pious; but all alive now, I must turn to." And so saying he went on deck, and we followed.

It was now clear sunrise. Soon the crew came on board in twos and threes; the riggers bestirred themselves; the mates were actively engaged; and several of the shore people were busy in bringing various last things on board. Meanwhile Captain Ahab remained invisibly enshrined within his cabin.

CHAPTER TWENTY TWO

Merry Christmas

AT LENGTH, towards noon, upon the final dismissal of the ship's riggers, and after the Pequod had been hauled out from the wharf, and after the ever-thoughtful Charity had come off in a whale-boat, with her last gift – a night-cap for Stubb, the second mate, her brother-in-law, and a spare Bible for the steward – after all this, the two Captains, Peleg and Bildad, issued from the cabin, and turning to the chief mate, Peleg said:

"Now, Mr. Starbuck, are you sure everything is right? Captain Ahab is all ready – just spoke to him – nothing more to be got from shore, eh? Well, call all hands, then. Muster 'em aft here – blast 'em!"

"No need of profane words, however great the hurry, Peleg," said Bildad, "but away with thee, friend Starbuck, and do our bidding."

How now! Here upon the very point of starting for the voyage, Captain Peleg and Captain Bildad were going it with a high hand on the quarter-deck, just as if they were to be joint-commanders at sea, as well as to all appearances in port. And, as for Captain Ahab, no sign of him was yet to be seen; only, they said he was in the cabin. But then, the idea was, that his presence was by no means necessary in getting the ship under weigh, and steering her well out to sea. Indeed, as that was not at all his proper business, but the pilot's; and as he was not yet completely recovered – so they said –

therefore, Captain Ahab stayed below. And all this seemed natural enough; especially as in the merchant service many captains never show themselves on deck for a considerable time after heaving up the anchor, but remain over the cabin table, having a farewell merry-making with their shore friends, before they quit the ship for good with the pilot.

But there was not much chance to think over the matter, for Captain Peleg was now all alive. He seemed to do most of the talking and commanding, and not Bildad.

"Aft here, ye sons of bachelors," he cried, as the sailors lingered at the main-mast. "Mr. Starbuck, drive'em aft."

"Strike the tent there!" – was the next order. As I hinted before, this whalebone marquee was never pitched except in port; and on board the Pequod, for thirty years, the order to strike the tent was well known to be the next thing to heaving up the anchor.

"Man the capstan! Blood and thunder! – jump!" – was the next command, and the crew sprang for the handspikes.

Now in getting under weigh, the station generally occupied by the pilot is the forward part of the ship. And here Bildad, who, with Peleg, be it known, in addition to his other officers, was one of the licensed pilots of the port – he being suspected to have got himself made a pilot in order to save the Nantucket pilot-fee to all the ships he was concerned in, for he never piloted any other craft – Bildad, I say, might now be seen actively engaged in looking over the bows for the approaching anchor, and at intervals singing what seemed a dismal stave of psalmody, to cheer the hands at the windlass, who roared forth some sort of a chorus about the girls in Booble Alley, with hearty good will. Nevertheless, not three days previous, Bildad had told them that no profane songs would be allowed on board the Pequod, particularly in getting under weigh; and Charity, his sister, had placed a small choice copy of Watts in each seaman's berth.

Meantime, overseeing the other part of the ship, Captain Peleg ripped and swore astern in the most frightful manner. I almost thought he would sink the ship before the anchor could be got up; involuntarily I paused on my handspike, and told Queequeg to do the same, thinking of the perils we both ran, in starting on the voyage with such a devil for a pilot. I was comforting myself, however, with the thought that in pious Bildad might be found some salvation, spite of his seven hundred and seventy-seventh lay; when I felt a sudden sharp poke in my rear, and turning round, was horrified at the apparition of Captain Peleg in the act of withdrawing his leg from my immediate vicinity. That was my first kick.

"Is that the way they heave in the marchant service?" he roared. "Spring, thou sheep-head; spring, and break thy backbone! Why don't ye spring, I say, all of ye – spring! Quohog! spring, thou chap with the red whiskers; spring there, Scotch-cap; spring, thou green pants. Spring, I say, all of ye, and spring your eyes out!" And so saying, he moved along the windlass, here and there using his leg very freely, while imperturbable Bildad kept leading off with his psalmody. Thinks I, Captain Peleg must have been drinking something to-day.

At last the anchor was up, the sails were set, and off we glided. It was a short, cold Christmas; and as the short northern day merged into night, we found ourselves almost broad upon the wintry ocean, whose freezing spray cased us in ice, as in polished armor. The long rows of teeth on the bulwarks glistened in the moonlight; and like the white ivory tusks of some huge elephant, vast curving icicles depended from the bows.

Lank Bildad, as pilot, headed the first watch, and ever and anon, as the old craft deep dived into the green seas, and sent the shivering frost all over her, and the winds howled, and the cordage rang, his steady notes were heard, –

"Sweet fields beyond the swelling flood, Stand dressed in living green. So to the Jews old Canaan stood, While Jordan rolled between."

Never did those sweet words sound more sweetly to me than then. They were full of hope and fruition. Spite of this frigid winter night in the boisterous Atlantic, spite of my wet feet and wetter jacket, there was yet, it then seemed to me, many a pleasant haven in store; and meads and glades so eternally vernal, that the grass shot up by the spring, untrodden, unwilted, remains at midsummer.

At last we gained such an offing, that the two pilots were needed no longer. The stout sail-boat that had accompanied us began ranging alongside.

It was curious and not unpleasing, how Peleg and Bildad were affected at this juncture, especially Captain Bildad. For loath to depart, yet; very loath to leave, for good, a ship bound on so long and perilous a voyage – beyond both stormy Capes; a ship in which some thousands of his hard earned dollars were invested; a ship, in which an old shipmate sailed as captain; a man almost as old as he, once more starting to encounter all the terrors of the pitiless jaw; loath to say good-bye to a thing so every way brimful of every interest to him, – poor old Bildad lingered long; paced the deck with anxious strides; ran down into the cabin to speak another farewell word there; again came on deck, and looked to windward; looked towards the wide and endless waters, only bounded by the far-off unseen Eastern Continents; looked towards the land; looked aloft; looked right and left; looked everywhere and nowhere; and at last, mechanically coiling a rope upon its pin, convulsively grasped stout Peleg by the hand, and holding up a lantern, for a moment stood gazing heroically in his face, as much as to say, "Nevertheless, friend Peleg, I can stand it; yes, I can."

As for Peleg himself, he took it more like a philosopher; but for all his philosophy, there was a tear twinkling in his eye, when the lantern came too near. And he, too, did not a little run from cabin to deck – now a word below, and now a word with Starbuck, the chief mate.

But, at last, he turned to his comrade, with a final sort of look about him, – "Captain Bildad – come, old shipmate, we must go. Back the main-yard there! Boat ahoy! Stand by to come close alongside, now! Careful, careful! – come, Bildad, boy – say your last. Luck to ye, Starbuck – luck to ye, Mr. Stubb – luck to ye, Mr. Flask – good-bye and good luck to ye all – and this day three years I'll have a hot supper smoking for ye in old Nantucket. Hurrah and away!"

"God bless ye, and have ye in His holy keeping, men," murmured old Bildad, almost incoherently. "I hope ye'll have fine weather now, so that Captain Ahab may soon be moving among ye – a pleasant sun is all he needs, and ye'll have plenty of them in the tropic voyage ye go. Be careful in the hunt, ye mates. Don't stave the boats needlessly, ye harpooneers; good white cedar plank is raised full three per cent. within the year. Don't forget your prayers, either. Mr. Starbuck, mind that cooper don't waste the spare staves. Oh! the sail-needles are in the green locker! Don't whale it too much a' Lord's days, men; but don't miss a fair chance either, that's rejecting Heaven's good gifts. Have an eye to the molasses tierce, Mr. Stubb; it was a little leaky, I thought. If ye touch at the islands, Mr. Flask, beware of fornication. Good-bye, good-bye! Don't keep that cheese too long down in the hold, Mr. Starbuck; it'll spoil. Be careful with the butter – twenty cents the pound it was, and mind ye, if – "

"Come, come, Captain Bildad; stop palavering, – away!" and with that, Peleg hurried him over the side, and both dropt into the boat.

Ship and boat diverged; the cold, damp night breeze blew between; a screaming gull flew overhead; the two hulls wildly rolled; we gave three heavy-hearted cheers, and blindly plunged like fate into the lone Atlantic.

CHAPTER TWENTY THREE

The Lee Shore

SOME CHAPTERS BACK, one Bulkington was spoken of, a tall, newlanded mariner, encountered in New Bedford at the inn.

When on that shivering winter's night, the Pequod thrust her vindictive bows into the cold malicious waves, who should I see standing at her helm but Bulkington! I looked with sympathetic awe and fearfulness upon the man, who in mid-winter just landed from a four years' dangerous voyage, could so unrestingly push off again for still another tempestuous term. The land seemed scorching to his feet. Wonderfullest things are ever the unmentionable; deep memories yield no epitaphs; this six-inch chapter is the stoneless grave of Bulkington. Let me only say that it fared with him as with the storm-tossed ship, that miserably drives along the leeward land. The port would fain give succor; the port is pitiful; in the port is safety, comfort, hearthstone, supper, warm blankets, friends, all that's kind to our mortalities. But in that gale, the port, the land, is that ship's direst jeopardy; she must fly all hospitality; one touch of land, though it but graze the keel, would make her shudder through and through. With all her might she crowds all sail off shore; in so doing, fights 'gainst the very winds that fain would blow her homeward; seeks all the lashed sea's landlessness again; for refuge's sake forlornly rushing into peril; her only friend her bitterest foe!

Know ye now, Bulkington? Glimpses do ye seem to see of that mortally intolerable truth; that all deep, earnest thinking is but the intrepid effort of the soul to keep the open independence of her sea; while the wildest winds of heaven and earth conspire to cast her on the treacherous, slavish shore?

But as in landlessness alone resides highest truth, shoreless, indefinite as God – so, better is it to perish in that howling infinite, than be ingloriously dashed upon the lee, even if that were safety! For worm-like, then, oh! who would craven crawl to land! Terrors of the terrible! is all this agony so vain? Take heart, take heart, O Bulkington! Bear thee grimly, demigod! Up from the spray of thy ocean-perishing – straight up, leaps thy apotheosis!

CHAPTER TWENTY FOUR

The Advocate

AS QUEEQUEG and I are now fairly embarked in this business of whaling; and as this business of whaling has somehow come to be regarded among landsmen as a rather unpoetical and disreputable pursuit; therefore, I am all anxiety to convince ye, ye landsmen, of the injustice hereby done to us hunters of whales.

In the first place, it may be deemed almost

superfluous to establish the fact, that among people at large, the business of whaling is not accounted on a level with what are called the liberal professions. If a stranger were introduced into any miscellaneous metropolitan society, it would but slightly advance the general opinion of his merits, were he presented to the company as a harpooneer, say; and if in emulation of the naval officers he should append the initials S.W.F. (Sperm Whale Fishery) to his visiting card, such a procedure would be deemed pre-eminently presuming and ridiculous.

Doubtless one leading reason why the world declines honouring us whalemen, is this: they think that, at best, our vocation amounts to a butchering sort of business; and that when actively engaged therein, we are surrounded by all manner of defilements. Butchers we are, that is true. But butchers, also, and butchers of the bloodiest badge have been all Martial Commanders whom the world invariably delights to honour. And as for the matter of the alleged uncleanliness of our business, ye shall soon be initiated into certain facts hitherto pretty generally unknown, and which, upon the whole, will triumphantly plant the sperm whale-ship at least among the cleanliest things of this tidy earth. But even granting the charge in question to be true; what disordered slippery decks of a whale-ship are comparable to the unspeakable carrion of those battle-fields from which so many soldiers return to drink in all ladies' plaudits? And if the idea of peril so much enhances the popular conceit of the soldier's profession; let me assure ye that many a veteran who has freely marched up to a battery, would quickly recoil at the apparition of the sperm whale's vast tail, fanning into eddies the air over his head. For what are the comprehensible terrors of man compared with the interlinked terrors and wonders of God!

But, though the world scouts at us whale hunters, yet does it unwittingly pay us the profoundest homage; yea, an all-abounding adoration! for almost all the tapers, lamps, and candles that burn round the globe, burn, as before so many shrines, to our glory!

But look at this matter in other lights; weigh it in all sorts of scales; see what we whalemen are, and have been.

Why did the Dutch in De Witt's time have admirals of their whaling fleets? Why did Louis XVI. of France, at his own personal expense, fit out whaling ships from Dunkirk, and politely invite to that town some score or two of families from our own island of Nantucket? Why did Britain between the years 1750 and 1788 pay to her whalemen in bounties upwards of L1,000,000? And lastly, how comes it that we whalemen of America now outnumber all the rest of the banded whalemen in the world; sail a navy of upwards of seven hundred vessels; manned by eighteen thousand men; yearly consuming 4,000,000 of dollars; the ships worth, at the time of sailing, $20,000,000!

and every year importing into our harbors a well reaped harvest of $7,000,000. How comes all this, if there be not something puissant in whaling?

But this is not the half; look again.

I freely assert, that the cosmopolite philosopher cannot, for his life, point out one single peaceful influence, which within the last sixty years has operated more potentially upon the whole broad world, taken in one aggregate, than the high and mighty business of whaling. One way and another, it has begotten events so remarkable in themselves, and so continuously momentous in their sequential issues, that whaling may well be regarded as that Egyptian mother, who bore offspring themselves pregnant from her womb. It would be a hopeless, endless task to catalogue all these things. Let a handful suffice. For many years past the whale-ship has been the pioneer in ferreting out the remotest and least known parts of the earth. She has explored seas and archipelagoes which had no chart, where no Cook or Vancouver had ever sailed. If American and European men-of-war now peacefully ride in once savage harbors, let them fire salutes to the honour and glory of the whale-ship, which originally showed them the way, and first interpreted between them and the savages. They may celebrate as they will the heroes of Exploring Expeditions, your Cooks, your Krusensterns; but I say that scores of anonymous Captains have sailed out of Nantucket, that were as great, and greater than your Cook and your Krusenstern. For in their succourless empty-handedness, they, in the heathenish sharked waters, and by the beaches of unrecorded, javelin islands, battled with virgin wonders and terrors that Cook with all his marines and muskets would not willingly have dared. All that is made such a flourish of in the old South Sea Voyages, those things were but the life-time commonplaces of our heroic Nantucketers. Often, adventures which

Vancouver dedicates three chapters to, these men accounted unworthy of being set down in the ship's common log. Ah, the world! Oh, the world!

Until the whale fishery rounded Cape Horn, no commerce but colonial, scarcely any intercourse but colonial, was carried on between Europe and the long line of the opulent Spanish provinces on the Pacific coast. It was the whaleman who first broke through the jealous policy of the Spanish crown, touching those colonies; and, if space permitted, it might be distinctly shown how from those whalemen at last eventuated the liberation of Peru, Chili, and Bolivia from the yoke of Old Spain, and the establishment of the eternal democracy in those parts.

That great America on the other side of the sphere, Australia, was given to the enlightened world by the whaleman. After its first blunder-born discovery by a Dutchman, all other ships long shunned those shores as pestiferously barbarous; but the whale-ship touched there. The whale-ship is the true mother of that now mighty colony. Moreover, in the infancy of the first Australian settlement, the emigrants were several times saved from starvation by the benevolent biscuit of the whale-ship luckily dropping an anchor in their waters. The uncounted isles of all Polynesia confess the same truth, and do commercial homage to the whale-ship, that cleared the way for the missionary and the merchant, and in many cases carried the primitive missionaries to their first destinations. If that double-bolted land, Japan, is ever to become hospitable, it is the whale-ship alone to whom the credit will be due; for already she is on the threshold.

But if, in the face of all this, you still declare that whaling has no aesthetically noble associations connected with it, then am I ready to shiver fifty lances with you there, and unhorse you with a split helmet every time.

The whale has no famous author, and

whaling no famous chronicler, you will say.

The whale no famous author, and whaling no famous chronicler? Who wrote the first account of our Leviathan? Who but mighty Job! And who composed the first narrative of a whaling-voyage? Who, but no less a prince than Alfred the Great, who, with his own royal pen, took down the words from Other, the Norwegian whale-hunter of those times! And who pronounced our glowing eulogy in Parliament? Who, but Edmund Burke!

True enough, but then whalemen themselves are poor devils; they have no good blood in their veins.

No good blood in their veins? They have something better than royal blood there. The grandmother of Benjamin Franklin was Mary Morrel; afterwards, by marriage, Mary Folger, one of the old settlers of Nantucket, and the ancestress to a long line of Folgers and harpooneers – all kith and kin to noble Benjamin – this day darting the barbed iron from one side of the world to the other.

Good again; but then all confess that somehow whaling is not respectable.

Whaling not respectable? Whaling is imperial! By old English statutory law, the whale is declared "a royal fish."*

Oh, that's only nominal! The whale himself has never figured in any grand imposing way.

The whale never figured in any grand imposing way? In one of the mighty triumphs given to a Roman general upon his entering the world's capital, the bones of a whale, brought all the way from the Syrian coast, were the most conspicuous object in the cymballed procession.1

Grant it, since you cite it; but, say what you will, there is no real dignity in whaling.

No dignity in whaling? The dignity of our calling the very heavens attest. Cetus is a constellation in the South! No more! Drive

---

1 See subsequent chapters for something more on this head.

down your hat in presence of the Czar, and take it off to Queequeg! No more! I know a man that, in his lifetime, has taken three hundred and fifty whales. I account that man more honourable than that great captain of antiquity who boasted of taking as many walled towns.

And, as for me, if, by any possibility, there be any as yet undiscovered prime thing in me; if I shall ever deserve any real repute in that small but high hushed world which I might not be unreasonably ambitious of; if hereafter I shall do anything that, upon the whole, a man might rather have done than to have left undone; if, at my death, my executors, or more properly my creditors, find any precious MSS. in my desk, then here I prospectively ascribe all the honour and the glory to whaling; for a whale-ship was my Yale College and my Harvard.

CHAPTER TWENTY FIVE

Postscript

IN BEHALF of the dignity of whaling, I would fain advance naught but substantiated facts. But after embattling his facts, an advocate who should wholly suppress a not unreasonable surmise, which might tell eloquently upon his cause – such an advocate, would he not be blameworthy?

It is well known that at the coronation of kings and queens, even modern ones, a certain curious process of seasoning them for their functions is gone through. There is a saltcellar of state, so called, and there may be a castor of state. How they use the salt, precisely – who knows? Certain I am, however, that a king's head is solemnly oiled at his coronation, even as a head of salad. Can it be, though, that they anoint it with a view of making its interior run well, as they anoint machinery? Much might be ruminated here, concerning the essential dignity of this regal process, because in common life we esteem but meanly and contemptibly a fellow who anoints his hair, and palpably smells of that anointing. In truth, a mature man who uses hair-oil, unless medicinally, that man has probably got a quoggy spot in him somewhere. As a general rule, he can't amount to much in his totality.

But the only thing to be considered here, is this – what kind of oil is used at coronations? Certainly it cannot be olive oil, nor macassar oil, nor castor oil, nor bear's oil, nor train oil, nor cod-liver oil. What then can it possibly be, but sperm oil in its unmanufactured, unpolluted state, the sweetest of all oils?

Think of that, ye loyal Britons! we whalemen supply your kings and queens with coronation stuff!

CHAPTER TWENTY SIX

Knights and Squires

THE CHIEF MATE of the Pequod was Starbuck, a native of Nantucket, and a Quaker by descent. He was a long, earnest man, and though born on an icy coast, seemed well adapted to endure hot latitudes, his flesh being hard as twice-baked biscuit. Transported to the Indies, his live blood would not spoil like bottled ale. He must have been born in some time of general drought and famine, or upon one of those fast days for which his state is famous. Only some thirty arid summers had he seen; those summers had dried up all his physical superfluousness. But this, his thinness, so to speak, seemed no more the token of wasting anxieties and cares, than it seemed the indication of any bodily blight. It was merely the condensation of the man. He was by no means ill-looking; quite the contrary. His pure tight skin was an excellent fit; and closely wrapped up in it, and embalmed with inner health and strength, like a revivified Egyptian, this Starbuck seemed prepared to endure for long ages to come, and to endure always, as now; for be it Polar snow or torrid sun, like a patent chronometer, his interior vitality was warranted to do well in all climates. Looking into his eyes, you seemed to see there the yet lingering images of those thousand-fold perils he had calmly confronted through life. A staid, steadfast man, whose life for the most part was a telling pantomime of action, and not a tame chapter of sounds. Yet, for all his hardy sobriety and fortitude, there were certain qualities in him which at times affected, and in some cases seemed well nigh to overbalance all the rest. Uncommonly conscientious for a seaman, and endued with a deep natural reverence, the wild watery loneliness of his life did therefore strongly incline him to superstition; but to that sort of superstition, which in some organizations seems rather to spring, somehow, from intelligence than from ignorance. Outward portents and inward presentiments were his. And if at times these things bent the welded iron of his soul, much more did his far-away domestic memories of his young Cape wife and child, tend to bend him still more from the original ruggedness of his nature, and open him still further to those latent influences which, in some honest-hearted men, restrain the gush of dare-devil daring, so often evinced by others in the more perilous vicissitudes of the fishery. “I will have no man in my boat,” said Starbuck, “who is not afraid of a whale.” By this, he seemed to mean, not only that the most reliable and useful courage was that which arises from the fair estimation of the encountered peril, but that an utterly fearless man is a far more dangerous comrade than a coward.

“Aye, aye,” said Stubb, the second mate, “Starbuck, there, is as careful a man as you’ll find anywhere in this fishery.” But we shall ere long see what that word “careful” precisely means when used by a man like Stubb, or almost any other whale hunter.

Starbuck was no crusader after perils; in him courage was not a sentiment; but a thing simply useful to him, and always at hand upon all mortally practical occasions. Besides, he thought, perhaps, that in this business of whaling, courage was one of the great staple outfits of the ship, like her beef and her bread, and not to be foolishly wasted. Wherefore he had no fancy for lowering for whales after sun-down; nor for persisting in fighting a fish that too much persisted in fighting him. For, thought Starbuck, I am here in this critical ocean to kill whales for my living, and not to be killed by them for theirs; and that hundreds of men had been so killed Starbuck well knew. What doom was his own father's? Where, in the bottomless deeps, could he find the torn limbs of his brother?

With memories like these in him, and, moreover, given to a certain superstitiousness, as has been said; the courage of this Starbuck which could, nevertheless, still flourish, must indeed have been extreme. But it was not in reasonable nature that a man so organized, and with such terrible experiences and remembrances as he had; it was not in nature that these things should fail in latently engendering an element in him, which, under suitable circumstances, would break out from its confinement, and burn all his courage up. And brave as he might be, it was that sort of bravery chiefly, visible in some intrepid men, which, while generally abiding firm in the conflict with seas, or winds, or whales, or any of the ordinary irrational horrors of the world, yet cannot withstand those more terrific, because more spiritual terrors, which sometimes menace you from the concentrating brow of an enraged and mighty man.

But were the coming narrative to reveal in any instance, the complete abasement of poor Starbuck's fortitude, scarce might I have the heart to write it; for it is a thing most sorrowful, nay shocking, to expose the fall of valour in the soul. Men may seem detestable as joint stock-companies and nations; knaves, fools, and murderers there may be; men may have mean and meagre faces; but man, in the ideal, is so noble and so sparkling, such a grand and glowing creature, that over any ignominious blemish in him all his fellows should run to throw their costliest robes. That immaculate manliness we feel within ourselves, so far within us, that it remains intact though all the outer character seem gone; bleeds with keenest anguish at the undraped spectacle of a valor-ruined man. Nor can piety itself, at such a shameful sight, completely stifle her upbraidings against the permitting stars. But this august dignity I treat of, is not the dignity of kings and robes, but that abounding dignity which has no robed investiture. Thou shalt see it shining in the arm that wields a pick or drives a spike; that democratic dignity which, on all hands, radiates without end from God; Himself! The great God absolute! The centre and circumference of all democracy! His omnipresence, our divine equality!

If, then, to meanest mariners, and renegades and castaways, I shall hereafter ascribe high qualities, though dark; weave round them tragic graces; if even the most mournful, perchance the most abased, among them all, shall at times lift himself to the exalted mounts; if I shall touch that workman's arm with some ethereal light; if I shall spread a rainbow over his disastrous set of sun; then against all mortal critics bear me out in it, thou Just Spirit of Equality, which hast spread one royal mantle of humanity over all my kind! Bear me out in it, thou great democratic God! who didst not refuse to the swart convict, Bunyan, the pale, poetic pearl; Thou who didst clothe with doubly hammered leaves of finest gold, the stumped and paupered arm of old Cervantes; Thou who didst pick up Andrew Jackson from the pebbles; who didst hurl him upon a war-horse; who didst thunder him higher than a throne! Thou who, in all Thy mighty, earthly marchings, ever cullest Thy selectest champions from the kingly commons; bear me out in it, O God!

CHAPTER TWENTY SEVEN

Knights and Squires

STUBB WAS THE second mate. He was a native of Cape Cod; and hence, according to local usage, was called a Cape-Cod-man. A happy-go-lucky; neither craven nor valiant; taking perils as they came with an indifferent air; and while engaged in the most imminent crisis of the chase, toiling away, calm and collected as a journeyman joiner engaged for the year. Good-humored, easy, and careless, he presided over his whaleboat as if the most deadly encounter were but a dinner, and his crew all invited guests. He was as particular about the comfortable arrangement of his part of the boat, as an old stage-driver is about the snugness of his box. When close to the whale, in the very death-lock of the fight, he handled his unpitying lance coolly and off-handedly, as a whistling tinker his hammer. He would hum over his old rigadig tunes while flank and flank with the most exasperated monster. Long usage had, for this Stubb, converted the jaws of death into an easy chair. What he thought of death itself, there is no telling. Whether he ever thought of it at all, might be a question; but, if he ever did chance to cast his mind that way after a comfortable dinner, no doubt, like a good sailor, he took it to be a sort of call of the watch to tumble aloft, and bestir themselves there, about something which he would find out when he obeyed the order, and not sooner.

What, perhaps, with other things, made Stubb such an easy-going, unfearing man, so cheerily trudging off with the burden of life in a world full of grave pedlars, all bowed to the ground with their packs; what helped to bring about that almost impious good-humor of his; that thing must have been his pipe. For, like his nose, his short, black little pipe was one of the regular features of his face. You would almost as soon have expected him to turn out of his bunk without his nose as without his pipe. He kept a whole row of pipes there ready loaded, stuck in a rack, within easy reach of his hand; and, whenever he turned in, he smoked them all out in succession, lighting one from the other to the end of the chapter; then loading them again to be in readiness anew. For, when Stubb dressed, instead of first putting his legs into his trowsers, he put his pipe into his mouth.

I say this continual smoking must have been one cause, at least, of his peculiar disposition; for every one knows that this earthly air, whether ashore or afloat, is terribly infected with the nameless miseries of the numberless mortals who have died exhaling it; and as in time of the cholera, some people go about with a camphorated handkerchief to their mouths; so, likewise, against all mortal tribulations, Stubb's tobacco smoke might have operated as a sort of disinfecting agent.

The third mate was Flask, a native of Tisbury, in Martha's Vineyard. A short, stout, ruddy young fellow, very pugnacious concerning whales, who somehow seemed to think that the great leviathans had personally and hereditarily affronted him; and therefore it was a sort of point of honour with him, to destroy them whenever encountered. So utterly lost was he to all sense of reverence for the many marvels of their majestic bulk and mystic ways; and so dead to anything like an apprehension of any possible danger from encountering them;

that in his poor opinion, the wondrous whale was but a species of magnified mouse, or at least water-rat, requiring only a little circumvention and some small application of time and trouble in order to kill and boil. This ignorant, unconscious fearlessness of his made him a little waggish in the matter of whales; he followed these fish for the fun of it; and a three years' voyage round Cape Horn was only a jolly joke that lasted that length of time. As a carpenter's nails are divided into wrought nails and cut nails; so mankind may be similarly divided. Little Flask was one of the wrought ones; made to clinch tight and last long. They called him King-Post on board of the Pequod; because, in form, he could be well likened to the short, square timber known by that name in Arctic whalers; and which by the means of many radiating side timbers inserted into it, serves to brace the ship against the icy concussions of those battering seas.

Now these three mates – Starbuck,

Stubb, and Flask, were momentous men. They it was who by universal prescription commanded three of the Pequod's boats as headsmen. In that grand order of battle in which Captain Ahab would probably marshal his forces to descend on the whales, these three headsmen were as captains of companies. Or, being armed with their long keen whaling spears, they were as a picked trio of lancers; even as the harpooneers were flingers of javelins.

And since in this famous fishery, each mate or headsman, like a Gothic Knight of old, is always accompanied by his boat-steerer or harpooneer, who in certain conjunctures provides him with a fresh lance, when the former one has been badly twisted, or elbowed in the assault; and moreover, as there generally subsists between the two, a close intimacy and friendliness; it is therefore but meet, that in this place we set down who the Pequod's harpooneers were, and to what headsman each of them belonged.

First of all was Queequeg, whom Starbuck, the chief mate, had selected for his squire. But Queequeg is already known.

Next was Tashtego, an unmixed Indian from Gay Head, the most westerly promontory of Martha's Vineyard, where there still exists the last remnant of a village of red men, which has long supplied the neighboring island of Nantucket with many of her most daring harpooneers. In the fishery, they usually go by the generic name of Gay-Headers. Tashtego's long, lean, sable hair, his high cheek bones, and black rounding eyes – for an Indian, Oriental in their largeness, but Antarctic in their glittering expression – all this sufficiently proclaimed him an inheritor of the unvitiated blood of those proud warrior hunters, who, in quest of the great New England moose, had scoured, bow in hand, the aboriginal forests of the main. But no longer snuffing in the trail of the wild beasts of the woodland, Tashtego now hunted in the wake of the great whales of the sea; the unerring harpoon of the son fitly replacing the infallible arrow of the sires. To look at the tawny brawn of his lithe snaky limbs, you would almost have credited the superstitions of some of the earlier Puritans, and half-believed this wild Indian to be a son of the Prince of the Powers of the Air. Tashtego was Stubb the second mate's squire.

Third among the harpooneers was Daggoo, a gigantic, coal-black negro-savage, with a lion-like tread – an Ahasuerus to behold. Suspended from his ears were two golden hoops, so large that the sailors called them ring-bolts, and would talk of securing the top-sail halyards to them. In his youth Daggoo had voluntarily shipped on board of a whaler, lying in a lonely bay on his native coast. And never having been anywhere in the world but in Africa, Nantucket, and the pagan harbors most frequented by whalemen; and having now led for many years the bold life of the fishery in the ships of owners uncommonly heedful of what manner of men they shipped; Daggoo retained all his barbaric virtues, and erect as a giraffe, moved about the decks in all the pomp of six feet five in his socks. There was a corporeal humility in looking up at him; and a white man standing before him seemed a white flag come to beg truce of a fortress. Curious to tell, this imperial negro, Ahasuerus Daggoo, was the Squire of little Flask, who looked like a chess-man beside him. As for the residue of the Pequod's company, be it said, that at the present day not one in two of the many thousand men before the mast employed in the American whale fishery, are Americans born, though pretty nearly all the officers are. Herein it is the same with the American whale fishery as with the American army and military and merchant navies, and the engineering forces employed in the construction of the American Canals and Railroads. The same,

I say, because in all these cases the native American liberally provides the brains, the rest of the world as generously supplying the muscles. No small number of these whaling seamen belong to the Azores, where the outward bound Nantucket whalers frequently touch to augment their crews from the hardy peasants of those rocky shores. In like manner, the Greenland whalers sailing out of Hull or London, put in at the Shetland Islands, to receive the full complement of their crew. Upon the passage homewards, they drop them there again. How it is, there is no telling, but Islanders seem to make the best whalemen. They were nearly all Islanders in the Pequod, **Isolatoes** too, I call such, not acknowledging the common continent of men, but each **Isolato** living on a separate continent of his own. Yet now, federated along one keel, what a set these Isolatoes were! An Anacharsis Clootz deputation from all the isles of the sea, and all the ends of the earth, accompanying

Old Ahab in the Pequod to lay the world's grievances before that bar from which not very many of them ever come back. Black Little Pip – he never did – oh, no! he went before. Poor Alabama boy! On the grim Pequod's forecastle, ye shall ere long see him, beating his tambourine; prelusive of the eternal time, when sent for, to the great quarter-deck on high, he was bid strike in with angels, and beat his tambourine in glory; called a coward here, hailed a hero there!

CHAPTER TWENTY EIGHT

Ahab

FOR SEVERAL DAYS after leaving Nantucket, nothing above hatches was seen of Captain Ahab. The mates regularly relieved each other at the watches, and for aught that could be seen to the contrary, they seemed to be the only commanders of the ship; only they sometimes issued from the cabin with orders so sudden and peremptory, that after all it was plain they but commanded vicariously. Yes, their supreme lord and dictator was there, though hitherto unseen by any eyes not permitted to penetrate into the now sacred retreat of the cabin.

Every time I ascended to the deck from my watches below, I instantly gazed aft to mark if any strange face were visible; for my first vague disquietude touching the unknown captain, now in the seclusion of the sea, became almost a perturbation. This was strangely heightened at times by the ragged Elijah's diabolical incoherences uninvitedly recurring to me, with a subtle energy I could not have before conceived of. But poorly could I withstand them, much as in other moods I was almost ready to smile at the solemn whimsicalities of that outlandish prophet of the wharves. But whatever it was of apprehensiveness or uneasiness – to call it so – which I felt, yet whenever I came to look about me in the ship, it seemed against all warrantry to cherish such emotions. For though the harpooneers, with the great body of the crew, were a far more barbaric, heathenish, and motley set than any of the tame merchant-ship companies which my previous experiences had made me acquainted with, still I ascribed this – and rightly ascribed it – to the fierce uniqueness of the very nature of that wild Scandinavian vocation in which I had so abandonedly embarked. But it was especially the aspect of the three chief officers of the ship, the mates, which was most forcibly calculated to allay these colourless misgivings, and induce confidence and cheerfulness in every presentment of the voyage. Three better, more likely sea-officers and men, each in his own different way, could not readily be found, and they were every one of them Americans; a Nantucketer, a Vineyarder, a Cape man. Now, it being Christmas when the ship shot from out her harbor, for a space we had biting Polar weather, though all the time running away from it to the southward; and by every degree and minute of latitude which we sailed, gradually leaving that merciless winter, and all its intolerable weather behind us. It was one of those less lowering, but still grey and gloomy enough mornings of the transition, when with a fair wind the ship was rushing through the water with a vindictive sort of leaping and melancholy rapidity, that as I mounted to the deck at the call of the forenoon watch, so soon as I levelled my glance towards the taffrail, foreboding shivers ran over me. Reality outran apprehension; Captain Ahab stood upon his quarter-deck.

There seemed no sign of common bodily illness about him, nor of the recovery from any. He looked like a man cut away from the stake, when the fire has overrunningly wasted all the limbs without consuming them, or taking away one particle from their compacted aged robustness. His whole high, broad form, seemed made of solid bronze, and shaped in an unalterable mould, like Cellini's cast Perseus. Threading its way out from among his grey hairs, and continuing right down one side of his tawny scorched face and neck, till it disappeared in his clothing, you saw a slender rod-like mark, lividly whitish. It resembled that perpendicular seam sometimes made in the straight, lofty trunk of a great tree, when the upper lightning tearingly darts down it, and without wrenching a single twig, peels and grooves out the bark from top to bottom, ere running off into the soil, leaving the tree still greenly alive, but branded. Whether that mark was born with him, or whether it was the scar left by some desperate wound, no one could certainly say. By some tacit consent, throughout the voyage little or no allusion was made to it, especially by the mates. But once Tashtego's senior, an old Gay-Head Indian among the crew, superstitiously asserted that not till he was full forty years old did Ahab become that way branded, and then it came upon him, not in the fury of any mortal fray, but in an elemental strife at sea. Yet, this wild hint seemed inferentially negatived, by what a grey Manxman insinuated, an old sepulchral man, who, having never before sailed out of Nantucket, had never ere this laid eye upon wild Ahab. Nevertheless, the old sea-traditions, the immemorial credulities, popularly invested this old Manxman with preternatural powers of discernment. So that no white sailor seriously contradicted him when he said that if ever Captain Ahab should be tranquilly laid out – which might hardly come to pass, so he muttered – then, whoever should do that last office for the dead, would find a birth-mark on him from crown to sole.

So powerfully did the whole grim aspect of Ahab affect me, and the livid brand which streaked it, that for the first few moments I hardly noted that not a little of this overbearing grimness was owing to the barbaric white leg upon which he partly stood. It had previously come to me that this ivory leg had at sea been fashioned from the polished bone of the sperm whale's jaw. "Aye, he was dismasted off Japan," said the old Gay-Head Indian once; "but like his dismasted craft, he shipped another mast without coming home for it. He has a quiver of 'em."

I was struck with the singular posture he maintained. Upon each side of the Pequod's quarter deck, and pretty close to the mizzen shrouds, there was an auger hole, bored about half an inch or so, into the plank. His bone leg steadied in that hole; one arm elevated, and holding by a shroud; Captain Ahab stood erect, looking straight out beyond the ship's ever-pitching prow. There was an infinity of firmest fortitude, a determinate, unsurrenderable wilfulness, in the fixed and fearless, forward dedication of that glance. Not a word he spoke; nor did his officers say aught to him; though by all their minutest gestures and expressions, they plainly showed the uneasy, if not painful, consciousness of being under a troubled master-eye. And not only that, but moody stricken Ahab stood before them with a crucifixion in his face; in all the nameless regal overbearing dignity of some mighty woe.

Ere long, from his first visit in the air, he withdrew into his cabin. But after that morning, he was every day visible to the crew; either standing in his pivot-hole, or seated upon an ivory stool he had; or heavily walking the deck. As the sky grew less gloomy; indeed, began to grow a little genial, he became still less and less a recluse; as if, when the ship had sailed from home, nothing but the dead wintry bleakness of the sea had then kept him so secluded. And, by and by, it came to pass, that he was almost continually in the air; but, as yet, for all that he said, or perceptibly did, on the at last sunny deck, he seemed as unnecessary there as another mast. But the Pequod was only making a passage now; not regularly cruising; nearly all whaling preparatives needing supervision the mates were fully competent to, so that there was little or nothing, out of himself, to employ or excite Ahab, now; and thus chase away, for that one interval, the clouds that layer upon layer were piled upon his brow, as ever all clouds choose the loftiest peaks to pile themselves upon.

Nevertheless, ere long, the warm, warbling persuasiveness of the pleasant, holiday weather we came to, seemed gradually to charm him from his mood. For, as when the red-cheeked, dancing girls, April and May, trip home to the wintry, misanthropic woods; even the barest, ruggedest, most thunder-cloven old oak will at least send forth some few green sprouts, to welcome such glad-hearted visitants; so Ahab did, in the end, a little respond to the playful allurings of that girlish air. More than once did he put forth the faint blossom of a look, which, in any other man, would have soon flowered out in a smile.

CHAPTER TWENTY NINE

Enter Ahab; to Him, Stubb

SOME DAYS ELAPSED, and ice and icebergs all astern, the Pequod now went rolling through the bright Quito spring, which, at sea, almost perpetually reigns on the threshold of the eternal August of the Tropic. The warmly cool, clear, ringing, perfumed, overflowing, redundant days, were as crystal goblets of Persian sherbet, heaped up – flaked up, with rose-water snow. The starred and stately nights seemed haughty dames in jewelled velvets, nursing at home in lonely pride, the memory of their absent conquering Earls, the golden helmeted suns! For sleeping man, 'twas hard to choose between such winsome days and such seducing nights. But all the witcheries of that unwaning weather did not merely lend new spells and potencies to the outward world. Inward they turned upon the soul, especially when the still mild hours of eve came on; then, memory shot her crystals as the clear ice most forms of noiseless twilights. And all these subtle agencies, more and more they wrought on Ahab's texture.

Old age is always wakeful; as if, the longer linked with life, the less man has to do with aught that looks like death. Among sea-commanders, the old greybeards will oftenest leave their berths to visit the night-cloaked deck. It was so with Ahab; only that now, of late, he seemed so much to live in the open air, that truly speaking, his visits were more to the cabin, than from the cabin to the planks. "It feels like going down into one's tomb," – he would mutter to himself – "for an old captain like me to be descending this narrow scuttle, to go to my grave-dug berth."

So, almost every twenty-four hours, when the watches of the night were set, and the band on deck sentinelled the slumbers of the band below; and when if a rope was to be hauled upon the forecastle, the sailors flung it not rudely down, as by day, but with some cautiousness dropt it to its place for fear of disturbing their slumbering shipmates; when this sort of steady quietude would begin to prevail, habitually, the silent steersman would watch the cabin-scuttle; and ere long the old man would emerge, gripping at the iron banister, to help his crippled way. Some considering touch of humanity was in him; for at times like these, he usually abstained from patrolling the quarter-deck; because to his wearied mates, seeking repose within six inches of his ivory heel, such would have been the reverberating crack and din of that bony step, that their dreams would have been on the crunching teeth of sharks. But once, the mood was on him too deep for common regardings; and as with heavy, lumber-like pace he was measuring the ship from taffrail to mainmast, Stubb, the old second mate, came up from below, with a certain unassured, deprecating humorousness, hinted that if Captain Ahab was pleased to walk the planks, then, no one could say nay; but there might be some way of muffling the noise; hinting something indistinctly and hesitatingly about a globe of tow, and the insertion into it, of the ivory heel. Ah! Stubb, thou didst not know Ahab then.

"Am I a cannon-ball, Stubb," said Ahab, "that thou wouldst wad me that fashion? But go thy ways; I had forgot. Below to thy nightly grave; where such as ye sleep between shrouds, to use ye to the filling one at last. – Down, dog, and kennel!"

Starting at the unforseen concluding exclamation of the so suddenly scornful old man, Stubb was speechless a moment; then said excitedly, "I am not used to be spoken to that way, sir; I do but less than half like it, sir."

"Avast! gritted Ahab between his set teeth, and violently moving away, as if to avoid some passionate temptation.

"No, sir; not yet," said Stubb, emboldened, "I will not tamely be called a dog, sir."

"Then be called ten times a donkey, and a mule, and an ass, and begone, or I'll clear the world of thee!"

As he said this, Ahab advanced upon him with such overbearing terrors in his aspect, that Stubb involuntarily retreated.

"I was never served so before without giving a hard blow for it," muttered Stubb, as he found himself descending the cabin-scuttle. "It's very queer. Stop, Stubb; somehow, now,

I don't well know whether to go back and strike him, or – what's that? – down here on my knees and pray for him? Yes, that was the thought coming up in me; but it would be the first time I ever **did** pray. It's queer; very queer; and he's queer too; aye, take him fore and aft, he's about the queerest old man Stubb ever sailed with. How he flashed at me! – his eyes like powder-pans! is he mad? Anyway there's something on his mind, as sure as there must be something on a deck when it cracks. He aint in his bed now, either, more than three hours out of the twenty-four; and he don't sleep then. Didn't that Dough-Boy, the steward, tell me that of a morning he always finds the old man's hammock clothes all rumpled and tumbled, and the sheets down at the foot, and the coverlid almost tied into knots, and the pillow a sort of frightful hot, as though a baked brick had been on it? A hot old man! I guess he's got what some folks ashore call a conscience; it's a kind of Tic-Dollyrow they say – worse nor a toothache. Well, well; I don't know what it is, but the Lord keep me from catching it. He's full of riddles; I wonder what he goes into the after hold for, every night, as Dough-Boy tells me he suspects; what's that for, I should like to know? Who's made appointments with him in the hold? Ain't that queer, now? But there's no telling, it's the old game – Here goes for a snooze. Damn me, it's worth a fellow's while to be born into the world, if only to fall right asleep. And now that I think of it, that's about the first thing babies do, and that's a sort of queer, too. Damn me, but all things are queer, come to think of 'em. But that's against my principles. Think not, is my eleventh commandment; and sleep when you can, is my twelfth – So here goes again. But how's that? didn't he call me a dog? blazes! he called me ten times a donkey, and piled a lot of jackasses on top of **that!** He might as well have kicked me, and done with it. Maybe he **did** kick me, and I didn't observe it, I was so taken all aback with his brow, somehow. It flashed like a bleached bone. What the devil's the matter with me? I don't stand right on my legs. Coming afoul of that old man has a sort of turned me wrong side out. By the Lord, I must have been dreaming, though – How? how? how? – but the only way's to stash it; so here goes to hammock again; and in the morning, I'll see how this plaguey juggling thinks over by daylight."

CHAPTER THIRTY

The Pipe

WHEN STUBB had departed, Ahab stood for a while leaning over the bulwarks; and then, as had been usual with him of late, calling a sailor of the watch, he sent him below for his ivory stool, and also his pipe. Lighting the pipe at the binnacle lamp and planting the stool on the weather side of the deck, he sat and smoked.

In old Norse times, the thrones of the sea-loving Danish kings were fabricated, saith tradition, of the tusks of the narwhale. How could one look at Ahab then, seated on that tripod of bones, without bethinking him of the royalty it symbolized? For a Khan of the plank, and a king of the sea, and a great lord of Leviathans was Ahab.

Some moments passed, during which the thick vapour came from his mouth in quick and constant puffs, which blew back again into his face. "How now," he soliloquized at last, withdrawing the tube, "this smoking no longer soothes. Oh, my pipe! hard must it go with me if thy charm be gone! Here have I been unconsciously toiling, not pleasuring – aye, and ignorantly smoking to windward all the while; to windward, and with such nervous whiffs, as if, like the dying whale, my final jets were the strongest and fullest of trouble. What business have I with this pipe? This thing that is meant for sereneness, to send up mild white vapours among mild white hairs, not among torn iron-grey locks like mine. I'll smoke no more – "

He tossed the still lighted pipe into the sea. The fire hissed in the waves; the same instant the ship shot by the bubble the sinking pipe made. With slouched hat, Ahab lurchingly paced the planks.

CHAPTER THIRTY ONE

Queen Mab

NEXT MORNING Stubb accosted Flask.

"Such a queer dream, King-Post, I never had. You know the old man's ivory leg, well I dreamed he kicked me with it; and when I tried to kick back, upon my soul, my little man, I kicked my leg right off! And then, presto! Ahab seemed a pyramid, and I, like a blazing fool, kept kicking at it. But what was still more curious, Flask – you know how curious all dreams are – through all this rage that I was in, I somehow seemed to be thinking to myself, that after all, it was not much of an insult, that kick from Ahab. 'Why,' thinks I, 'what's the row? It's not a real leg, only a false leg.' And there's a mighty difference between a living thump and a dead thump. That's what makes a blow from the hand, Flask, fifty times more savage to bear than a blow from a cane. The living member – that makes the living insult, my little man. And thinks I to myself all the while, mind, while I was stubbing my silly toes against that cursed pyramid – so confoundedly contradictory was it all, all the while, I say, I was thinking to myself, 'what's his leg now, but a cane – a whalebone cane. Yes,' thinks I, 'it was only a playful cudgelling – in fact, only a whaleboning that he gave me – not a base kick. Besides,' thinks I, 'look at it once; why, the end of it – the foot part – what a small sort of end it is; whereas, if a broad footed farmer kicked me, **there's** a devilish broad insult. But this insult is whittled down to a point only.' But now comes the greatest joke of the dream, Flask. While I was battering away at the pyramid, a sort of badger-haired old merman, with a hump on his back, takes me by the shoulders, and slews me round. 'What are you 'bout?' says he. Slid! man, but I was frightened. Such a phiz! But, somehow, next moment I was over the fright. 'What am I about?' says I at last. 'And what business is that of yours, I should like to know, Mr. Humpback? Do **you** want a kick?' By the lord, Flask, I had no sooner said that, than he turned round his stern to me, bent over, and dragging up a lot of seaweed he had for a clout – what do you think, I saw? – why thunder alive, man, his stern was stuck full of marlinspikes, with the points out. Says I, on second thoughts, 'I guess I won't kick you, old fellow.' 'Wise Stubb,' said he, 'wise Stubb;' and kept muttering it all the time, a sort of eating of his own gums like a chimney hag. Seeing he wasn't going to stop saying over his 'wise Stubb, wise Stubb,' I thought I might as well fall to kicking the pyramid again. But I had only just lifted my foot for it, when he roared out, 'Stop that kicking!' 'Halloa,' says I, 'what's the matter now, old fellow?' 'Look ye here,' says he; 'let's argue the insult. Captain Ahab kicked ye, didn't he?' 'Yes, he did,' says I – 'right **here** it was.' 'Very good,' says he – 'he used his ivory leg, didn't he?' 'Yes, he did,' says I. 'Well then,' says he, 'wise Stubb, what have you to complain of? Didn't he kick with right good will? it wasn't a common pitch pine leg he kicked with, was it? No, you were kicked by a great man, and with a beautiful ivory leg, Stubb. It's an honour; I consider it an honour. Listen, wise Stubb. In old England the greatest lords think it great glory to be slapped by a queen, and made garter-knights of; but, be **your** boast, Stubb, that ye were kicked by old Ahab, and made a wise man of. Remember what I say; **be** kicked by him; account his kicks honours; and on no account kick back; for you can't help yourself, wise Stubb. Don't you see that pyramid?' With that, he all of a sudden seemed somehow, in some queer fashion, to swim off into the air. I snored; rolled over; and there I was in my hammock! Now, what do you think of that dream, Flask?"

"I don't know; it seems a sort of foolish to me, tho.'"

"May be; may be. But it's made a wise man of me, Flask. D'ye see Ahab standing there, sideways looking over the stern? Well, the best thing you can do, Flask, is to let the old man alone; never speak to him, whatever he says. Halloa! What's that he shouts? Hark!"

"Mast-head, there! Look sharp, all of ye! There are whales hereabouts!

"If ye see a white one, split your lungs for him!

"What do you think of that now, Flask? ain't there a small drop of something queer about that, eh? A white whale – did ye mark that, man? Look ye – there's something special in the wind. Stand by for it, Flask. Ahab has that that's bloody on his mind. But, mum; he comes this way."

CHAPTER THIRTY TWO

Cetology

ALREADY WE ARE boldly launched upon the deep; but soon we shall be lost in its unshored, harbourless immensities. Ere that come to pass; ere the Pequod's weedy hull rolls side by side with the barnacled hulls of the leviathan; at the outset it is but well to attend to a matter almost indispensable to a thorough appreciative understanding of the more special leviathanic revelations and allusions of all sorts which are to follow.

It is some systematized exhibition of the whale in his broad genera, that I would now fain put before you. Yet is it no easy task. The classification of the constituents of a chaos, nothing less is here essayed. Listen to what the best and latest authorities have laid down.

"No branch of Zoology is so much involved as that which is entitled Cetology," says Captain Scoresby, A.D. 1820.

"It is not my intention, were it in my power, to enter into the inquiry as to the true method of dividing the cetacea into groups and families.... Utter confusion exists among the historians of this animal" (sperm whale), says Surgeon Beale, A.D. 1839.

"Unfitness to pursue our research in the unfathomable waters." "Impenetrable veil covering our knowledge of the cetacea." "A field strewn with thorns." "All these incomplete indications but serve to torture us naturalists."

Thus speak of the whale, the great Cuvier, and John Hunter, and Lesson, those lights of zoology and anatomy. Nevertheless, though of real knowledge there be little, yet of books there are a plenty; and so in some small degree, with cetology, or the science of whales. Many are the men, small and great, old and new, landsmen and seamen, who have at large or in little, written of the whale. Run over a few: – The Authors of the Bible; Aristotle; Pliny; Aldrovandi; Sir Thomas Browne; Gesner; Ray; Linnaeus; Rondeletius; Willoughby; Green; Artedi; Sibbald; Brisson; Marten; Lacepede; Bonneterre; Desmarest; Baron Cuvier; Frederick Cuvier; John Hunter; Owen; Scoresby; Beale; Bennett; J. Ross Browne; the Author of Miriam Coffin; Olmstead; and the Rev. T. Cheever. But to what ultimate generalizing purpose all these have written, the above cited extracts will show.

Of the names in this list of whale authors, only those following Owen ever saw living whales; and but one of them was a real professional harpooneer and whaleman. I mean Captain Scoresby. On the separate subject of the Greenland or right-whale, he is the best existing authority. But Scoresby knew nothing and says nothing of the great sperm whale, compared with which the Greenland whale is almost unworthy mentioning. And here be it said, that the Greenland whale is an usurper upon the throne of the seas. He is not even by any means the largest of the whales. Yet, owing to the long priority of his claims, and the profound ignorance which, till some seventy years back, invested the then fabulous or utterly unknown sperm-whale, and which ignorance to this present day still reigns in all but some few scientific retreats and whale-ports; this usurpation has been every way complete. Reference to nearly all the leviathanic allusions in the great poets of past days, will satisfy you that the Greenland whale, without one rival, was to them the monarch of the seas. But the time has at last come for a new proclamation. This is Charing Cross; hear ye! good people all, – the Greenland whale is deposed, – the great sperm whale now reigneth!

There are only two books in being which at all pretend to put the living sperm whale before you, and at the same time, in the remotest degree succeed in the attempt. Those books are Beale's and Bennett's; both in their time surgeons to English South-Sea whale-ships, and both exact and reliable men. The original matter touching the sperm whale to be found in their volumes is necessarily small; but so far as it goes, it is of excellent quality, though mostly confined to scientific description. As yet, however, the sperm whale, scientific or poetic, lives not complete in any literature. Far above all other hunted whales, his is an unwritten life.

Now the various species of whales need some sort of popular comprehensive classification, if only an easy outline one for the present, hereafter to be filled in all its departments by subsequent laborers. As no better man advances to take this matter in hand, I hereupon offer my own poor endeavors. I promise nothing complete; because any human thing supposed to be complete, must for that very reason infallibly be faulty. I shall not pretend to a minute anatomical description of the various species, or – in this place at least – to much of any description. My object here is simply to project the draught of a systematization of cetology. I am the architect, not the builder.

But it is a ponderous task; no ordinary letter-sorter in the Post-Office is equal to it. To grope down into the bottom of the sea after them; to have one's hands among the unspeakable foundations, ribs, and very pelvis of the world; this is a fearful thing. What am I that I should essay to hook the nose of this leviathan! The awful tauntings in Job might well appal me. Will he (the leviathan) make a covenant with thee?

Behold the hope of him is vain! But I have swam through libraries and sailed through oceans; I have had to do with whales with these visible hands; I am in earnest; and I will try. There are some preliminaries to settle.

First: The uncertain, unsettled condition of this science of Cetology is in the very vestibule attested by the fact, that in some quarters it still remains a moot point whether a whale be a fish. In his System of Nature, A.D. 1776, Linnaeus declares, "I hereby separate the whales from the fish." But of my own knowledge, I know that down to the year 1850, sharks and shad, alewives and herring, against Linnaeus's express edict, were still found dividing the possession of the same seas with the Leviathan.

The grounds upon which Linnaeus would fain have banished the whales from the waters, he states as follows: "On account of their warm bilocular heart, their lungs, their movable eyelids, their hollow ears, penem intrantem feminam mammis lactantem," and finally, "ex lege naturae jure meritoque." I submitted all this to my friends Simeon Macey and Charley Coffin, of Nantucket, both messmates of mine in a certain voyage, and they united in the opinion that the reasons set forth were altogether insufficient. Charley profanely hinted they were humbug.

Be it known that, waiving all argument, I take the good old fashioned ground that the whale is a fish, and call upon holy Jonah to back me. This fundamental thing settled, the next point is, in what internal respect does the whale differ from other fish. Above, Linnaeus has given you those items. But in brief, they are these: lungs and warm blood; whereas, all other fish are lungless and cold blooded.

Next: how shall we define the whale, by his obvious externals, so as conspicuously to label him for all time to come? To be short, then, a whale is **a spouting fish**

with a horizontal tail. There you have him. However contracted, that definition is the result of expanded meditation. A walrus spouts much like a whale, but the walrus is not a fish, because he is amphibious. But the last term of the definition is still more cogent, as coupled with the first. Almost any one must have noticed that all the fish familiar to landsmen have not a flat, but a vertical, or up-and-down tail. Whereas, among spouting fish the tail, though it may be similarly shaped, invariably assumes a horizontal position.

By the above definition of what a whale is, I do by no means exclude from the leviathanic brotherhood any sea creature hitherto identified with the whale by the best informed Nantucketers; nor, on the other hand, link with it any fish hitherto authoritatively regarded as alien.* Hence, all the smaller, spouting, and horizontal tailed fish must be included in this ground-plan of Cetology. Now, then, come the grand divisions of the entire whale host.

*I am aware that down to the present time, the fish styled Lamatins and Dugongs (Pig-fish and Sow-fish of the Coffins of Nantucket) are included by many naturalists among the whales. But as these pig-fish are a noisy, contemptible set, mostly lurking in the mouths of rivers, and feeding on wet hay, and especially as they do not spout, I deny their credentials as whales; and have presented them with their passports to quit the Kingdom of Cetology.

First: According to magnitude I divide the whales into three primary BOOKS (subdivisible into CHAPTERS), and these shall comprehend them all, both small and large.

I. THE FOLIO WHALE; II. the OCTAVO WHALE; III. the DUODECIMO WHALE.

As the type of the FOLIO I present the **Sperm Whale**; of the OCTAVO, the **Grampus**; of the DUODECIMO, the **Porpoise**.

FOLIOS. Among these I here include the

following chapters: – I. The **Sperm Whale**; II. the **Right Whale**; III. the **Fin-Back Whale**; IV. the **Hump-backed Whale**; V. the **Razor-Back Whale**; VI. the **Sulphur-Bottom Whale**.

BOOK I. (**Folio**), CHAPTER I. (**Sperm Whale**). – This whale, among the English of old vaguely known as the Trumpa whale, and the Physeter whale, and the Anvil Headed whale, is the present Cachalot of the French, and the Pottsfich of the Germans, and the Macrocephalus of the Long Words. He is, without doubt, the largest inhabitant of the globe; the most formidable of all whales to encounter; the most majestic in aspect; and lastly, by far the most valuable in commerce; he being the only creature from which that valuable substance, spermaceti, is obtained. All his peculiarities will, in many other places, be enlarged upon. It is chiefly with his name that I now have to do. Philologically considered, it is absurd. Some centuries ago, when the Sperm whale was almost wholly unknown in his own proper individuality, and when his oil was only accidentally obtained from the stranded fish; in those days spermaceti, it would seem, was popularly supposed to be derived from a creature identical with the one then known in England as the Greenland or Right Whale. It was the idea also, that this same spermaceti was that quickening humor of the Greenland Whale which the first syllable of the word literally expresses. In those times, also, spermaceti was exceedingly scarce, not being used for light, but only as an ointment and medicament. It was only to be had from the druggists as you nowadays buy an ounce of rhubarb. When, as I opine, in the course of time, the true nature of spermaceti became known, its original name was still retained by the dealers; no doubt to enhance its value by a notion so strangely significant of its scarcity. And so the appellation must at last have come to be bestowed upon the whale from which this spermaceti was really derived.

BOOK I. (**Folio**), CHAPTER II. (**Right Whale**). – In one respect this is the most venerable of the leviathans, being the one first regularly hunted by man. It yields the article commonly known as whalebone or baleen; and the oil specially known as "whale oil," an inferior article in commerce. Among the fishermen, he is indiscriminately designated by all the following titles: The Whale; the Greenland Whale; the Black Whale; the Great Whale; the True Whale; the Right Whale. There is a deal of obscurity concerning the identity of the species thus multitudinously baptised. What then is the whale, which I include in the second species of my Folios? It is the Great Mysticetus of the English naturalists; the Greenland Whale of the English whalemen; the Baleine Ordinaire of the French whalemen; the Growlands Walfish of the Swedes. It is the whale which for more than two centuries past has been hunted by the Dutch and

English in the Arctic seas; it is the whale which the American fishermen have long pursued in the Indian ocean, on the Brazil Banks, on the Nor' West Coast, and various other parts of the world, designated by them Right Whale Cruising Grounds.

Some pretend to see a difference between the Greenland whale of the English and the right whale of the Americans. But they precisely agree in all their grand features; nor has there yet been presented a single determinate fact upon which to ground a radical distinction. It is by endless subdivisions based upon the most inconclusive differences, that some departments of natural history become so repellingly intricate. The right whale will be elsewhere treated of at some length, with reference to elucidating the sperm whale.

BOOK I. (**Folio**), CHAPTER III. (**Fin-Back**). – Under this head I reckon a monster which, by the various names of Fin-Back, Tall-Spout, and Long-John, has been seen almost in every sea and is commonly the whale whose distant jet is so often descried by passengers crossing the Atlantic, in the New York packet-tracks. In the length he attains, and in his baleen, the Fin-back resembles the right whale, but is of a less portly girth, and a lighter colour, approaching to olive. His great lips present a cable-like aspect, formed by the intertwisting, slanting folds of large wrinkles. His grand distinguishing feature, the fin, from which he derives his name, is often a conspicuous object. This fin is some three or four feet long, growing vertically from the hinder part of the back, of an angular shape, and with a very sharp pointed end. Even if not the slightest other part of the creature be visible, this isolated fin will, at times, be seen plainly projecting from the surface. When the sea is moderately calm, and slightly marked with spherical ripples, and this gnomon-like fin stands up and casts shadows upon the wrinkled surface, it may well be supposed that the watery circle surrounding it somewhat resembles a dial, with its style and wavy hour-lines graved on it. On that Ahaz-dial the shadow often goes back. The Fin-Back is not gregarious. He seems a whale-hater, as some men are man-haters. Very shy; always going solitary; unexpectedly rising to the surface in the remotest and most sullen waters; his straight and single lofty jet rising like a tall misanthropic spear upon a barren plain; gifted with such wondrous power and velocity in swimming, as to defy all present pursuit from man; this leviathan seems the banished and unconquerable Cain of his race, bearing for his mark that style upon his back. From having the baleen in his mouth, the Fin-Back is sometimes included with the right whale, among a theoretic species denominated **Whalebone Whales**, that is, whales with baleen. Of these so called Whalebone whales, there would seem to be several varieties, most of which, however, are little known. Broad-nosed whales and beaked whales; pike-headed whales;

bunched whales; under-jawed whales and rostrated whales, are the fishermen's names for a few sorts.

In connection with this appellative of "Whalebone whales," it is of great importance to mention, that however such a nomenclature may be convenient in facilitating allusions to some kind of whales, yet it is in vain to attempt a clear classification of the Leviathan, founded upon either his baleen, or hump, or fin, or teeth; notwithstanding that those marked parts or features very obviously seem better adapted to afford the basis for a regular system of Cetology than any other detached bodily distinctions, which the whale, in his kinds, presents. How then? The baleen, hump, back-fin, and teeth; these are things whose peculiarities are indiscriminately dispersed among all sorts of whales, without any regard to what may be the nature of their structure in other and more essential particulars. Thus, the sperm whale and the humpbacked whale, each has a hump; but there the similitude ceases. Then, this same humpbacked whale and the Greenland whale, each of these has baleen; but there again the similitude ceases. And it is just the same with the other parts above mentioned. In various sorts of whales, they form such irregular combinations; or, in the case of any one of them detached, such an irregular isolation; as utterly to defy all general methodization formed upon such a basis. On this rock every one of the whale-naturalists has split.

But it may possibly be conceived that, in the internal parts of the whale, in his anatomy – there, at least, we shall be able to hit the right classification. Nay; what thing, for example, is there in the Greenland whale's anatomy more striking than his baleen? Yet we have seen that by his baleen it is impossible correctly to classify the Greenland whale. And if you descend into the bowels of the various leviathans, why there you will not find distinctions a fiftieth part as available to the systematizer as those external ones already enumerated. What then remains? nothing but to take hold of the whales bodily, in their entire liberal volume, and boldly sort them that way. And this is the Bibliographical system here adopted; and it is the only one that can possibly succeed, for it alone is practicable. To proceed.

BOOK I. (**Folio**) CHAPTER IV. (**Hump-Back**). – This whale is often seen on the northern American coast. He has been frequently captured there, and towed into harbor. He has a great pack on him like a peddler; or you might call him the Elephant and Castle whale. At any rate, the popular name for him does not sufficiently distinguish him, since the sperm whale also has a hump though a smaller one. His oil is not very valuable. He has baleen. He is the most gamesome and light-hearted of all the whales, making more gay foam and white water generally than any other of them.

BOOK I. (**Folio**), CHAPTER V. (**Razor-**

Back). – Of this whale little is known but his name. I have seen him at a distance off Cape Horn. Of a retiring nature, he eludes both hunters and philosophers. Though no coward, he has never yet shown any part of him but his back, which rises in a long sharp ridge. Let him go. I know little more of him, nor does anybody else.

BOOK I. (**Folio**), CHAPTER VI. (**Sulphur-Bottom**). – Another retiring gentleman, with a brimstone belly, doubtless got by scraping along the Tartarian tiles in some of his profounder divings. He is seldom seen; at least I have never seen him except in the remoter southern seas, and then always at too great a distance to study his countenance. He is never chased; he would run away with rope-walks of line. Prodigies are told of him. Adieu, Sulphur Bottom! I can say nothing more that is true of ye, nor can the oldest Nantucketer.

Thus ends BOOK I. (**Folio**), and now begins BOOK II. (**Octavo**).

OCTAVOES.* – These embrace the whales of middling magnitude, among which present may be numbered: – I., the **Grampus**; II., the **Black Fish**; III., the **Narwhale**; IV., the **Thrasher**; V., the **Killer**.

*Why this book of whales is not denominated the Quarto is very plain. Because, while the whales of this order, though smaller than those of the former order, nevertheless retain a proportionate likeness to them in figure, yet the bookbinder's Quarto volume in its dimensioned form does not preserve the shape of the Folio volume, but the Octavo volume does.

BOOK II. (**Octavo**), CHAPTER I. (**Grampus**). – Though this fish, whose loud sonorous breathing, or rather blowing, has furnished a proverb to landsmen, is so well known a denizen of the deep, yet is he not popularly classed among whales. But possessing all the grand distinctive features of the leviathan, most naturalists have recognised him for one. He is of moderate octavo size, varying from fifteen to twenty-five feet in length, and of corresponding dimensions round the waist. He swims in herds; he is never regularly hunted, though his oil is considerable in quantity, and pretty good for light. By some fishermen his approach is regarded as premonitory of the advance of the great sperm whale.

BOOK II. (**Octavo**), CHAPTER II. (**Black Fish**). – I give the popular fishermen's names for all these fish, for generally they are the best. Where any name happens to be vague or inexpressive, I shall say so, and suggest another. I do so now, touching the Black Fish, so-called, because blackness is the rule among almost all whales. So, call him the Hyena Whale, if you please. His voracity is well known, and from the circumstance that the inner angles of his lips are curved upwards, he carries an everlasting Mephistophelean grin on his face. This whale averages some sixteen or eighteen feet in length. He is found in almost all latitudes. He has a peculiar way of showing his dorsal hooked fin in swimming, which looks something like a Roman nose. When not more profitably employed, the sperm whale hunters sometimes capture the Hyena whale, to keep up the supply of cheap oil for domestic employment – as some frugal housekeepers, in the absence of company, and quite alone by themselves, burn unsavory tallow instead of odorous wax. Though their blubber is very thin, some of these whales will yield you upwards of thirty gallons of oil.

BOOK II. (**Octavo**), CHAPTER III. (**Narwhale**), that is, **Nostril whale**. –Another instance of a curiously named whale, so named I suppose from his peculiar horn being originally mistaken for a peaked nose. The creature is some sixteen feet in length, while its horn averages five feet, though some exceed ten, and even attain to fifteen feet. Strictly speaking, this horn is but a lengthened tusk, growing out from the jaw in a line a little depressed from the horizontal.

But it is only found on the sinister side, which has an ill effect, giving its owner something analogous to the aspect of a clumsy left-handed man. What precise purpose this ivory horn or lance answers, it would be hard to say. It does not seem to be used like the blade of the sword-fish and bill-fish; though some sailors tell me that the Narwhale employs it for a rake in turning over the bottom of the sea for food. Charley Coffin said it was used for an ice-piercer; for the Narwhale, rising to the surface of the Polar Sea, and finding it sheeted with ice, thrusts his horn up, and so breaks through. But you cannot prove either of these surmises to be correct. My own opinion is, that however this one-sided horn may really be used by the Narwhale – however that may be – it would certainly be very convenient to him for a folder in reading pamphlets. The Narwhale I have heard called the Tusked whale, the Horned whale, and the Unicorn whale. He is certainly a curious example of the Unicornism to be found in almost every kingdom of animated nature. From certain cloistered old authors I have gathered that this same sea-unicorn's horn was in ancient days regarded as the great antidote against poison, and as such, preparations of it brought immense prices. It was also distilled to a volatile salts for fainting ladies, the same way that the horns of the male deer are manufactured into hartshorn. Originally it was in itself accounted an object of great curiosity. Black Letter tells me that Sir Martin Frobisher on his return from that voyage, when Queen Bess did gallantly wave her jewelled hand to him from a window of Greenwich Palace, as his bold ship sailed down the Thames; "when Sir Martin returned from that voyage," saith Black Letter, "on bended knees he presented to her highness a prodigious long horn of the Narwhale, which for a long period after hung in the castle at Windsor." An Irish author avers that the Earl of Leicester, on bended knees, did likewise present to her highness another horn, pertaining to a land beast of the unicorn nature.

The Narwhale has a very picturesque, leopard-like look, being of a milk-white ground colour, dotted with round and oblong spots of black. His oil is very superior, clear and fine; but there is little of it, and he is seldom hunted. He is mostly found in the circumpolar seas.

BOOK II. (**Octavo**), CHAPTER IV. (**Killer**). – Of this whale little is precisely known to the Nantucketer, and nothing at all to the professed naturalist. From what I have seen of him at a distance, I should say that he was about the bigness of a grampus. He is very savage – a sort of Feegee fish. He sometimes takes the great Folio whales by the lip, and hangs there like a leech, till the mighty brute is worried to death. The Killer is never hunted. I never heard what sort of oil he has. Exception might be taken to the name bestowed upon this whale, on the ground of its indistinctness. For we are all killers, on land and on sea; Bonapartes and Sharks included.

BOOK II. (**Octavo**), CHAPTER V. (**Thrasher**). – This gentleman is famous for his tail, which he uses for a ferule in thrashing his foes. He mounts the Folio whale's back, and as he swims, he works his passage by flogging him; as some schoolmasters get along in the world by a similar process. Still less is known of the Thrasher than of the Killer. Both are outlaws, even in the lawless seas.

Thus ends BOOK II. (**Octavo**), and begins BOOK III. (**Duodecimo**).

DUODECIMOES. – These include the smaller whales. I. The Huzza Porpoise. II. The Algerine Porpoise. III. The Mealy-mouthed Porpoise.

To those who have not chanced specially to study the subject, it may possibly seem strange, that fishes not commonly exceeding four or five feet should be marshalled among WHALES – a word, which, in the popular sense, always conveys an idea of hugeness. But the creatures set down above as Duodecimoes are infallibly whales, by the terms of my definition of what a whale is – **i.e.** a spouting fish, with a horizontal tail.

BOOK III. (**Duodecimo**), CHAPTER 1. (**Huzza Porpoise**). – This is the common porpoise found almost all over the globe. The name is of my own bestowal; for there are more than one sort of porpoises, and something must be done to distinguish them. I call him thus, because he always swims in hilarious shoals, which upon the broad sea keep tossing themselves to heaven like caps in a Fourth-of-July crowd. Their appearance is generally hailed with delight by the mariner. Full of fine spirits, they invariably come from the breezy billows to windward. They are the lads that always live before the wind. They are accounted a lucky omen. If you yourself can withstand three cheers at beholding these vivacious fish, then heaven help ye; the spirit of godly gamesomeness is not in ye.

A well-fed, plump Huzza Porpoise will yield you one good gallon of good oil. But the fine and delicate fluid extracted from his jaws is exceedingly valuable. It is in request among jewellers and watchmakers. Sailors put it on their hones. Porpoise meat is good eating, you know. It may never have occurred to you that a porpoise spouts. Indeed, his spout is so small that it is not very readily discernible. But the next time you have a chance, watch him; and you will then see the great Sperm whale himself in miniature.

BOOK III. (**Duodecimo**), CHAPTER II. (**Algerine Porpoise**). – A pirate. Very savage. He is only found, I think, in the Pacific. He is somewhat larger than the Huzza Porpoise, but much of the same general make. Provoke him, and he will buckle to a shark. I have lowered for him many times, but never yet saw him captured.

BOOK III. (**Duodecimo**), CHAPTER III. (**Mealy-mouthed Porpoise**). – The largest kind of Porpoise; and only found in the Pacific, so far as it is known. The only English name, by which he has hitherto been designated, is that of the fishers – Right-Whale Porpoise, from the circumstance that he is chiefly found in the vicinity of that Folio. In shape, he differs in some degree from the Huzza Porpoise, being of a less rotund and jolly girth; indeed, he is of quite a neat and gentleman-like figure. He has no fins on his back (most other porpoises have), he has a lovely tail, and sentimental Indian eyes of a hazel hue. But his mealy-mouth spoils all. Though his entire back down to his side fins is of a deep sable, yet a boundary line, distinct as the mark in a ship's hull, called the "bright waist," that line streaks him from stem to stern, with two separate colours, black above and white below. The white comprises part of his head, and the whole of his mouth, which makes him look as if he had just escaped from a felonious visit to a meal-bag. A most mean and mealy aspect! His oil is much like that of the common porpoise.

Beyond the DUODECIMO, this system does not proceed, inasmuch as the Porpoise is the smallest of the whales. Above, you have all the Leviathans of note. But there are a rabble of uncertain, fugitive, half-fabulous whales, which, as an American whaleman, I know by reputation, but not personally. I shall enumerate them by their fore-castle appellations; for possibly such a list may be valuable to future investigators, who may complete what I have here but begun. If any of the following whales, shall hereafter be caught and marked, then he can readily be incorporated into this System, according to his Folio, Octavo, or Duodecimo magnitude: – The Bottle-Nose Whale; the Junk Whale; the Pudding-Headed Whale; the Cape Whale; the Leading Whale; the Cannon Whale; the Scragg Whale; the Coppered Whale; the Elephant Whale; the Iceberg Whale; the Quog Whale; the Blue Whale; etc. From Icelandic, Dutch, and old English authorities, there might be quoted other lists of uncertain whales, blessed with all manner of uncouth names. But I omit them as altogether obsolete; and can hardly help suspecting them for mere sounds, full of Leviathanism, but signifying nothing.

Finally: It was stated at the outset, that this system would not be here, and at once, perfected. You cannot but plainly see that I have kept my word. But I now leave my cetological System standing thus unfinished, even as the great Cathedral of Cologne was left, with the crane still standing upon the top of the uncompleted tower. For small erections may be finished by their first architects; grand ones, true ones, ever leave the copestone to posterity. God keep me from ever completing anything. This whole book is but a draught – nay, but the draught of a draught. Oh, Time, Strength, Cash, and Patience!

CHAPTER THIRTY THREE

The Specksnyder

CONCERNING THE officers of the whale-craft, this seems as good a place as any to set down a little domestic peculiarity on ship-board, arising from the existence of the harpooneer class of officers, a class unknown of course in any other marine than the whale-fleet.

The large importance attached to the harpooneer's vocation is evinced by the fact, that originally in the old Dutch Fishery, two centuries and more ago, the command of a whale ship was not wholly lodged in the person now called the captain, but was divided between him and an officer called the Specksnyder. Literally this word means Fat-Cutter; usage, however, in time made it equivalent to Chief Harpooneer. In those days, the captain's authority was restricted to the navigation and general management of the vessel; while over the whale-hunting department and all its concerns, the Specksnyder or Chief Harpooneer reigned supreme. In the British Greenland Fishery, under the corrupted title of Specksioneer, this old Dutch official is still retained, but his former dignity is sadly abridged. At present he ranks simply as senior Harpooneer; and as such, is but one of the captain's more inferior subalterns. Nevertheless, as upon the good conduct of the harpooneers the success of a whaling voyage largely depends, and since in the American Fishery he is not only an important officer in the boat, but under certain circumstances (night watches on a whaling ground) the command of the ship's deck is also his; therefore the grand political maxim of the sea demands, that he should nominally live apart from the men before the mast, and be in some way distinguished as their professional superior; though always, by them, familiarly regarded as their social equal.

Now, the grand distinction drawn between officer and man at sea, is this – the first lives aft, the last forward. Hence, in whale-ships and merchantmen alike, the mates have their quarters with the captain; and so, too, in most of the American whalers the harpooneers are lodged in the after part of the ship. That is to say, they take their meals in the captain's cabin, and sleep in a place indirectly communicating with it.

Though the long period of a Southern whaling voyage (by far the longest of all voyages now or ever made by man), the peculiar perils of it, and the community of interest prevailing among a company, all of whom, high or low, depend for their profits, not upon fixed wages, but upon their common luck, together with their common vigilance, intrepidity, and hard work; though all these things do in some cases tend to beget a less rigorous discipline than in merchantmen generally; yet, never mind how much like an old Mesopotamian family these whalemen may, in some primitive instances, live together; for all that, the punctilious externals, at least, of the quarter-deck are seldom materially relaxed, and in no instance done away. Indeed, many are the Nantucket ships in which you will see the skipper parading his quarter-deck with an elated grandeur not surpassed in any military navy; nay, extorting almost as much outward homage as if he wore the imperial purple, and not the shabbiest of pilot-cloth.

And though of all men the moody captain of the Pequod was the least given to that sort of shallowest assumption; and though the only homage he ever exacted, was implicit, instantaneous obedience; though he required no man to remove the shoes from his feet ere stepping upon the quarter-deck; and though there were times when, owing to peculiar circumstances connected with events hereafter to be detailed, he addressed them in unusual terms, whether of condescension or **in terrorem**, or otherwise; yet even Captain Ahab was by no means unobservant of the paramount forms and usages of the sea.

Nor, perhaps, will it fail to be eventually perceived, that behind those forms and usages, as it were, he sometimes masked himself; incidentally making use of them for other and more private ends than they were legitimately intended to subserve. That certain sultanism of his brain, which had otherwise in a good degree remained unmanifested; through those forms that same sultanism became incarnate in an irresistible dictatorship. For be a man's intellectual superiority what it will, it can never assume the practical, available supremacy over other men, without the aid of some sort of external arts and entrenchments, always, in themselves, more or less paltry and base. This it is, that for ever keeps God's true princes of the Empire from the world's hustings; and leaves the highest honours that this air can give, to those men who become famous more through their infinite inferiority to the choice hidden handful of the Divine Inert, than through their undoubted superiority over the dead level of the mass. Such large virtue lurks in these small things when extreme political superstitions invest them, that in some royal instances even to idiot imbecility they have imparted potency. But when, as in the case of Nicholas the Czar, the ringed crown of geographical empire encircles an imperial brain; then, the plebeian herds crouch abased before the tremendous centralization. Nor, will the tragic dramatist who would depict mortal indomitableness in its fullest sweep and direct swing, ever forget a hint, incidentally so important in his art, as the one now alluded to.

But Ahab, my Captain, still moves before me in all his Nantucket grimness and shagginess; and in this episode touching Emperors and Kings, I must not conceal that I have only to do with a poor old whale-hunter like him; and, therefore, all outward majestical trappings and housings are denied me. Oh, Ahab! what shall be grand in thee, it must needs be plucked at from the skies, and dived for in the deep, and featured in the unbodied air!

CHAPTER THIRTY FOUR

The Cabin-Table

IT IS NOON; and Dough-Boy, the steward, thrusting his pale loaf-of-bread face from the cabin-scuttle, announces dinner to his lord and master; who, sitting in the lee quarter-boat, has just been taking an observation of the sun; and is now mutely reckoning the latitude on the smooth, medallion-shaped tablet, reserved for that daily purpose on the upper part of his ivory leg. From his complete inattention to the tidings, you would think that moody Ahab had not heard his menial. But presently, catching hold of the mizen shrouds, he swings himself to the deck, and in an even, unexhilarated voice, saying, "Dinner, Mr. Starbuck," disappears into the cabin.

When the last echo of his sultan's step has died away, and Starbuck, the first Emir, has every reason to suppose that he is seated, then Starbuck rouses from his quietude, takes a few turns along the planks, and, after a grave peep into the binnacle, says, with some touch of pleasantness, "Dinner, Mr. Stubb," and descends the scuttle. The second Emir lounges about the rigging awhile, and then slightly shaking the main brace, to see whether it will be all right with that important rope, he likewise takes up the old burden, and with a rapid "Dinner, Mr. Flask," follows after his predecessors.

But the third Emir, now seeing himself all alone on the quarter-deck, seems to feel relieved from some curious restraint; for, tipping all sorts of knowing winks in all sorts of directions, and kicking off his shoes, he strikes into a sharp but noiseless squall of a hornpipe right over the Grand Turk's head; and then, by a dexterous sleight, pitching his cap up into the mizentop for a shelf, he goes down rollicking so far at least as he remains visible from the deck, reversing all other processions, by bringing up the rear with music. But ere stepping into the cabin doorway below, he pauses, ships a new face altogether, and, then, independent, hilarious little Flask enters King Ahab's presence, in the character of Abjectus, or the Slave.

It is not the least among the strange things bred by the intense artificialness of sea-usages, that while in the open air of the deck some officers will, upon provocation, bear themselves boldly and defyingly enough towards their commander; yet, ten to one, let those very officers the next moment go down to their customary dinner in that same commander's cabin, and straightway their inoffensive, not to say deprecatory and humble air towards him, as he sits at the head of the table; this is marvellous, sometimes most comical. Wherefore this difference? A problem? Perhaps not. To have been Belshazzar, King of Babylon; and to have been Belshazzar, not haughtily but courteously, therein certainly must have been some touch of mundane grandeur. But he who in the rightly regal and intelligent spirit presides over his own private dinner-table of invited guests, that man's unchallenged power and dominion of individual influence for the time; that man's royalty of state transcends Belshazzar's, for Belshazzar was not the greatest. Who has but once dined his friends, has tasted what it is to be Caesar. It is a witchery of social czarship which there is no withstanding. Now, if to this consideration you superadd the official supremacy of a ship-master, then, by inference, you will derive the cause of that peculiarity of sea-life just mentioned.

Over his ivory-inlaid table, Ahab presided like a mute, maned sea-lion on the white coral beach, surrounded by his warlike but still deferential cubs. In his own proper turn, each officer waited to be served. They were as little children before Ahab; and yet, in Ahab, there seemed not to lurk the smallest social arrogance. With one mind, their intent eyes all fastened upon the old man's knife, as he carved the chief dish before him. I do not suppose that for the world they would have profaned that moment with the slightest observation, even upon so neutral a topic as the weather. No! And when reaching out his knife and fork, between which the slice of beef was locked, Ahab thereby motioned Starbuck's plate towards him, the mate received his meat as though receiving alms; and cut it tenderly; and a little started if, perchance, the knife grazed against the plate; and chewed it noiselessly; and swallowed it, not without circumspection. For, like the Coronation banquet at Frankfort, where the German Emperor profoundly dines with the seven Imperial Electors, so these cabin meals were somehow solemn meals, eaten in awful silence; and yet at table old Ahab forbade not conversation; only he himself was dumb. What a relief it was to choking Stubb, when a rat made a sudden racket in the hold below. And poor little Flask, he was the youngest son, and little boy of this weary family party. His were the shinbones of the saline beef; his would have been the drumsticks. For Flask to have presumed to help himself, this must have seemed to him tantamount to larceny in the first degree. Had he helped himself at that table, doubtless, never more would he have been able to hold his head up in this honest world; nevertheless, strange to say, Ahab never forbade him. And had Flask helped himself, the chances were Ahab had never so much as noticed it. Least of all, did Flask presume to help himself to butter. Whether he thought the owners of the ship denied it to him, on account of its clotting his clear, sunny complexion; or whether he deemed that, on so long a voyage in such marketless waters, butter was at a premium, and therefore was not for him, a subaltern; however it was, Flask, alas! was a butterless man!

Another thing. Flask was the last person down at the dinner, and Flask is the first man up. Consider! For hereby Flask's dinner was badly jammed in point of time. Starbuck and Stubb both had the start of him; and yet they also have the privilege of lounging in the rear. If Stubb even, who is but a peg higher than Flask, happens to have but a small appetite, and soon shows symptoms of concluding his repast, then Flask must bestir himself, he will not get more than three mouthfuls that day; for it is against holy usage for Stubb to precede Flask to the deck. Therefore it was that Flask once admitted in private, that ever since he had arisen to the dignity of an officer, from that moment he had never known what it was to be otherwise than hungry, more or less. For what he ate did not so much relieve his hunger, as keep it immortal in him. Peace and satisfaction, thought Flask, have for ever departed from my stomach. I am an officer; but, how I wish I could fish a bit of old-fashioned beef in the forecastle, as I used to when I was before the mast. There's the fruits of promotion now; there's the vanity of glory: there's the insanity of life! Besides, if it were so that any mere sailor of the Pequod had a grudge against Flask in Flask's official capacity, all that sailor had to do, in order to obtain ample vengeance, was to go aft at dinner-time, and get a peep at Flask through the cabin sky-light, sitting silly and dumfoundered before awful Ahab.

Now, Ahab and his three mates formed what may be called the first table in the Pequod's cabin. After their departure, taking place in inverted order to their arrival, the canvas cloth was cleared, or rather was restored to some hurried order by the pallid steward. And then the three harpooneers were bidden to the feast, they being its residuary legatees. They made a sort of temporary servants' hall of the high and mighty cabin.

In strange contrast to the hardly tolerable constraint and nameless invisible domineerings of the captain's table, was the entire care-free license and ease, the almost frantic democracy of those inferior fellows the harpooneers. While their masters, the mates, seemed afraid of the sound of the hinges of their own jaws, the harpooneers chewed their food with such a relish that there was a report to it. They dined like lords; they filled their bellies like Indian ships all day loading with spices. Such portentous appetites had Queequeg and Tashtego, that to fill out the vacancies made by the previous repast, often the pale Dough-Boy was fain to bring on a great baron of salt-junk, seemingly quarried out of the solid ox. And if he were not lively about it, if he did not go with a nimble hop-skip-and-jump, then Tashtego had an ungentlemanly way of accelerating him by darting a fork at his back, harpoon-wise. And once Daggoo, seized with a sudden humor, assisted Dough-Boy's memory by snatching him up bodily, and thrusting his head into a great empty wooden trencher, while Tashtego, knife in hand, began laying out the circle preliminary to scalping him. He was naturally a very nervous, shuddering sort of little fellow, this bread-faced steward; the progeny of a bankrupt baker and a hospital nurse. And what with the standing spectacle of the black terrific Ahab, and the periodical tumultuous visitations of these three savages, Dough-Boy's whole life was one continual lip-quiver. Commonly, after seeing the harpooneers furnished with all things they demanded, he would escape from their clutches into his little pantry adjoining, and fearfully peep out at them through the blinds of its door, till all was over.

It was a sight to see Queequeg seated over against Tashtego, opposing his filed teeth to the Indian's: crosswise to them, Daggoo seated on the floor, for a bench would have brought his hearse-plumed head to the low carlines; at every motion of his colossal limbs, making the low cabin framework to shake, as when an African elephant goes passenger in a ship. But for all this, the great negro was wonderfully abstemious, not to say dainty. It seemed hardly possible that by such comparatively small mouthfuls he could keep up the vitality diffused through so broad, baronial, and superb a person. But, doubtless, this noble savage fed strong and drank deep of the abounding element of air; and through his dilated nostrils snuffed in the sublime life of the worlds. Not by beef or by bread, are giants made or nourished. But Queequeg, he had a mortal, barbaric smack of the lip in eating – an ugly sound enough – so much so, that the trembling Dough-Boy almost looked to see whether any marks of teeth lurked in his own lean arms. And when he would hear Tashtego singing out for him to produce himself, that his bones might be picked, the simple-witted steward all but shattered the crockery hanging round him in the pantry, by his sudden fits of the palsy. Nor did the whetstone which the harpooneers carried in their pockets, for their lances and other weapons; and with which whetstones, at dinner, they would ostentatiously sharpen their knives; that grating sound did not at all tend to tranquillize poor Dough-Boy. How could he forget that in his Island days, Queequeg, for one, must certainly have been guilty of some murderous, convivial indiscretions. Alas! Dough-Boy! hard fares the white waiter who waits upon cannibals. Not a napkin should he carry on his arm, but a buckler. In good time, though, to his great delight, the three salt-sea warriors would rise and depart; to his credulous, fable-mongering ears, all their martial bones jingling in them at every step, like Moorish scimetars in scabbards.

But, though these barbarians dined in the cabin, and nominally lived there; still, being anything but sedentary in their habits, they were scarcely ever in it except at mealtimes, and just before sleeping-time, when they passed through it to their own peculiar quarters.

In this one matter, Ahab seemed no exception to most American whale captains, who, as a set, rather incline to the opinion that by rights the ship's cabin belongs to them; and that it is by courtesy alone that anybody else is, at any time, permitted there. So that, in real truth, the mates and harpooneers of the Pequod might more properly be said to have lived out of the cabin than in it. For when they did enter it, it was something as a street-door enters a house; turning inwards for a moment, only to be turned out the next;

and, as a permanent thing, residing in the open air. Nor did they lose much hereby; in the cabin was no companionship; socially, Ahab was inaccessible. Though nominally included in the census of Christendom, he was still an alien to it. He lived in the world, as the last of the Grisly Bears lived in settled Missouri. And as when Spring and Summer had departed, that wild Logan of the woods, burying himself in the hollow of a tree, lived out the winter there, sucking his own paws; so, in his inclement, howling old age, Ahab's soul, shut up in the caved trunk of his body, there fed upon the sullen paws of its gloom!

CHAPTER THIRTY FIVE

The Mast-Head

IT WAS DURING the more pleasant weather, that in due rotation with the other seamen my first mast-head came round.

In most American whalemen the mast-heads are manned almost simultaneously with the vessel's leaving her port; even though she may have fifteen thousand miles, and more, to sail ere reaching her proper cruising ground. And if, after a three, four, or five years' voyage she is drawing nigh home with anything empty in her – say, an empty vial even – then, her mast-heads are kept manned to the last; and not till her skysail-poles sail in among the spires of the port, does she altogether relinquish the hope of capturing one whale more.

Now, as the business of standing mast-heads, ashore or afloat, is a very ancient and interesting one, let us in some measure expatiate here. I take it, that the earliest standers of mast-heads were the old Egyptians; because, in all my researches, I find none prior to them. For though their progenitors, the builders of Babel, must doubtless, by their tower, have intended to rear the loftiest mast-head in all Asia, or Africa either; yet (ere the final truck was put to it) as that great stone mast of theirs may be said to have gone by the board, in the dread gale of God's wrath; therefore, we cannot give these Babel builders priority over the Egyptians. And that the Egyptians were a nation of mast-head standers, is an assertion based upon the general belief among archaeologists, that the first pyramids were founded for astronomical purposes: a theory singularly supported by the peculiar stair-like formation of all four sides of those edifices; whereby, with prodigious long upliftings of their legs, those old astronomers were wont to mount to the apex, and sing out for new stars; even as the look-outs of a modern ship sing out for a sail, or a whale just bearing in sight. In Saint Stylites, the famous Christian hermit of old times, who built him a lofty stone pillar in the desert and spent the whole latter portion of his life on its summit, hoisting his food from the ground with a tackle; in him we have a remarkable instance of a dauntless stander-of-mast-heads; who was not to be driven from his place by fogs or frosts, rain, hail, or sleet; but valiantly facing everything out to the last, literally died at his post. Of modern standers-of-mast-heads we have but a lifeless set; mere stone, iron, and bronze men; who, though well capable of facing out a stiff gale, are still entirely incompetent to the business of singing out upon discovering any strange sight. There is Napoleon; who, upon the top of the column of Vendome, stands with arms folded, some one hundred and fifty feet in the air; careless, now, who rules the decks below; whether Louis Philippe, Louis Blanc, or Louis the Devil. Great Washington, too, stands high aloft on his towering main-mast in Baltimore, and like one of Hercules' pillars, his column marks that point of human grandeur beyond which few mortals will go. Admiral Nelson, also, on a capstan of gun-metal, stands his mast-head in Trafalgar Square; and ever when most obscured by that London smoke, token is yet given that a hidden hero is there; for where there is smoke, must be fire. But neither great Washington, nor Napoleon, nor Nelson, will answer a single hail from below, however madly invoked to befriend by their counsels the distracted decks upon which they gaze; however it may be surmised, that their spirits penetrate through the thick haze of the future, and descry what shoals and what rocks must be shunned.

It may seem unwarrantable to couple in any respect the mast-head standers of the land with those of the sea; but that in truth it is not so, is plainly evinced by an item for which Obed Macy, the sole historian of Nantucket, stands accountable. The worthy Obed tells us, that in the early times of the whale fishery, ere ships were regularly launched in pursuit of the game, the people of that island erected lofty spars along the sea-coast, to which the look-outs ascended by means of nailed cleats, something as fowls go upstairs in a hen-house. A few years ago this same plan was adopted by the Bay whalemen of New Zealand, who, upon descrying the game, gave notice to the ready-manned boats nigh the beach. But this custom has now become obsolete; turn we then to the one proper mast-head, that of a whale-ship at sea. The three mast-heads are kept manned from sun-rise to sun-set; the seamen taking their regular turns (as at the helm), and relieving each other every two hours. In the serene weather of the tropics it is exceedingly pleasant the mast-head; nay, to a dreamy meditative man it is delightful. There you stand, a hundred feet above the silent decks, striding along the deep, as if the masts were gigantic stilts, while beneath you and between your legs, as it were, swim the hugest monsters of the sea, even as ships once sailed between the boots of the famous Colossus at old Rhodes. There you stand, lost in the infinite series of the sea, with nothing ruffled but the waves. The tranced ship indolently rolls; the drowsy trade winds blow; everything resolves you into languor. For the most part, in this tropic whaling life, a sublime uneventfulness invests you; you hear no news; read no gazettes; extras with startling accounts of commonplaces never delude you into unnecessary excitements; you hear of no domestic afflictions; bankrupt securities; fall of stocks; are never troubled with the thought of what you shall have for dinner – for all your meals for three years and more are snugly stowed in casks, and your bill of fare is immutable.

In one of those southern whalesmen, on a long three or four years' voyage, as often happens, the sum of the various hours you spend at the mast-head would amount to several entire months. And it is much to be deplored that the place to which you devote so considerable a portion of the whole term of your natural life, should be so sadly destitute of anything approaching to a cosy inhabitiveness, or adapted to breed a comfortable localness of feeling, such as pertains to a bed, a hammock, a hearse, a sentry box, a pulpit, a coach, or any other of those small and snug contrivances in which men temporarily isolate themselves. Your most usual point of perch is the head of the t' gallant-mast, where you stand upon two thin parallel sticks (almost peculiar to whalemen) called the t' gallant cross-trees. Here, tossed about by the sea, the beginner feels about as cosy as he would standing on a bull's horns. To be sure, in cold weather you may carry your house aloft with you, in the shape of a watch-coat; but properly speaking the thickest watch-coat is no more of a house than the unclad body; for as the soul is glued inside of its fleshy tabernacle, and cannot freely move about in it, nor even move out of it, without running great risk of perishing (like an ignorant pilgrim crossing the snowy Alps in winter); so a watch-coat is not so much of a house as it is a mere envelope, or additional skin encasing you. You cannot put a shelf or chest of drawers in your body, and no more can you make a convenient closet of your watch-coat.

Concerning all this, it is much to be deplored

that the mast-heads of a southern whale ship are unprovided with those enviable little tents or pulpits, called **crow's-nests**, in which the look-outs of a Greenland whaler are protected from the inclement weather of the frozen seas. In the fireside narrative of Captain Sleet, entitled "A Voyage among the Icebergs, in quest of the Greenland Whale, and incidentally for the re-discovery of the Lost Icelandic Colonies of Old Greenland;" in this admirable volume, all standers of mast-heads are furnished with a charmingly circumstantial account of the then recently invented **crow's-nest** of the Glacier, which was the name of Captain Sleet's good craft. He called it the **Sleet's crow's-nest**, in honour of himself; he being the original inventor and patentee, and free from all ridiculous false delicacy, and holding that if we call our own children after our own names (we fathers being the original inventors and patentees), so likewise should we denominate after ourselves any other apparatus we may beget. In shape, the Sleet's crow's-nest is something like a large tierce or pipe; it is open above, however, where it is furnished with a movable side-screen to keep to windward of your head in a hard gale. Being fixed on the summit of the mast, you ascend into it through a little trap-hatch in the bottom. On the after side, or side next the stern of the ship, is a comfortable seat, with a locker underneath for umbrellas, comforters, and coats. In front is a leather rack, in which to keep your speaking trumpet, pipe, telescope, and other nautical conveniences. When Captain Sleet in person stood his mast-head in this crow's-nest of his, he tells us that he always had a rifle with him (also fixed in the rack), together with a powder flask and shot, for the purpose of popping off the stray narwhales, or vagrant sea unicorns infesting those waters; for you cannot successfully shoot at them from the deck owing to the resistance of the water, but to shoot down upon them is a very different thing. Now, it was plainly a labor of love for Captain Sleet to describe, as he does, all the little detailed conveniences of his crow's-nest; but though he so enlarges upon many of these, and though he treats us to a very scientific account of his experiments in this crow's-nest, with a small compass he kept there for the purpose of counteracting the errors resulting from what is called the "local attraction" of all binnacle magnets; an error ascribable to the horizontal vicinity of the iron in the ship's planks, and in the Glacier's case, perhaps, to there having been so many broken-down blacksmiths among her crew; I say, that though the Captain is very discreet and scientific here, yet, for all his learned "binnacle deviations," "azimuth compass observations," and "approximate errors," he knows very well, Captain Sleet, that he was not so much immersed in those profound magnetic meditations, as to fail being attracted occasionally towards that well replenished little case-bottle, so nicely tucked in on one side of his crow's nest, within easy reach of his hand. Though, upon the whole, I greatly admire and even love the brave, the honest, and learned Captain; yet I take it very ill of him that he should so utterly ignore that case-bottle, seeing what a faithful friend and comforter it must have been, while with mittened fingers and hooded head he was studying the mathematics aloft there in that bird's nest within three or four perches of the pole.

But if we Southern whale-fishers are not so snugly housed aloft as Captain Sleet and his Greenlandmen were; yet that disadvantage is greatly counter-balanced by the widely contrasting serenity of those seductive seas in which we South fishers mostly float. For one, I used to lounge up the rigging very leisurely, resting in the top to have a chat with Queequeg, or any one else off duty whom I might find there; then ascending a little way further, and throwing a lazy leg over the top-sail yard, take a preliminary view of the watery pastures, and so at last mount to my ultimate destination.

Let me make a clean breast of it here, and frankly admit that I kept but sorry guard. With the problem of the universe revolving in me, how could I – being left completely to myself at such a thought-engendering altitude – how could I but lightly hold my obligations to observe all whale-ships' standing orders, "Keep your weather eye open, and sing out every time."

And let me in this place movingly admonish you, ye ship-owners of Nantucket! Beware of enlisting in your vigilant fisheries any lad with lean brow and hollow eye; given to unseasonable meditativeness; and who offers to ship with the Phaedon instead of Bowditch in his head. Beware of such an one, I say; your whales must be seen before they can be killed; and this sunken-eyed young Platonist will tow you ten wakes round the world, and never make you one pint of sperm the richer. Nor are these monitions at all unneeded. For nowadays, the whale-fishery furnishes an asylum for many romantic, melancholy, and absent-minded young men, disgusted with the carking cares of earth, and seeking sentiment in tar and blubber. Childe Harold not unfrequently perches himself upon the mast-head of some luckless disappointed whale-ship, and in moody phrase ejaculates: –

"Roll on, thou deep and dark blue ocean, roll! Ten thousand blubber-hunters sweep over thee in vain."

Very often do the captains of such ships take those absent-minded young philosophers to task, upbraiding them with not feeling sufficient "interest" in the voyage; half-hinting that they are so hopelessly lost to all honourable ambition, as that in their secret souls they would rather not see whales than otherwise. But all in vain; those young Platonists have a notion that their vision is imperfect; they are short-sighted; what use, then, to strain the visual nerve? They have left their opera-glasses at home.

"Why, thou monkey," said a harpooneer to one of these lads, "we've been cruising now hard upon three years, and thou hast not raised a whale yet. Whales are scarce as hen's teeth whenever thou art up here." Perhaps they were; or perhaps there might have been shoals of them in the far horizon; but lulled into such an opium-like listlessness of vacant, unconscious reverie is this absent-minded youth by the blending cadence of waves with thoughts, that at last he loses his identity; takes the mystic ocean at his feet for the visible image of that deep, blue, bottomless soul, pervading mankind and nature; and every strange, half-seen, gliding, beautiful thing that eludes him; every dimly-discovered, uprising fin of some undiscernible form, seems to him the embodiment of those elusive thoughts that only people the soul by continually flitting through it. In this enchanted mood, thy spirit ebbs away to whence it came; becomes diffused through time and space; like Crammer's (Thomas Cranmer) sprinkled Pantheistic ashes, forming at last a part of every shore the round globe over.

There is no life in thee, now, except that rocking life imparted by a gently rolling ship; by her, borrowed from the sea; by the sea, from the inscrutable tides of God. But while this sleep, this dream is on ye, move your foot or hand an inch; slip your hold at all; and your identity comes back in horror. Over Descartian vortices you hover. And perhaps, at mid-day, in the fairest weather, with one half-throttled shriek you drop through that transparent air into the summer sea, no more to rise for ever. Heed it well, ye Pantheists!

CHAPTER THIRTY SIX

The Quarter-Deck

(**Enter Ahab: Then, all**)

IT WAS NOT a great while after the affair of the pipe, that one morning shortly after breakfast, Ahab, as was his wont, ascended the cabin-gangway to the deck. There most sea-captains usually walk at that hour, as country gentlemen, after the same meal, take a few turns in the garden.

Soon his steady, ivory stride was heard,

as to and fro he paced his old rounds, upon planks so familiar to his tread, that they were all over dented, like geological stones, with the peculiar mark of his walk. Did you fixedly gaze, too, upon that ribbed and dented brow; there also, you would see still stranger foot-prints – the foot-prints of his one unsleeping, ever-pacing thought.

But on the occasion in question, those dents looked deeper, even as his nervous step that morning left a deeper mark. And, so full of his thought was Ahab, that at every uniform turn that he made, now at the main-mast and now at the binnacle, you could almost see that thought turn in him as he turned, and pace in him as he paced; so completely possessing him, indeed, that it all but seemed the inward mould of every outer movement.

"D'ye mark him, Flask?" whispered Stubb; "the chick that's in him pecks the shell. 'Twill soon be out."

The hours wore on; – Ahab now shut up

within his cabin; anon, pacing the deck, with the same intense bigotry of purpose in his aspect.

It drew near the close of day. Suddenly he came to a halt by the bulwarks, and inserting his bone leg into the auger-hole there, and with one hand grasping a shroud, he ordered Starbuck to send everybody aft.

"Sir!" said the mate, astonished at an order seldom or never given on ship-board except in some extraordinary case.

"Send everybody aft," repeated Ahab. "Mast-heads, there! come down!"

When the entire ship's company were assembled, and with curious and not wholly unapprehensive faces, were eyeing him, for he looked not unlike the weather horizon when a storm is coming up, Ahab, after rapidly glancing over the bulwarks, and then darting his eyes among the crew, started from his standpoint; and as though not a soul were nigh him resumed his heavy turns upon the deck. With bent head and half-slouched hat he continued to pace, unmindful of the wondering whispering among the men; till Stubb cautiously whispered to Flask, that Ahab must have summoned them there for the purpose of witnessing a pedestrian feat. But this did not last long. Vehemently pausing, he cried: –

"What do ye do when ye see a whale, men?"

"Sing out for him!" was the impulsive rejoinder from a score of clubbed voices.

"Good!" cried Ahab, with a wild approval in his tones; observing the hearty animation into which his unexpected question had so magnetically thrown them.

"And what do ye next, men?"

"Lower away, and after him!"

"And what tune is it ye pull to, men?"

"A dead whale or a stove boat!"

More and more strangely and fiercely glad and approving, grew the countenance of the old man at every shout; while the mariners began to gaze curiously at each other, as if marvelling how it was that they themselves became so excited at such seemingly purposeless questions.

But, they were all eagerness again, as Ahab, now half-revolving in his pivot-hole, with one hand reaching high up a shroud, and tightly, almost convulsively grasping it, addressed them thus: –

“All ye mast-headers have before now heard me give orders about a white whale. Look ye! d’ye see this Spanish ounce of gold?” – holding up a broad bright coin to the sun – “it is a sixteen dollar piece, men. D’ye see it? Mr. Starbuck, hand me yon top-maul.”

While the mate was getting the hammer, Ahab, without speaking, was slowly rubbing the gold piece against the skirts of his jacket, as if to heighten its lustre, and without using any words was meanwhile lowly humming to himself, producing a sound so strangely muffled and inarticulate that it seemed the mechanical humming of the wheels of his vitality in him.

Receiving the top-maul from Starbuck, he advanced towards the main-mast with the hammer uplifted in one hand, exhibiting the gold with the other, and with a high raised voice exclaiming: “Whosoever of ye raises me a white-headed whale with a wrinkled brow and a crooked jaw; whosoever of ye raises me that white-headed whale, with three holes punctured in his starboard fluke – look ye, whosoever of ye raises me that same white whale, he shall have this gold ounce, my boys!”

“Huzza! huzza!” cried the seamen, as with swinging tarpaulins they hailed the act of nailing the gold to the mast.

“It’s a white whale, I say,” resumed Ahab, as he threw down the topmaul: “a white whale. Skin your eyes for him, men; look sharp for white water; if ye see but a bubble, sing out.”

All this while Tashtego, Daggoo, and

Queequeg had looked on with even more intense interest and surprise than the rest, and at the mention of the wrinkled brow and crooked jaw they had started as if each was separately touched by some specific recollection.

"Captain Ahab," said Tashtego, "that white whale must be the same that some call Moby Dick."

"Moby Dick?" shouted Ahab. "Do ye know the white whale then, Tash?"

"Does he fan-tail a little curious, sir, before he goes down?" said the Gay-Header deliberately.

"And has he a curious spout, too," said Daggoo, "very bushy, even for a parmacetty, and mighty quick, Captain Ahab?"

"And he have one, two, three – oh! good many iron in him hide, too, Captain," cried Queequeg disjointedly, "all twiske-tee be-twisk, like him – him – " faltering hard for a word, and screwing his hand round and round as though uncorking a bottle – "like him – him – “

“Corkscrew!” cried Ahab, “aye, Queequeg, the harpoons lie all twisted and wrenched in him; aye, Daggoo, his spout is a big one, like a whole shock of wheat, and white as a pile of our Nantucket wool after the great annual sheep-shearing; aye, Tashtego, and he fan-tails like a split jib in a squall. Death and devils! men, it is Moby Dick ye have seen – Moby Dick – Moby Dick!”

“Captain Ahab,” said Starbuck, who, with Stubb and Flask, had thus far been eyeing his superior with increasing surprise, but at last seemed struck with a thought which somewhat explained all the wonder. “Captain Ahab, I have heard of Moby Dick – but it was not Moby Dick that took off thy leg?”

“Who told thee that?” cried Ahab; then pausing, “Aye, Starbuck; aye, my hearties all round; it was Moby Dick that dismasted me; Moby Dick that brought me to this dead stump I stand on now. Aye, aye,” he shouted with a terrific, loud, animal sob, like that of a heart-stricken moose; "Aye, aye! it was that accursed white whale that razed me; made a poor pegging lubber of me for ever and a day!" Then tossing both arms, with measureless imprecations he shouted out: "Aye, aye! and I'll chase him round Good Hope, and round the Horn, and round the Norway Maelstrom, and round perdition's flames before I give him up. And this is what ye have shipped for, men! to chase that white whale on both sides of land, and over all sides of earth, till he spouts black blood and rolls fin out. What say ye, men, will ye splice hands on it, now? I think ye do look brave."

"Aye, aye!" shouted the harpooneers and seamen, running closer to the excited old man: "A sharp eye for the white whale; a sharp lance for Moby Dick!"

"God bless ye," he seemed to half sob and half shout. "God bless ye, men. Steward! go draw the great measure of grog. But what's this long face about, Mr. Starbuck; wilt thou not chase the white whale? art not game for Moby Dick?"

"I am game for his crooked jaw, and for the jaws of Death too, Captain Ahab, if it fairly comes in the way of the business we follow; but I came here to hunt whales, not my commander's vengeance. How many barrels will thy vengeance yield thee even if thou gettest it, Captain Ahab? it will not fetch thee much in our Nantucket market."

"Nantucket market! Hoot! But come closer, Starbuck; thou requirest a little lower layer. If money's to be the measurer, man, and the accountants have computed their great counting-house the globe, by girdling it with guineas, one to every three parts of an inch; then, let me tell thee, that my vengeance will fetch a great premium **here!**"

"He smites his chest," whispered Stubb, "what's that for? methinks it rings most vast, but hollow."

"Vengeance on a dumb brute!" cried

Starbuck, “that simply smote thee from blindest instinct! Madness! To be enraged with a dumb thing, Captain Ahab, seems blasphemous.”

“Hark ye yet again – the little lower layer. All visible objects, man, are but as pasteboard masks. But in each event – in the living act, the undoubted deed – there, some unknown but still reasoning thing puts forth the mouldings of its features from behind the unreasoning mask. If man will strike, strike through the mask! How can the prisoner reach outside except by thrusting through the wall? To me, the white whale is that wall, shoved near to me. Sometimes I think there’s naught beyond. But ‘tis enough. He tasks me; he heaps me; I see in him outrageous strength, with an inscrutable malice sinewing it. That inscrutable thing is chiefly what I hate; and be the white whale agent, or be the white whale principal, I will wreak that hate upon him. Talk not to me of blasphemy, man; I’d strike the sun if it insulted me. For could the sun do that, then could I do the other; since there is ever a sort of fair play herein, jealousy presiding over all creations. But not my master, man, is even that fair play. Who's over me? Truth hath no confines. Take off thine eye! more intolerable than fiends' glarings is a doltish stare! So, so; thou reddenest and palest; my heat has melted thee to anger-glow. But look ye, Starbuck, what is said in heat, that thing unsays itself. There are men from whom warm words are small indignity. I meant not to incense thee. Let it go. Look! see yonder Turkish cheeks of spotted tawn – living, breathing pictures painted by the sun. The Pagan leopards – the unrecking and unworshipping things, that live; and seek, and give no reasons for the torrid life they feel! The crew, man, the crew! Are they not one and all with Ahab, in this matter of the whale? See Stubb! he laughs! See yonder Chilian! he snorts to think of it. Stand up amid the general hurricane, thy one tost sapling cannot, Starbuck! And what is it? Reckon it. 'Tis but to help strike a fin; no wondrous feat for Starbuck. What is it more? From this one poor hunt, then, the best lance out of all Nantucket, surely he will not hang back, when every foremast-hand has clutched a whetstone? Ah! constrainings seize thee; I see! the billow lifts thee! Speak, but speak! – Aye, aye! thy silence, then, **that** voices thee. (**Aside**) Something shot from my dilated nostrils, he has inhaled it in his lungs. Starbuck now is mine; cannot oppose me now, without rebellion."

"God keep me! – keep us all!" murmured Starbuck, lowly.

But in his joy at the enchanted, tacit acquiescence of the mate, Ahab did not hear his foreboding invocation; nor yet the low laugh from the hold; nor yet the presaging vibrations of the winds in the cordage; nor yet the hollow flap of the sails against the masts, as for a moment their hearts sank in. For again Starbuck's downcast eyes lighted up with the stubbornness of life; the subterranean laugh died away; the winds blew on; the sails filled out; the ship heaved and rolled as before. Ah, ye admonitions and warnings! why stay ye not when ye come? But rather are ye predictions than warnings, ye shadows! Yet not so much predictions from without, as verifications of the foregoing things within. For with little external to constrain us, the innermost necessities in our being, these still drive us on.

"The measure! the measure!" cried Ahab.

Receiving the brimming pewter, and turning to the harpooneers, he ordered them to produce their weapons. Then ranging them before him near the capstan, with their harpoons in their hands, while his three mates stood at his side with their lances, and the rest of the ship's company formed a circle round the group; he stood for an instant searchingly eyeing every man of his crew. But those wild eyes met his, as the bloodshot eyes of the prairie wolves meet the eye of their leader, ere he rushes on at their head in the trail of the bison; but, alas! only to fall into the hidden snare of the Indian.

"Drink and pass!" he cried, handing the heavy charged flagon to the nearest seaman. "The crew alone now drink. Round with it, round! Short draughts – long swallows, men; 'tis hot as Satan's hoof. So, so; it goes round excellently. It spiralizes in ye; forks out at the serpent-snapping eye. Well done; almost drained. That way it went, this way it comes. Hand it me – here's a hollow! Men, ye seem the years; so brimming life is gulped and gone. Steward, refill!

"Attend now, my braves. I have mustered ye all round this capstan; and ye mates, flank me with your lances; and ye harpooneers, stand there with your irons; and ye, stout mariners, ring me in, that I may in some sort revive a noble custom of my fisherman fathers before me. O men, you will yet see that – Ha! boy, come back? bad pennies come not sooner. Hand it me. Why, now, this pewter had run brimming again, were't not thou St. Vitus' imp – away, thou ague!

"Advance, ye mates! Cross your lances full before me. Well done! Let me touch the axis." So saying, with extended arm, he grasped the three level, radiating lances at their crossed centre; while so doing, suddenly and nervously twitched them; meanwhile, glancing intently from Starbuck to Stubb; from Stubb to Flask. It seemed as though, by some nameless, interior volition, he would fain have shocked into them the same fiery emotion accumulated within the Leyden jar of his own magnetic life. The three mates quailed before his strong, sustained, and mystic aspect. Stubb and Flask looked sideways from him; the honest eye of Starbuck fell downright.

"In vain!" cried Ahab; "but, maybe, 'tis well. For did ye three but once take the full-forced shock, then mine own electric thing, **that** had perhaps expired from out me. Perchance, too, it would have dropped ye dead. Perchance ye need it not. Down lances! And now, ye mates, I do appoint ye three cupbearers to my three pagan kinsmen there – yon three most honourable gentlemen and noblemen, my valiant harpooneers. Disdain the task? What, when the great Pope washes the feet of beggars, using his tiara for ewer? Oh, my sweet cardinals! your own condescension, **that** shall bend ye to it. I do not order ye; ye will it. Cut your seizings and draw the poles, ye harpooneers!"

Silently obeying the order, the three harpooneers now stood with the detached iron part of their harpoons, some three feet long, held, barbs up, before him.

"Stab me not with that keen steel! Cant them; cant them over! know ye not the goblet end? Turn up the socket! So, so; now, ye cup-bearers, advance. The irons!

take them; hold them while I fill!” Forthwith, slowly going from one officer to the other, he brimmed the harpoon sockets with the fiery waters from the pewter.

“Now, three to three, ye stand. Commend the murderous chalices! Bestow them, ye who are now made parties to this indissoluble league. Ha! Starbuck! but the deed is done! Yon ratifying sun now waits to sit upon it. Drink, ye harpooneers! drink and swear, ye men that man the deathful whaleboat’s bow – Death to Moby Dick! God hunt us all, if we do not hunt Moby Dick to his death!” The long, barbed steel goblets were lifted; and to cries and maledictions against the white whale, the spirits were simultaneously quaffed down with a hiss. Starbuck paled, and turned, and shivered. Once more, and finally, the replenished pewter went the rounds among the frantic crew; when, waving his free hand to them, they all dispersed; and Ahab retired within his cabin.

CHAPTER THIRTY SEVEN

Sunset

The cabin; by the stern windows; Ahab sitting alone, and gazing out.

I LEAVE A WHITE and turbid wake; pale waters, paler cheeks, where'er I sail. The envious billows sidelong swell to whelm my track; let them; but first I pass.

Yonder, by ever-brimming goblet's rim, the warm waves blush like wine. The gold brow plumbs the blue. The diver sun – slow dived from noon – goes down; my soul mounts up! she wearies with her endless hill. Is, then, the crown too heavy that I wear? this Iron Crown of Lombardy. Yet is it bright with many a gem; I the wearer, see not its far flashings; but darkly feel that I wear that, that dazzlingly confounds. 'Tis iron – that I know – not gold. 'Tis split, too – that I feel; the jagged edge galls me so, my brain seems to beat against the solid metal; aye, steel skull, mine; the sort that needs no helmet in the most brain-battering fight!

Dry heat upon my brow? Oh! time was, when as the sunrise nobly spurred me, so the sunset soothed. No more. This lovely light, it lights not me; all loveliness is anguish to me, since I can ne'er enjoy. Gifted with the high perception, I lack the low, enjoying power; damned, most subtly and most malignantly! damned in the midst of Paradise! Good night – good night! (**waving his hand, he moves from the**

window.)

'Twas not so hard a task. I thought to find one stubborn, at the least; but my one cogged circle fits into all their various wheels, and they revolve. Or, if you will, like so many ant-hills of powder, they all stand before me; and I their match. Oh, hard! that to fire others, the match itself must needs be wasting! What I've dared, I've willed; and what I've willed, I'll do! They think me mad – Starbuck does; but I'm demoniac, I am madness maddened! That wild madness that's only calm to comprehend itself! The prophecy was that I should be dismembered; and – Aye! I lost this leg. I now prophesy that I will dismember my dismemberer. Now, then, be the prophet and the fulfiller one. That's more than ye, ye great gods, ever were. I laugh and hoot at ye, ye cricket-players, ye pugilists, ye deaf Burkes and blinded Bendigoes! I will not say as schoolboys do to bullies – Take some one of your own size; don't pommel **me!** No, ye've knocked me down, and I am up again; but **ye** have run and hidden. Come forth from behind your cotton bags! I have no long gun to reach ye. Come, Ahab's compliments to ye; come and see if ye can swerve me. Swerve me? ye cannot swerve me, else ye swerve yourselves! man has ye there. Swerve me? The path to my fixed purpose is laid with iron rails, whereon my soul is grooved to run. Over unsounded gorges, through the rifled hearts of mountains, under torrents' beds, unerringly I rush! Naught's an obstacle, naught's an angle to the iron way!

CHAPTER THIRTY EIGHT

Dusk

By the mainmast; Starbuck leaning against it.

MY SOUL is more than matched; she's overmanned; and by a madman! Insufferable sting, that sanity should ground arms on such a field! But he drilled deep down, and blasted all my reason out of me! I think I see his impious end; but feel that I must help him to it. Will I, nill I, the ineffable thing has tied me to him; tows me with a cable I have no knife to cut. Horrible old man! Who's over him, he cries; – aye, he would be a democrat to all above; look, how he lords it over all below! Oh! I plainly see my miserable office, – to obey, rebelling; and worse yet, to hate with touch of pity! For in his eyes I read some lurid woe would shrivel me up, had I it. Yet is there hope. Time and tide flow wide. The hated whale has the round watery world to swim in, as the small gold-fish has its glassy globe. His heaven-insulting purpose, God may wedge aside. I would up heart, were it not like lead. But my whole clock's run down; my heart the all-controlling weight, I have no key to lift again.

[**A burst of revelry from the forecastle**.]

Oh, God! to sail with such a heathen crew that have small touch of human mothers in them! Whelped somewhere by the sharkish sea. The white whale is their demigorgon. Hark! the infernal orgies! that revelry is forward! mark the unfaltering silence aft! Methinks it pictures life. Foremost through the sparkling sea shoots on the gay, embattled, bantering bow, but only to drag dark Ahab after it, where he broods within his sternward cabin, builded over the dead water of the wake, and further on, hunted by its wolfish gurglings. The long howl thrills me through! Peace! ye revellers, and set the watch! Oh, life! 'tis in an hour like this, with soul beat down and held to knowledge, – as wild, untutored things are forced to feed – Oh, life! 'tis now that I do feel the latent horror in thee! but 'tis not me! that horror's out of me! and with the soft feeling of the human in me, yet will I try to fight ye, ye grim, phantom futures! Stand by me, hold me, bind me, O ye blessed influences!

CHAPTER THIRTY NINE

First Night Watch.

Fore-Top.

(**Stubb solus, and mending a brace**.)

HA! HA! HA! HA! hem! clear my throat! – I've been thinking over it ever since, and that ha, ha's the final consequence. Why so? Because a laugh's the wisest, easiest answer to all that's queer; and come what will, one comfort's always left – that unfailing comfort is, it's all predestinated. I heard not all his talk with Starbuck; but to my poor eye Starbuck then looked something as I the other evening felt. Be sure the old Mogul has fixed him, too. I twigged it, knew it; had had the gift, might readily have prophesied it – for when I clapped my eye upon his skull I saw it. Well, Stubb, **wise** Stubb – that's my title – well, Stubb, what of it, Stubb? Here's a carcase. I know not all that may be coming, but be it what it will, I'll go to it laughing. Such a waggish leering as lurks in all your horribles! I feel funny. Fa, la! lirra, skirra! What's my juicy little pear at home doing now? Crying its eyes out? – Giving a party to the last arrived harpooneers, I dare say, gay as a frigate's pennant, and so am I – fa, la! lirra, skirra! Oh –

We'll drink to-night with hearts as light, To love, as gay and fleeting As bubbles that swim, on the beaker's brim, And break on the lips while meeting.

A brave stave that – who calls? Mr. Starbuck? Aye, aye, sir – (**Aside**) he's my superior, he has his too, if I’m not mistaken. – Aye, aye, sir, just through with this job – coming.

CHAPTER FOURTY

Midnight, Forecastle. Harpooneers and Sailors

(Foresail rises and discovers the watch standing, lounging, leaning, and lying in various attitudes, all singing in chorus.)

Farewell and adieu to you, Spanish ladies!
Farewell and adieu to you, ladies of Spain!
Our captain's commanded. –

1ST NANTUCKET SAILOR. Oh, boys, don't

be sentimental; it's bad for the digestion! Take a tonic, follow me! (**Sings, and all follow**)

Our captain stood upon the deck,
A spy-glass in his hand,
A viewing of those gallant whales
That blew at every strand.
Oh, your tubs in your boats, my boys,
And by your braces stand,
And we'll have one of those fine whales,
Hand, boys, over hand!
So, be cheery, my lads! may your hearts
never fail!
While the bold harpooner is striking the
whale!

MATE'S VOICE FROM THE QUARTER-DECK. Eight bells there, forward!

2ND NANTUCKET SAILOR. Avast the chorus! Eight bells there! d'ye hear, bell-boy? Strike the bell eight, thou Pip! thou blackling! and let me call the watch. I've the sort of mouth for that – the hogshead mouth. So, so, (**thrusts his head down the scuttle**,) Star-bo-l-e-e-n-s, a-h-o-y! Eight bells there below! Tumble up!

DUTCH SAILOR. Grand snoozing to-night, maty; fat night for that. I mark this in our old Mogul's wine; it's quite as deadening to some as filliping to others. We sing; they sleep – aye, lie down there, like ground-tier butts. At 'em again! There, take this copper-pump, and hail 'em through it. Tell 'em to avast dreaming of their lasses. Tell 'em it's the resurrection; they must kiss their last, and come to judgment. That's the way – **that's** it; thy throat ain't spoiled with eating Amsterdam butter.

FRENCH SAILOR. Hist, boys! let's have a jig or two before we ride to anchor in Blanket Bay. What say ye? There comes the other watch. Stand by all legs! Pip! little Pip! hurrah with your tambourine!

PIP. (**Sulky and sleepy**) Don't know where it is.

FRENCH SAILOR. Beat thy belly, then, and wag thy ears. Jig it, men, I say; merry's the word; hurrah! Damn me, won't you dance? Form, now, Indian-file, and gallop into the double-shuffle? Throw yourselves! Legs! legs!

ICELAND SAILOR. I don't like your floor, maty; it's too springy to my taste. I'm used to ice-floors. I'm sorry to throw cold water on the subject; but excuse me.

MALTESE SAILOR. Me too; where's your girls? Who but a fool would take his left hand by his right, and say to himself, how d'ye do? Partners! I must have partners!

SICILIAN SAILOR. Aye; girls and a green! – then I'll hop with ye; yea, turn grasshopper!

LONG-ISLAND SAILOR. Well, well, ye sulkies, there's plenty more of us. Hoe corn when you may, say I. All legs go to harvest soon. Ah! here comes the music; now for it!

AZORE SAILOR. (**Ascending, and pitching the tambourine up the scuttle**.) Here you are, Pip; and there's the windlassbitts; up you mount! Now, boys! (**The half of them dance to the tambourine; some go below; some sleep or lie among the coils of rigging. Oaths a-plenty**.)

AZORE SAILOR. (**Dancing**) Go it, Pip! Bang it, bell-boy! Rig it, dig it, stig it, quig it, bell-boy! Make fire-flies; break the jinglers!

PIP. Jinglers, you say?–there goes another, dropped off; I pound it so.

CHINA SAILOR. Rattle thy teeth, then, and pound away; make a pagoda of thyself.

FRENCH SAILOR. Merry-mad! Hold up thy hoop, Pip, till I jump through it! Split jibs! tear yourselves!

TASHTEGO. (**Quietly smoking**) That's a white man; he calls that fun: humph! I save my sweat.

OLD MANX SAILOR. I wonder whether those jolly lads bethink them of what they are dancing over. I'll dance over your grave, I will – that's the bitterest threat of your night-women, that beat head-winds round corners. O Christ! to think of the green navies and the green-skulled crews! Well, well; belike the whole world's a ball, as you scholars have it; and so 'tis right to make one ballroom of it. Dance on, lads, you're young; I was once.

3D NANTUCKET SAILOR. Spell oh! – whew! this is worse than pulling after whales in a calm – give us a whiff, Tash.

(**They cease dancing, and gather in clusters. Meantime the sky darkens – the wind rises**.)

LASCAR SAILOR. By Brahma! boys, it'll be douse sail soon. The sky-born, high-tide Ganges turned to wind! Thou showest thy black brow, Seeva!

MALTESE SAILOR. (**Reclining and shaking his cap**.) It's the waves – the snow's caps turn to jig it now. They'll shake their tassels soon. Now would all the waves were women, then I'd go drown, and chassee with them evermore! There's naught so sweet on earth – heaven may not match it! – as those swift glances of warm, wild bosoms in the dance, when the over-arboring arms hide such ripe, bursting grapes.

SICILIAN SAILOR. (**Reclining**.) Tell me not of it! Hark ye, lad – fleet interlacings of the limbs – lithe swayings – coyings – flutterings! lip! heart! hip! all graze: unceasing touch and go! not taste, observe ye, else come satiety. Eh, Pagan? (**Nudging**.)

TAHITAN SAILOR. (**Reclining on a mat**.) Hail, holy nakedness of our dancing girls! – the Heeva-Heeva! Ah! low veiled, high palmed Tahiti! I still rest me on thy mat, but the soft soil has slid! I saw thee woven in the wood, my mat! green the first day I brought ye thence; now worn and wilted quite. Ah me! – not thou nor I can bear the change! How then, if so be transplanted to yon sky? Hear I the roaring streams from Pirohitee's peak of spears, when they leap down the crags and drown the villages? – The blast! the blast! Up, spine, and meet it! (**Leaps to his feet**.)

PORTUGUESE SAILOR. How the sea rolls swashing 'gainst the side! Stand by for reefing, hearties! the winds are just crossing swords, pell-mell they'll go lunging presently.

DANISH SAILOR. Crack, crack, old ship! so long as thou crackest, thou holdest! Well done! The mate there holds ye to it stiffly. He's no more afraid than the isle fort at Cattegat, put there to fight the Baltic with storm-lashed guns, on which the sea-salt cakes!

4TH NANTUCKET SAILOR. He has his orders, mind ye that. I heard old Ahab tell him he must always kill a squall, something as they burst a waterspout with a pistol – fire your ship right into it!

ENGLISH SAILOR. Blood! but that old man's a grand old cove! We are the lads to hunt him up his whale!

ALL. Aye! aye!

OLD MANX SAILOR. How the three pines shake! Pines are the hardest sort of tree to live when shifted to any other soil, and here there's none but the crew's cursed clay. Steady, helmsman! steady. This is the sort of weather when brave hearts snap ashore, and keeled hulls split at sea. Our captain has his birthmark; look yonder, boys, there's another in the sky – lurid-like, ye see, all else pitch black.

DAGGOO. What of that? Who's afraid of black's afraid of me! I'm quarried out of it!

SPANISH SAILOR. (**Aside**.) He wants to bully, ah! – the old grudge makes me touchy (**Advancing**.) Aye, harpooneer, thy race is the undeniable dark side of mankind – devilish dark at that. No offence.

DAGGOO (**grimly**). None.

ST. JAGO'S SAILOR. That Spaniard's mad or drunk. But that can't be, or else in his one case our old Mogul's fire-waters are somewhat long in working.

5TH NANTUCKET SAILOR. What's that I saw – lightning? Yes.

SPANISH SAILOR. No; Daggoo showing

his teeth.

DAGGOO (**springing**). Swallow thine, mannikin! White skin, white liver!

SPANISH SAILOR (**meeting him**). Knife thee heartily! big frame, small spirit!

ALL. A row! a row! a row!

TASHTEGO (**with a whiff**). A row a'low, and a row aloft – Gods and men – both brawlers! Humph!

BELFAST SAILOR. A row! arrah a row! The Virgin be blessed, a row! Plunge in with ye!

ENGLISH SAILOR. Fair play! Snatch the Spaniard's knife! A ring, a ring!

OLD MANX SAILOR. Ready formed. There! the ringed horizon. In that ring Cain struck Abel. Sweet work, right work! No? Why then, God, mad'st thou the ring?

MATE'S VOICE FROM THE QUARTER-DECK. Hands by the halyards! in top-gallant sails! Stand by to reef topsails!

ALL. The squall! the squall! jump, my jollies! (**They scatter**.)

PIP (**shrinking under the windlass**). Jollies? Lord help such jollies! Crish, crash! there goes the jib-stay! Blang-whang! God! Duck lower, Pip, here comes the royal yard! It's worse than being in the whirled woods, the last day of the year! Who'd go climbing after chestnuts now? But there they go, all cursing, and here I don't. Fine prospects to 'em; they're on the road to heaven. Hold on hard! Jimmini, what a squall! But those chaps there are worse yet – they are your white squalls, they. White squalls? white whale, shirr! shirr! Here have I heard all their chat just now, and the white whale – shirr! shirr! – but spoken of once! and only this evening – it makes me jingle all over like my tambourine – that anaconda of an old man swore 'em in to hunt him! Oh, thou big white God aloft there somewhere in yon darkness, have mercy on this small black boy down here; preserve him from all men that have no bowels to feel fear!

CHAPTER FOURTY ONE

Moby Dick

I, ISHMAEL, was one of that crew; my shouts had gone up with the rest; my oath had been welded with theirs; and stronger I shouted, and more did I hammer and clinch my oath, because of the dread in my soul. A wild, mystical, sympathetical feeling was in me; Ahab's quenchless feud seemed mine. With greedy ears I learned the history of that murderous monster against whom I and all the others had taken our oaths of violence and revenge.

For some time past, though at intervals only, the unaccompanied, secluded White Whale had haunted those uncivilized seas mostly frequented by the Sperm Whale fishermen. But not all of them knew of his existence; only a few of them, comparatively, had knowingly seen him; while the number who as yet had actually and knowingly given battle to him, was small indeed. For, owing to the large number of whale-cruisers; the disorderly way they were sprinkled over the entire watery circumference, many of them adventurously pushing their quest along solitary latitudes, so as seldom or never for a whole twelvemonth or more on a stretch, to encounter a single news-telling sail of any sort; the inordinate length of each separate voyage; the irregularity of the times of sailing from home; all these, with other circumstances, direct and indirect, long obstructed the spread through the whole world-wide whaling-fleet of the special individualizing tidings concerning Moby Dick. It was hardly to be doubted, that several vessels reported to have encountered, at such or such a time, or on such or such a meridian, a Sperm Whale of uncommon magnitude and malignity, which whale, after doing great mischief to his assailants, had completely escaped them; to some minds it was not an unfair presumption, I say, that the whale in question must have been no other than Moby Dick. Yet as of late the Sperm Whale fishery had been marked by various and not unfrequent instances of great ferocity, cunning, and malice in the monster attacked; therefore it was, that those who by accident ignorantly gave battle to Moby Dick; such hunters, perhaps, for the most part, were content to ascribe the peculiar terror he bred, more, as it were, to the perils of the Sperm Whale fishery at large, than to the individual cause. In that way, mostly, the disastrous encounter between Ahab and the whale had hitherto been popularly regarded.

And as for those who, previously hearing of the White Whale, by chance caught sight of him; in the beginning of the thing they had every one of them, almost, as boldly and fearlessly lowered for him, as for any other whale of that species. But at length, such calamities did ensue in these assaults – not restricted to sprained wrists and ankles, broken limbs, or devouring amputations – but fatal to the last degree of fatality; those repeated disastrous repulses, all accumulating and piling their terrors upon Moby Dick; those things had gone far to shake the fortitude of many brave hunters, to whom the story of the White Whale had eventually come.

Nor did wild rumors of all sorts fail to exaggerate, and still the more horrify the true histories of these deadly encounters. For not only do fabulous rumors naturally grow out of the very body of all surprising terrible events, – as the smitten tree gives birth to its fungi; but, in maritime life, far more than in that of terra firma, wild rumors abound, wherever there is any adequate reality for them to cling to. And as the sea surpasses the land in this matter, so the whale fishery surpasses every other sort of maritime life, in the wonderfulness and fearfulness of the rumors which sometimes circulate there. For not only are whalemen as a body unexempt from that ignorance and superstitiousness hereditary to all sailors; but of all sailors, they are by all odds the most directly brought into contact with whatever is appallingly astonishing in the sea; face to face they not only eye its greatest marvels, but, hand to jaw, give battle to them. Alone, in such remotest waters, that though you sailed a thousand miles, and passed a thousand shores, you would not come to any chiseled hearth-stone, or aught hospitable beneath that part of the sun; in such latitudes and longitudes, pursuing too such a calling as he does, the whaleman is wrapped by influences all tending to make his fancy pregnant with many a mighty birth.

No wonder, then, that ever gathering volume from the mere transit over the widest watery spaces, the outblown rumors of the White Whale did in the end incorporate with themselves all manner of morbid hints, and half-formed foetal suggestions of supernatural agencies, which eventually invested Moby Dick with new terrors unborrowed from anything that visibly appears. So that in many cases such a panic did he finally strike, that few who by those rumors, at least, had heard of the White Whale, few of those hunters were willing to encounter the perils of his jaw.

But there were still other and more vital practical influences at work. Not even at the present day has the original prestige of the Sperm Whale, as fearfully distinguished from all other species of the leviathan, died out of the minds of the whalemen as a body. There are those this day among them, who, though intelligent and courageous enough in offering battle to the

Greenland or Right whale, would perhaps – either from professional inexperience, or incompetency, or timidity, decline a contest with the Sperm Whale; at any rate, there are plenty of whalemen, especially among those whaling nations not sailing under the American flag, who have never hostilely encountered the Sperm Whale, but whose sole knowledge of the leviathan is restricted to the ignoble monster primitively pursued in the North; seated on their hatches, these men will hearken with a childish fireside interest and awe, to the wild, strange tales of Southern whaling. Nor is the pre-eminent tremendousness of the great Sperm Whale anywhere more feelingly comprehended, than on board of those prows which stem him.

And as if the now tested reality of his might had in former legendary times thrown its shadow before it; we find some book naturalists – Olassen and Povelson – declaring the Sperm Whale not only to be a consternation to every other creature in the sea, but also to be so incredibly ferocious as continually to be athirst for human blood. Nor even down to so late a time as Cuvier's, were these or almost similar impressions effaced. For in his Natural History, the Baron himself affirms that at sight of the Sperm Whale, all fish (sharks included) are "struck with the most lively terrors," and "often in the precipitancy of their flight dash themselves against the rocks with such violence as to cause instantaneous death." And however the general experiences in the fishery may amend such reports as these; yet in their full terribleness, even to the bloodthirsty item of Povelson, the superstitious belief in them is, in some vicissitudes of their vocation, revived in the minds of the hunters.

So that overawed by the rumors and portents concerning him, not a few of the fishermen recalled, in reference to Moby Dick, the earlier days of the Sperm Whale fishery, when it was oftentimes hard to induce long practised Right whalemen to embark in the perils of this new and daring warfare; such men protesting that although other leviathans might be hopefully pursued, yet to chase and point lance at such an apparition as the Sperm Whale was not for mortal man. That to attempt it, would be inevitably to be torn into a quick eternity. On this head, there are some remarkable documents that may be consulted.

Nevertheless, some there were, who even in the face of these things were ready to give chase to Moby Dick; and a still greater number who, chancing only to hear of him distantly and vaguely, without the specific details of any certain calamity, and without superstitious accompaniments, were sufficiently hardy not to flee from the battle if offered.

One of the wild suggestions referred to, as at last coming to be linked with the White Whale in the minds of the superstitiously inclined, was the unearthly conceit that Moby Dick was ubiquitous; that he had actually been encountered in opposite latitudes at one and the same instant of time.

Nor, credulous as such minds must have been, was this conceit altogether without some faint show of superstitious probability. For as the secrets of the currents in the seas have never yet been divulged, even to the most erudite research; so the hidden ways of the Sperm Whale when beneath the surface remain, in great part, unaccountable to his pursuers; and from time to time have originated the most curious and contradictory speculations regarding them, especially concerning the mystic modes whereby, after sounding to a great depth, he transports himself with such vast swiftness to the most widely distant points.

It is a thing well known to both American and English whale-ships, and as well a thing placed upon authoritative record years ago by Scoresby, that some whales have been captured far north in the Pacific, in whose bodies have been found the barbs of harpoons darted in the Greenland seas. Nor is it to be gainsaid, that in some of these instances it has been declared that the interval of time between the two assaults could not have exceeded very many days. Hence, by inference, it has been believed by some whalemen, that the Nor' West Passage, so long a problem to man, was never a problem to the whale. So that here, in the real living experience of living men, the prodigies related in old times of the inland Strello mountain in Portugal (near whose top there was said to be a lake in which the wrecks of ships floated up to the surface); and that still more wonderful story of the Arethusa fountain near Syracuse (whose waters were believed to have come from the Holy Land by an underground passage); these fabulous narrations are almost fully equalled by the realities of the whalemen.

Forced into familiarity, then, with such

prodigies as these; and knowing that after repeated, intrepid assaults, the White Whale had escaped alive; it cannot be much matter of surprise that some whalemen should go still further in their superstitions; declaring Moby Dick not only ubiquitous, but immortal (for immortality is but ubiquity in time); that though groves of spears should be planted in his flanks, he would still swim away unharmed; or if indeed he should ever be made to spout thick blood, such a sight would be but a ghastly deception; for again in unensanguined billows hundreds of leagues away, his unsullied jet would once more be seen.

But even stripped of these supernatural surmisings, there was enough in the earthly make and incontestable character of the monster to strike the imagination with unwonted power. For, it was not so much his uncommon bulk that so much distinguished him from other sperm whales, but, as was elsewhere thrown out—a peculiar snow-white wrinkled forehead, and a high, pyramidical white hump. These were his prominent features; the tokens whereby, even in the limitless, uncharted seas, he revealed his identity, at a long distance, to those who knew him.

The rest of his body was so streaked, and spotted, and marbled with the same shrouded hue, that, in the end, he had gained his distinctive appellation of the White Whale; a name, indeed, literally justified by his vivid aspect, when seen gliding at high noon through a dark blue sea, leaving a milky-way wake of creamy foam, all spangled with golden gleamings.

Nor was it his unwonted magnitude, nor his remarkable hue, nor yet his deformed lower jaw, that so much invested the whale with natural terror, as that unexampled, intelligent malignity which, according to specific accounts, he had over and over again evinced in his assaults. More than all, his treacherous retreats struck more of dismay than perhaps aught else. For, when swimming before his exulting pursuers, with every apparent symptom of alarm, he had several times been known to turn round suddenly, and, bearing down upon them, either stave their boats to splinters, or drive them back in consternation to their ship.

Already several fatalities had attended his chase. But though similar disasters, however little bruited ashore, were by no means unusual in the fishery; yet, in most instances, such seemed the White Whale's infernal aforethought of ferocity, that every dismembering or death that he caused, was not wholly regarded as having been inflicted by an unintelligent agent.

Judge, then, to what pitches of inflamed, distracted fury the minds of his more desperate hunters were impelled, when amid the chips of chewed boats, and the sinking limbs of torn comrades, they swam out of the white curds of the whale's direful wrath into the serene, exasperating sunlight, that smiled on, as if at a birth or a bridal.

His three boats stove around him, and oars and men both whirling in the eddies; one captain, seizing the line-knife from his broken prow, had dashed at the whale, as an Arkansas duellist at his foe, blindly seeking with a six inch blade to reach the fathom-deep life of the whale. That captain was Ahab. And then it was, that suddenly sweeping his sickle-shaped lower jaw beneath him, Moby Dick had reaped away Ahab's leg, as a mower a blade of grass in the field. No turbaned Turk, no hired Venetian or Malay, could have smote him with more seeming malice. Small reason was there to doubt, then, that ever since that almost fatal encounter, Ahab had cherished a wild vindictiveness against the whale, all the more fell for that in his frantic morbidness he at last came to identify with him, not only all his bodily woes, but all his intellectual and spiritual exasperations. The White Whale swam before him as the monomaniac incarnation of all those malicious agencies which some deep men feel eating in them, till they are left living on with half a heart and half a lung. That intangible malignity which has been from the beginning; to whose dominion even the modern Christians ascribe one-half of the worlds; which the ancient Ophites of the east reverenced in their statue devil; – Ahab did not fall down and worship it like them; but deliriously transferring its idea to the abhorred white whale, he pitted himself, all mutilated, against it. All that most maddens and torments; all that stirs up the lees of things; all truth with malice in it; all that cracks the sinews and cakes the brain; all the subtle demonisms of life and thought; all evil, to crazy Ahab, were visibly personified, and made practically assailable in Moby Dick. He piled upon the whale's white hump the sum of all the general rage and hate felt by his whole race from Adam down; and then, as if his chest had been a mortar, he burst his hot heart's shell upon it.

It is not probable that this monomania in him took its instant rise at the precise time of his bodily dismemberment. Then, in darting at the monster, knife in hand, he had but given loose to a sudden, passionate, corporal animosity; and when he received the stroke that tore him, he probably but felt the agonizing bodily laceration, but nothing more. Yet, when by this collision forced to turn towards home, and for long months of days and weeks, Ahab and anguish lay stretched together in one hammock, rounding in mid winter that dreary, howling Patagonian Cape; then it was, that his torn body and gashed soul bled into one another; and so interfusing, made him mad. That it was only then, on the homeward voyage, after the encounter, that the final monomania seized him, seems all but certain from the fact that, at intervals during the passage, he was a raving lunatic; and, though unlimbed of a leg, yet such vital strength yet lurked in his Egyptian chest, and was moreover intensified by his delirium, that his mates were forced to lace him fast, even there, as he sailed, raving in his hammock. In a strait-jacket, he swung to the mad rockings of the gales. And, when running into more sufferable latitudes, the ship, with mild stun'sails spread, floated across the tranquil tropics, and, to all appearances, the old man's delirium seemed left behind him with the Cape Horn swells, and he came forth from his dark den into the blessed light and air; even then, when he bore that firm, collected front, however pale, and issued his calm orders once again; and his mates thanked God the direful madness was now gone; even then, Ahab, in his hidden self, raved on. Human madness is oftentimes a cunning and most feline thing. When you think it fled, it may have but become transfigured into some still subtler form. Ahab's full lunacy subsided not, but deepeningly contracted; like the unabated Hudson, when that noble Northman flows narrowly, but unfathomably through the Highland gorge. But, as in his narrow-flowing monomania, not one jot of Ahab's broad madness had been left behind; so in that broad madness, not one jot of his great natural intellect had perished. That before living agent, now became the living instrument. If such a furious trope may stand, his special lunacy stormed his general sanity, and carried it, and turned all its concentred cannon upon its own mad mark; so that far from having lost his strength, Ahab, to that one end, did now possess a thousand fold more potency than ever he had sanely brought to bear upon any one reasonable object.

This is much; yet Ahab's larger, darker, deeper part remains unhinted. But vain to popularize profundities, and all truth is profound. Winding far down from within the very heart of this spiked Hotel de Cluny where we here stand – however grand and wonderful, now quit it; – and take your way, ye nobler, sadder souls, to those vast Roman halls of Thermes; where far beneath the fantastic towers of man's upper earth, his root of grandeur, his whole awful essence sits in bearded state; an antique buried beneath antiquities, and throned on torsoes! So with a broken throne, the great gods mock that captive king; so like a Caryatid, he patient sits, upholding on his frozen brow the piled entablatures of ages. Wind ye down there, ye prouder, sadder souls! question that proud, sad king! A family likeness! aye, he did beget ye, ye young exiled royalties; and from your grim sire only will the old State-secret come.

Now, in his heart, Ahab had some glimpse of this, namely: all my means are sane, my motive and my object mad. Yet without power to kill, or change, or shun the fact; he likewise knew that to mankind he did long dissemble; in some sort, did still. But that thing of his dissembling was only subject to his perceptibility, not to his will determinate. Nevertheless, so well did he succeed in that dissembling, that when with ivory leg he stepped ashore at last, no Nantucketer thought him otherwise than but naturally grieved, and that to the quick, with the terrible casualty which had overtaken him.

The report of his undeniable delirium at sea was likewise popularly ascribed to a kindred cause. And so too, all the added moodiness which always afterwards, to the very day of sailing in the Pequod on the present voyage, sat brooding on his brow. Nor is it so very unlikely, that far from distrusting his fitness for another whaling voyage, on account of such dark symptoms, the calculating people of that prudent isle were inclined to harbor the conceit, that for those very reasons he was all the better qualified and set on edge, for a pursuit so full of rage and wildness as the bloody hunt of whales. Gnawed within and scorched without, with the infixed, unrelenting fangs of some incurable idea; such an one, could he be found, would seem the very man to dart his iron and lift his lance against the most appalling of all brutes. Or, if for any reason thought to be corporeally incapacitated for that, yet such an one would seem superlatively competent to cheer and howl on his underlings to the attack. But be all this as it may, certain it is, that with the mad secret of his unabated rage bolted up and keyed in him, Ahab had purposely sailed upon the present voyage with the one only and all-engrossing object of hunting the White Whale. Had any one of his old acquaintances on shore but half dreamed of what was lurking in him then, how soon would their aghast and righteous souls have wrenched the ship from such a fiendish man! They were bent on profitable cruises, the profit to be counted down in dollars from the mint. He was intent on an audacious, immitigable, and supernatural revenge.

Here, then, was this grey-headed, ungodly old man, chasing with curses a Job's whale round the world, at the head of a crew, too, chiefly made up of mongrel renegades, and castaways, and cannibals – morally enfeebled also, by the incompetence of mere unaided virtue or right-mindedness in Starbuck, the invulnerable jollity of indifference and recklessness in Stubb, and the pervading mediocrity in Flask. Such a crew, so officered, seemed specially picked and packed by some infernal fatality to help him to his monomaniac revenge. How it was that they so aboundingly responded to the old man's ire – by what evil magic their souls were possessed, that at times his hate seemed almost theirs; the White Whale as much their insufferable foe as his; how all this came to be – what the White Whale was to them, or how to their unconscious understandings, also, in some dim, unsuspected way, he might have seemed the gliding great demon of the seas of life, – all this to explain, would be to dive deeper than Ishmael can go. The subterranean miner that works in us all, how can one tell whither leads his shaft by the ever shifting, muffled sound of his pick? Who does not feel the irresistible arm drag? What skiff in tow of a seventy-four can stand still? For one, I gave myself up to the abandonment of the time and the place; but while yet all a-rush to encounter the whale, could see naught in that brute but the deadliest ill.

CONTINUES IN VOLUME TWO

GRANDTYPECLASSICS.COM

"There is no friend as loyal as a book." E. Hemingway

1984 BY G. ORWELL
20,000 Leagues Under the Sea BY J. VERNE
A Christmas Carol BY C. DICKENS
A Doll's House BY H. IBSEN
A Hero of Our Time BY M. LERMONTOV
A History of New York BY W. IRVING
A Little Princess BY . HODGSON BURNETT
A Journal of the Plague Year BY D. DEFOE
A Passage to India BY E. M. FORSTER
A Room with a View BY E. M. FORSTER
A Study in Scarlet BY A. C. DOYLE
A Tale of Two Cities BY C. DICKENS
Aesop's Fables BY AESOP
Agnes Grey BY A. BRONTË
Alice in Wonderland BY L. CARROLL
An American Tragedy BY T. DREISER
Anabasis BY XENOPHON
Animal Farm BY G. ORWELL
Anna Karenina BY L.TOLSTOY
Anne of Avonlea BY L. M. MONTGOMERY
Anne of Green Gables BY L. M. MONTGOMERY
Anthem BY A. RAND
Around the World in 80 Days BY J. VERNE

GT GRANDTYPECLASSICS.COM

"If a book is well written,
I always find it too short." J. Austen

As a Man Thinketh BY J. ALLEN
Au Bonheur des Dames BY É. ZOLA
Autobiography of a Yogi BY P. YOGANANDA
Barnaby Rudge BY C. DICKENS
Ben-Hur BY L. WALLACE
Beyond Good and Evil BY F. NIETZSCHE
Billy Budd, Sailor BY H. MELVILLE
Black Beauty BY A. SEWELL
Bleak House BY C. DICKENS
Candide BY VOLTAIRE
Captain Blood BY R. SABATINI
Captains Courageous BY R. KIPLING
Common Sense BY T. PAINE
Cousin Bette BY H. DE BALZAC
Cranford BY E. GASKELL
Crime and Punishment BY F. DOSTOEVSKY
Daphnis and Chloe BY LONGUS
David Copperfield BY C. DICKENS
Dead Souls BY N. GOGOL
Devils BY F. DOSTOEVSKY
Doctor Thorne BY A. TROLLOPE
Dombey and Son BY C. DICKENS
Don Quixote BY M. DE CERVANTES

GRANDTYPECLASSICS.COM

"A room without books is like a body without a soul." Cicero

Dracula BY B. STOKER
Dubliners BY J. JOYCE
Emily of New Moon BY L. M. MONTGOMERY
Emma BY J. AUSTEN
Ethan Frome BY E. WHARTON
Eugene Onegin BY A. PUSHKIN
Evelina BY F. BURNEY
Far from the Madding Crowd BY T. HARDY
Fathers and Sons BY I. TURGENEV
Fear and Trembling BY S. KIERKEGAARD
Five Children and It BY E. NESBIT
Flatland BY EDWIN A. ABBOTT
Frankenstein BY MARY SHELLEY
From the Earth to the Moon BY JULES VERNE
Gargantua and Pantagruel BY F. RABELAIS
Gone with the Wind BY M. MITCHELL
Gorgias BY PLATO
Great Expectations BY C. DICKENS
Grimm's Fairy Tales BY J. AND W. GRIMM
Gulliver's Travels BY J. SWIFT
Guy Mannering BY SIR W. SCOTT
Hamlet BY W. SHAKESPEARE
Hard Times BY CHARLES DICKENS

GT GRANDTYPECLASSICS.COM

"The man who doesn't read has no advantage over the man who can't read." M. Twain

Heart of Darkness by Joseph Conrad
Heidi by Johanna Spyri
Hellenica by Xenophon
Howards End by E. M. Forster
Idylls of the King by A. L. Tennyson
In Our Time by E. Hemingway
Interior Castle by St. T. Avila
Ivanhoe by Sir W. Scott
Jane Eyre by C. Brontë
Journey to the Center of the Earth by J. Verne
Jude the Obscure by T. Hardy
Just So Stories by R. Kipling
Kidnapped by R. L. Stevenson
Kim by R. Kipling
King Solomon's Mines by H. R. Haggard
Lady Audley's Secret by M. E. Braddon
Lady Chatterley's Lover by D. H. Lawrence
Le Morte d'Arthur: by Sir T. Malory
Leaves of Grass by W. Whitman
Les Misérables by V. Hugo
Letters from a Stoic by L. A. Seneca
Leviathan by T. Hobbes
And Many More...

www.ingramcontent.com/pod-product-compliance
Lightning Source LLC
Chambersburg PA
CBHW020917310726
48980CB00011B/930/J